the gospel according to
Johnny Bender

the gospel according to Johnny Bender

by
Dean Lilleyman

urbanepublications.com

First published in Great Britain in 2016 by Urbane Publications Ltd
Suite 3, Brown Europe House, 33/34 Gleaming Wood Drive, Chatham, Kent ME5 8RZ

A CIP catalogue record for this book is available from the British Library.

ISBN 978-1-911129-00-4
EPUB 978-1-911129-01-1
MOBI 978-1-911129-02-8

Design and Typeset by Julie Martin
Cover by Stephen Holmes and Julie Martin

Printed and bound by
CP Group (UK) Ltd, Croydon, CR0 4YY

urbanepublications.com

The publisher supports the Forest Stewardship Council® (FSC®), the leading international forest-certification organisation. This book is made from acid-free paper from an FSC®-certified provider. FSC is the only forest-certification scheme supported by the leading environmental organisations, including Greenpeace.

The illustrations in *The Gospel According to Johnny Bender*, including the cover art, are original pieces created by contemporary artist Stephen Holmes.

You can discover more about Stephen and his work at stephenholmesart.com

Photography of the author by
Scott Hukins and Meghan Lilleyman.

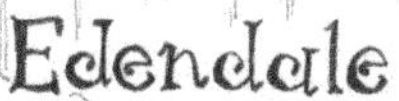
Edendale

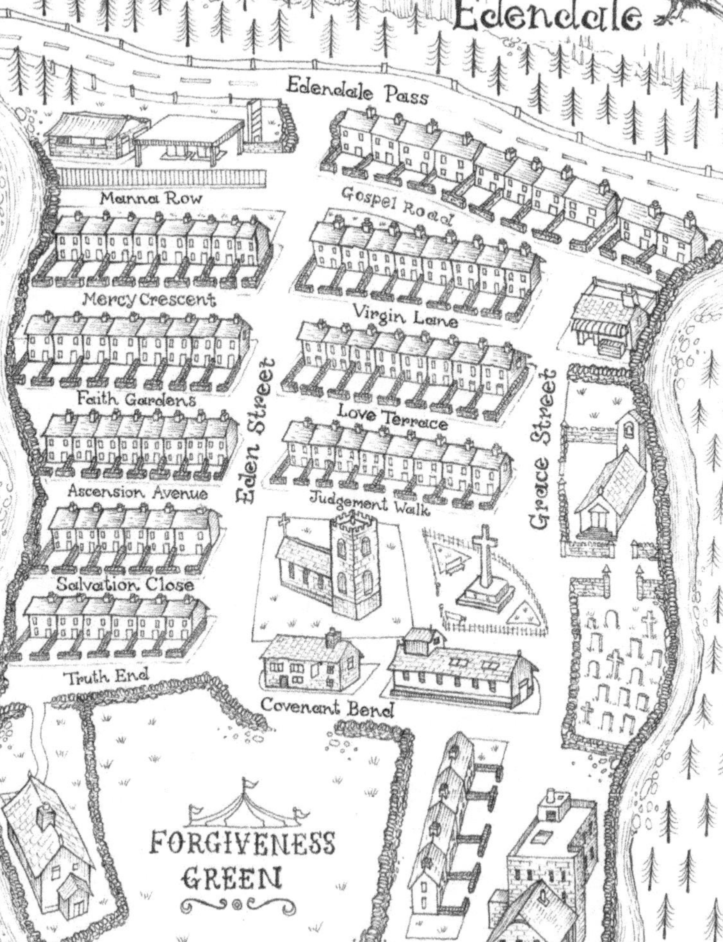
Edendale Pass
Manna Row
Gospel Road
Mercy Crescent
Virgin Lane
Faith Gardens
Love Terrace
Eden Street
Grace Street
Ascension Avenue
Judgement Walk
Salvation Close
Truth End
Covenant Bend
FORGIVENESS
GREEN

Blessed is he who reads aloud the words of the prophecy, and blessed are those who hear and who keep what is written therein, for the time is near.
(*The Book of Revelation*)

You lot'll not know what fuckin' day it is, so convincing will be my selection of tunes ... and time ... time, my friend ... will have no ... meaning ... at all ...
(*Disco Dennis*)

1.

I'll tell you what I know, so maybe you'll remember. It's forty-three minutes past seven o'clock. Some might say I'm wrong and right me, tell you me both it's seventeen minutes to eight. Today, I am eyes not mouth, so I won't answer back. Eyes tell things that mouth cannot. They see mattress, sleep bag, floorboards, that yellowy light through curtains that tell morning. They tell my fingernails are long, carry dark half-moons that scratch leg. Today, I am ears, hear scratch, see it, feel it. Ears tell things that mouth cannot. Today, I am ears and eyes, but never mouth. Ears hear tree birds outside singing on top, and always river below. Name given to river is Went. It runs by house, but doesn't say Went in people word. No. This river is a singing that washes body and belly. Dirt carried from skin by song. Off and away. It shouldn't come back, but it does.

Jeremiah Jones made this place from limestone dug from hills and called it Edendale. He said it would be happy on grass while Went made smile around us, while tor cliff held off cold wind from our doors. But tor gives shadow too, our sun always to be gone before it should, like night coming on too soon. He made a mill from hill stones. Dipped a big wheel into river. To turn and turn to keep other wheels turning inside. He said God was with us. One-hundred and twenty-two houses Jeremiah made, then one on its own, behind trees next to river, down at bottom for him. If you were a blackbird flying sky, you could see something from up there. Can you see it? He built these people-houses in shape of Adam's ribs. Look. Eyes tell it. Five ribs down left, four ribs down right. One missing that made an Eve. And there, a church where heart should lie. Some men broke top left rib years ago though, took nine people-houses away, put a garage there to suckle big road going past with petrol and oil and bars of chocolate, with maps and titty books. Are you still a blackbird? It's like Adam is turning away isn't it? Rolling over onto his side to face where our sun goes behind hills to bring night too soon. Can you see what eyes tell now? Eden Street down middle is straight down chest bone where ribs meet. Not backbone. See? Backbone is laid against Went on right side of smile as blackbird sees it ... Shop, school, graveyard ... and down, down, at root of it, a mill that isn't a mill anymore ... a limestone council office. Mouths say sometimes child ghosts who got killed working looms say boo inside broom cupboards. What do you think? Do you believe in ghosts?

Go wait by front door while I put coat on. Mind cat droppings in hall. Sometimes I forget to shut door and they come in, like you did. Have you been lost? Go take stairs.

I'll be down in a minute. And my name? They all call me Johnny Bender. I don't know why. We don't talk. That's not my name, not really.

You walk down the stairs, and each step has its own voice, each different from the last. You stand in the hall and see with eyes what the mouth cannot tell. This house is not clean. On the hall floor is a scatter of printed news. There are several small piles of cat droppings. The scatter of printed news is all the same kind. Low Peak Gazette. The eyes tell you that they fell through the letterbox but never got picked up. There is a swept half-circle shape where the door opens. The eyes see yellow morning light through the mottled glass panels of the black door. This light tells the eyes of summer. The letterbox is a mouth with a tongue of quarter-folded news. Pull it out. The brass lip clacks. Another Low Peak Gazette.

July 31st 1999
EDENDALE CARNIVAL 20TH ANNIVERSARY SPECIAL

The picture is a smiling young girl with curly blonde hair. Her teeth are small and white. She is dressed as a princess or … no … a fairy. Tips of pink wings above her shoulders.

The steps behind you each have their own voice, each different to the last. Johnny Bender is with you again. He says, *Let's go for a walk.*

2.

Listen. Church bell tells one, two, three, four, five, six, seven, eight. Mr Sun tells it too. Left to right as day tick-tocks, big white face that comes on from behind tor. And if you are that blackbird, you'd see not just Adam, you'd see Edendale as sundial too. Church steeple, a shadow that measures. Tick-tock, til night says stop. I was born in this house. Fifteen, Gospel Road. Mother is dead. Father went out for bread and never came back.

Come, let's go down path onto street. You'll see and hear and feel that today is different, but same. Like Christmas. People get tickles in belly and head. Makes electric that floats, joining everyone together because that's what they're asked to want. Do you feel it too? Let's walk. This is story that needs feet on ground to see it, hear it, for nose to smell it. Shut garden gate. Red, blue, white. They tied these triangles to string and hung them from roof gutters yesterday. It will be hot today. White, red, blue. They all agreed it. Did it.

Look. Didn't take long to reach chest bone did it? Eden

Street. And to your right, tor. Up, up, and up. There's garage over there. And there's road that takes people past us, or into us. Edendale Pass. They've even hung banner across mouth. Makes no sense backwards, from where we are. Not really. But if you think about it, it does. It's like something that was and then isn't. If only look from forward you see nothing of backward. The quick brown fox jumps over the lazy dog ... Turn around and look back down my street. Did you see numbers on houses when we were walking? Ten, eleven, twelve, thirteen, fourteen ... each number after last never repeating ... each window looking to a garden. Jeremiah wanted it like that. They say he liked things in order, each thing separate, each thing after other so he knew where it was, who it was ... one number one in village, one number two, on and on to number hundred and twenty-two. It's broken now though, since they built garage. No more number one, two, three, four, five, six, seven, eight, nine ... You understand what that banner says now, don't you? Jeremiah had no carnival. Jeremiah said hard work and prayer was only way to Eden. Never play. He had to be dead before they built drink house.

Let's walk. This story needs beginning, and beginning needs to know where it starts.

You walk down Eden Street with the sun to your left. You read the names of each street, each rib that leaves the chest bone. Manna Row. Virgin Lane. Mercy Crescent. Love Terrace. Faith Gardens. Judgement Walk. You see the church. Divinity Way. Ascension Avenue. Salvation Close.

A pub called The Fiddler's Rest. Covenant Bend.

Red, white and blue bunting is hung from every roof gutter, across every street, from lamp-post to lamp-post. You see the grey shadow of people-shapes behind windows, in doorways, busying themselves. Something is going to happen today. You can feel it, hear it in the singing of the river that seems to be underneath all the other sounds.

You are now stood before a low wall that pens a wide belly of grass. On the grass is a big blue marquee, as big as six houses ... bigger. There are other things on the grass too. A roped square the size of a small sheep field. Several small round tented stalls with signs that say HOOK-A-DUCK and FORTUNE TELLER and BAKED POTATOES. A larger tent that says MUSIC, and a bigger one still that says BAR. All around you, you can hear the sounds of things being readied, of things being set in motion, things that will happen today. Behind you, and in front, the grey shadows of people begin to gain flesh and face, body, arms and legs, and as the church bell rings one, two, three, the hands of the church clock tell your eyes it is half past eight.

Johnny Bender leans on the low wall, waving for you to come near, to listen.

Jeremiah called grass field Forgiveness Green. Our feet are on Truth End. Look behind you. You see street we have walked, tor cliff that watches, has seen it all from beginning. People are readying. Soon your eyes will see it, your ears will hear all that is said. Jeremiah said God is with this place. Do you believe, Blackbird? Come this way. One, two, three, four, five, six, seven, eight, nine, ten, eleven, twelve steps ... here. This is end of Truth End. Over that wall there, to your right, is river. You can hear it, so you know it. It has run longer than any clock, tick-tock. Look beyond gate. House down there on its own is where Jeremiah lived. It's a king's house, and it now belongs to Mr King. His, is beginning of it, a say of carnival twenty summers ago. River is clockwork before clockwork. Before looms, before mouths talked of ghost children. Close your eyes, Blackbird, listen to it. This is where you unlearn song. See. You're there already. Forwards, backwards, sing is babble to you, Blackbird. That is, unless you listen very carefully as river runs back way it came, a grain that can be planed backward as smoothly as it can forward by carpenter that holds plane. We are opening gate. We are walking path to where a king lives. It is not today, but it is. Read words from behind sign, Blackbird. King's window is open, and sign is this. Farmer has cut down trees to make way for more growing. An end that makes beginning. He has cut to stump three from nine. And now, he is burning stumps back into earth.

Open your eyes, Blackbird. It is 1979, and king is making speech.

3.

In his study, Mr King closes his window because the smell of burning is annoying him. He makes a mental note to check on the smell again in half-an-hour, and if it still persists he will telephone the police station in nearby Castletor and get a body on the situation. He suspects Rod Stanton is the culprit, clearing his land again. Mr King has no problem with this normally, in fact, at the last council meeting his was the authority that stamped the go ahead.

Local business should mean local success, as Mr King's motto goes, and money coming in means money coming in, as Mr King is also known to say.

But what kind of ignorant inbred illiterate arsehole makes a stink like that on a day like today? Does not the thick fucking peasant realise that today is carnival day? Is not the stupid shit-shovelling moron aware that today is the culmination of five months planning and meetings and handshakes and ...

Mr King moves away from his window and takes a deep

breath. He looks at the grandfather clock, and the hands tell Mr King that he has time for one more run through, that this needs to be right, perfect, the speech of a man whose words make things happen.

Mr King looks to his reflection in the full-length mirror by the grandfather clock. His brown leather shoes suggested by his London tailor do indeed give the air of a man well into his stride, rooting affably a plaid wool double-breasted four-button suit in earthy colours, that his tailor described as emanating power yet amiable accessibility to peer and serf alike.

Gentleman farmer? Mr King hopes not, more gentleman landowner, a down-to-earth success story, a man of the people to guide the people.

He studies the white shirt and brown plaid tie, fingering the double-Windsor knot between thumb and forefinger. A tad left, a tad right, middled. His tailor was right. Power, accessibility, a man trusted to lead.

He lifts the silver comb, an anniversary gift from his wife, from the oak vanity stand by the mirror, runs it once through his side-parted fringe, twice down either side of his head, twice behind. His barber has cut impeccably, again, understanding the importance of framing a face for public consumption ... persuasion. And, like his tailor, his barber is also situated in the heart of London. Some things just cannot be done cheaply, be it suit or shoe or haircut. They understand these things in the capital, of what makes a man of standing, of what differentiates a figure of ambition from the average Freddy Shit-Kicker.

Mr King clears his throat, walks the short distance from the mirror to the desk, drinks from the half glass of water, clears his throat again, leans towards the cassette player and presses play. Now standing shoulders-back and smiling as the C60 reels turn, imagining the expectant faces looking up at him in that peopled marquee of tonight, making that all-important eye-contact, hearing his own voice say from the machine: *Wait for the applause to taper but begin before it gets too sparse*, feeling that little skip of the heart knowing as he does that this delivery will be paperless, scriptless, to underline the genuine compassion of things said direct from the heart like all great orators do, speeches that go down in history from men who stand high above the herd as guiding light, this king hearing his own voice count a whispered *one two three* from the cassette recorder as he now joins himself in speech: Thank you ... thank you ... People of Edendale! of Castletor! and the surrounding Low Peak and beyond! What a day of celebration this has been!

(*Wait until applause dies down but not much ... two three four*)

Community is what we are, and community is what we celebrate.

(*Applause? two three four*)

Nearly two-hundred years ago, Jeremiah Jones built an industry, and a village around that industry, and he called it Edendale ...

(*Applause? two three four*)

... and here today, nearly two-hundred years later, the mill may not be a mill anymore, but the wheels of Edendale are still turning, because together we stand, for now the industry is community, is togetherness, is what you see around you right here and now.

(*Applause? two three four*)

In short, we ... you ... each and every one of us, have made this a celebration today, and with it, we celebrate each other!

(*Applause? two three four*)

Edendale ... a name given to us by Jeremiah for good reason. For we sit within a beautiful dale, surrounded by a beautiful river, in fact all around us, beauty is to be seen ... we are indeed blessed with our very own Eden. But ... it is not just this landscape that gives Edendale its beauty ... it is, above all things, the people, us, in our sense of community that make it so ... something that we have witnessed today in fruitful abundance.

(*Applause? two three four*)

And on that note, there are some people that I ... that we ... should thank for helping put together this very first Edendale Carnival. Firstly, the carnival committee ... a team of four, of which I myself am privileged to be part of ...

(*Applause? two three four*)

... alongside my long-suffering and saintly wife, Mrs King.

(*Laughter? Applause? two three four*)

And of course, our spiritual core, the pip of Edendale's apple if you will ...

(*Laughter? two three four*)

... the Reverend Haywire, a man ever on hand to hear

out our problems both spiritual and practical alike, offering a wisdom and a goodness that over the years many of us have benefitted from.

(*Applause? two three four*)

And last, but certainly not least, the man that keeps our shelves stocked here in Edendale, the man who makes sure we are never short of anything, from baked beans to bottled beer, and not to mention that very particular brand of off the shelf humour he so readily supplies ...

(*Laughter? two three four*)

Our very own Mr Alan Childlove!

(*Applause? two three four*)

I would also like to thank each and every one of you who participated in the parade, or helped with the stalls and displays here on Forgiveness Green and in the Church Hall, or by your very being here, you ... villagers and visitors alike ... who have made this a wonderful day of celebration! Thank you, thank you, thank you!

(*Applause? two three four*)

And so ... without further ado, because I can see you're all itching to get dancing again ... and may I say what a great job our resident Edendale DJ is doing tonight ... take a bow, Disco Dennis!

(*Applause? two three four*)

So let's turn down the lights, and get the party started again, as our first ever Edendale carnival queen takes to the floor ... Give us a little wave, Maggie ... isn't she beautiful, ladies and gentlemen ... and Maggie has a basket of special Edendale Carnival chocolates she'll be handing out for you all to enjoy, and remember, we have an extra special event as the clock strikes a quarter to midnight ... a fabulous firework extravaganza, organised by the Low Peak Council as a special commemorative marker of this, our very first carnival, of which we hope, will be the first of many more to come!

(*Applause? two three four*)

Now ... music if you will Mr DJ! Let's return to the dance!

Mr King smiles, waves to his imaginary audience and exits stage left, goes to press stop on the cassette recorder just as whatever was recorded on there before vomits something about love being confusing, stop, another of those silly fucking pop songs his daughter Rose likes so much (best destroy the tape lest she get mad at him for taping over it). And now walking across to the window, sliding it open, a frown as he sniffs the air ... *cunt* ... the sounds of Edendale sounding so very different today, like something's going to happen, which it will ... *cunt* ... Mr King's forefinger now turning the phone dial, *click, whirr, click, whirr,* then slamming the receiver back down, because he's way too fucking angry to make any reasonable request to Sergeant Harrison at Castletor Police Station to go stop that stupid peasant twat from stinking up the air, *CUNT* ... Mr King now heading out of his study and down the stairs to where he can hear Mrs King clank-banging the breakfast pots, stop, take a breath, You are Mr King, and you are in control, the double-Windsor knot between thumb and forefinger, a tad left, a tad right, middled ... *CUNT* ...

4.

Blackbird. Can you still smell burning? No? Good. Back and forth, back and forth. That was then, this is now … new things, old things, trippity-trip. Come sit by tree. Dog bite still hurts after bite. Teeth-holes stay showing like echo. Put your hand to trunk. You feel body, and through body, green leaves too high to touch … brown roots too deep to reach, but, you do. Like if you jumped in river. You'd be in all of it from first tick-tock to last. It's all same. Do you understand, Blackbird? Did cat ever catch mouse? Round and round clock it pretends, a space between teeth and tail never changing, yet chase is always chasing. Painter's hand painted want to get, painted fear of being gotten. Took brush to colour murder that never will, but might. Stupid cat … stupid mouse …

Voices from Forgiveness Green are more now, aren't they Blackbird. Still early, yet grass is warm. Look. Woman in that window. Old wife of a king. Suppose that makes her queen. King is on staircase growing wrinkles and belly and goosey grey hair, waiting for words to be ready, knows queen is sad. Twenty years gone, or one minute down staircase. Back and forth, back and forth. Woodcutter slices open belly of wolf and out jumps Little Red. Once upon a time there was a girl called ... Stupid mouse. Stupid cat. Are you still with me, Blackbird? King is on that bottom step, hand on door knob. Queen stands by sink. Calendar of days turned face down on window-ledge. Queen's finger is cut on broken glass, and she watches without seeing, blood drip-drip into dish water. We, are mouse, looking from mouse-alley between cupboards, while behind lays a trap, poised and delicate. Between table legs we see door open ...

Close your eyes, Blackbird. Watch.

5.

Mrs King feels herself tighten. She hears him make that annoyed sigh he makes when something isn't to his liking. He reaches past her to the window-sill, stands the calendar back up.

July 31st, 1999.

She feels his hand on her back. She sees blood on her finger. Blood in the dish water. Blood on her apron. She can't stop the sob that rises like a fist from her gut. CAN'T! is the sound that rooks from her mouth, and now she is held in his arms, and he is telling her careful, not to get blood on his suit, that it's alright, that they can do this, together, together.

He guides her towards the kitchen table, pulls a chair out, sits her down, glances to the floor, then kneels on one knee. Look at me, he says.

Her chin tilts, just. She opens her eyes.

You'll have to get your make-up sorted, he says. And probably get changed. There'll be blood on your dress.

She dabs both eyes with a tissue dug from her apron pocket, tells him again that she can't do this. She feels his hand tighten on her knee. He stands, quick-brushing his trousers where he knelt, pulls another chair out from under the table and sits square in front of her.

He strokes her hair once, twice, and she wants to tell him she is not a fucking dog.

Listen, he says, I know this is difficult, but it's difficult for both of us. And we have to do this. We can't show weakness. Do you understand?

She says that she does. She is looking at the tissue in her hand. Black streaks of mascara. Blood from her finger. She feels the sob punch itself up from her gut again, and she can't stop it. Head in her hands. CAN'T! CAN'T! CAN'T!

SanDRA! he barks, a hand now on each of her shoulders, the trace of a shake, and then: LOOK at me!

She looks. She sees anger. Then restraint. A softening then a smile, his grip becoming a stroke. A pat.

I am not. A fucking. Dog.

Sandra ... *listen* ... we *must* be strong. We have a position to maintain, and if we show weakness, we'll lose. *We* ... are Mr and Mrs King ... *Do you understand?*

She nods. The tissue is on the floor. Blood and mascara.

She takes a deep breath. Forces a smile and then a glance at his face. He's smiling the smile of a father to a child. The tissue is on the floor. He cups her hands in his.

Right, he says, in voice that has hardened, a switch flicked, all-too quick. In half-an-hour I will leave the house. You will go to your room and sort yourself out. And then, you will meet me in the marquee at eleven. *And* ... you will look strong, beautiful, in control, and the people will see that and admire you for it. And *Sandra?*

She glances up at his eyes. Blinks.

No-one will mention it after the church. And we, will get on with our day. He says this with a hand stroking hers.

I am not. A fucking. Dog.

And when you've got through this day ... when *we* have got through this day ... you will feel very, very, proud of yourself, Sandra.

She feels herself tense. The tissue is on the floor. She feels his fingers under her chin. A gentle pressure, upwards, smiling that smile of a father to a child.

Be strong, darling. It happened. And there isn't a day goes by where I don't think about her. But we have to carry on. And this carnival must, too. And it has done. Every year since. Twenty years, Sandra. It's part of her, of us, this village. Rose will always, *always* be with us. And the people of this village need to see us strong. We cannot ... *cannot* ... show weakness. The people look up to us, Sandra, and they *must* remain to do so.

She feels nothing. The tissue is on the floor. Blood, and mascara.

6.

Let's move on, Blackbird. Back up path to gate. Are you understanding it? Back and forth is sometimes muddle, isn't it? But better to watch it go past than stop it and ask. Questions is like talking over answer, not listening to it. La, la, la ... I go for a walk every day. Always same but different. You've been walking too, haven't you, Blackbird. Open gate. Let's walk some more.

And you walk. The river behind you, houses to your left, the grass to your right. The King's house is hidden behind trees now. People are more. The church clock chimes one, two, three, four, five, six, seven, eight, nine. On Forgiveness Green you see girls in brown clothes doing handstands, a scatter of blue-uniformed men with drums by feet and trumpets in hand. *Testing testing* wafts a voice, a man on a bunting-strung stage, *hello hello* an echo down a corridor not there, the bottom of Eden Street, the corner of Covenant Bend, The Fiddler's Rest, a woman placing chairs under tables out front. Divinity Way, the church, old ladies dressing little square tables with white cloths that misbehave in the breeze, and to your right, a long rectangle building labelled Church Hall, a painted banner saying LOW PEAK W.I. CRAFT AND JUMBLE SALE, and by the wall, a mosaic of flower petals dressed into an uncertain picture of the tor cliff it looks across at, *Edendale Carnival, 1979-1999*, blood red rose petals, stop.

Remember when you were that blackbird up there? Saw Adam turning onto his side? This here is backbone you saw. Grace Street. Dead people over there, buried under grass. King and queen have her in a jar though, a glass cabinet in a room little used. She has a stone in church, but no stone over there with others. Am I telling it? Maybe I shouldn't. But maybe it helps you understand, Blackbird. King and queen will pray by church stone today. Reverend and few others doing same. Flowers. Nothing else. That's what King wants. To go forward. And so should we. Come, Blackbird. Step, step, step...

Look, there's school, and further up, Mr Childlove's shop. The quick brown fox jumps over the lazy dog. Turn around. That's Love Terrace. Let me tell you about Michael. He lives there, right on end. Number seventy-eight. Michael never left. His mother and father did though. Went to live somewhere else. Michael lives alone. He's thought about leaving, but something stops him. He teaches books in town where they call him Mr Goodman.

Do you like poetry, Blackbird?

7.

Michael stares up at his bedroom ceiling, eyes following a crack that stems from the light fitting, cricks left, spawning a dozen thin roots like a badly-made tree that never branched, never grew leaves, never felt the sun's caress, never reached up to feel July's breath move it one single inch, *nothing*, just a hard crack of *nothing*, dead, *nothing*.

And of course, he is thinking of her sleep-breathing by his side, and when he turns over, he'll feel her breath on his skin, that warm-soft tide of her, in and out, as he traces the line of her lips with a forefinger, seeing her smile, a twitch, her eyes still closed but pretending sleep, his fingers now tracing the horizon of her neck, her shoulder, arm, his palm now on her hip bone, hand now a gentle pressure upon her thigh, the kiss, her lips soft and warm and sleep-dry, and between deeper kisses he will tell those closed eyes again and again that he loves her, he loves her, that he will *always* love her. And now her eyes are open, green like sea, green like corn grass … no … green, like … like …

Fuck.

He sits upright in bed, throws the pencil a short distance to where the notebook lies on the duvet, puts his hands on his head and ruffles his hair quick till it near hurts, makes a sound like a bike tyre being Stanley-knifed. Swings his legs out of bed, stands.

Fuck.

In the dressing table mirror, he is naked, cut off at the knees, decapitated at the mouth. He takes a step back, his calves pressing the bed, the mirrored self-portrait now sliced across forehead, across shins, cock still half-proud.

He hears the milk-truck an empty-bottled rattle in the street below. He blinks, staring into his own eyes as he begins to speak.

You don't love him, you love me.

I can make you happy.

Keep you happy.

I know you love me.

I know it by the way you kiss me.

I know it by the way you look at me.

I know it when we fuck.

It's too good not to be real.

I know this.

You know it too.

You don't feel that way with him.

He's a boy.

And I'm a man.

Michael closes his eyes, sits back down on the bed, elbows on knees, head in hands, fingers pressing hard into scalp.

FuckfuckFUCK.

He stares at his feet.

Hears the sound of his breath.

The birds singing.

The sound of a car.

Another.

The birds singing.

His breath.

A car.

The birds singing.

A bicycle bell.

His breath.

The birds.

And then, as though bitten by a midge, he twitches, turns quick, picks up the notebook and pencil from the bed.

8.

How easy it is to be sad, Blackbird. Some mouths say that having what you want for little time is better than never a time. What do you think? Come. Let's walk up and around bend. Enough time for a story in this story. When I was little I wanted a birthday. I was eight or nine or ten. Mother said no but Father told her I needed to learn some things. She helped me make letters to some people at school. We sat at kitchen table and put letters inside envelopes. She kept saying this is wrong this is wrong. She wrote names I said onto my envelopes and I drew birds and animals on them. When I gave them to people some of them laughed. Some of them made faces like what Mother did sometimes when Father took her upstairs to sleep. On birthday Mother made sandwiches and a cake. We sat at kitchen table waiting for people to come. No-one did, and Mother got sad and went to bed. I enjoyed eating sandwiches but cake was best. Father came home and laughed a lot. He said you have to light candle and make a wish and ask for something you really, really want. I told him I wanted to make more letters and he laughed again, walked around kitchen popping all my balloons that Mother had stuck to our walls, bang bang bang bang, one by one by one with his cigarette till all were gone. Then he went upstairs to see Mother and I ate cake. We never had a birthday after that one ...

This is Virgin Lane. In this house lives Mr Alcock and a daughter called Sarah. Mr Alcock cleans windows and fixes cars and paints people's houses for money in back pocket. Some people call him Odd-job Alcock. Or Paul. It's easy to be sad. Sarah looks happy today. Her friend Natalie is with her. They're dressing up for carnival and laughing at it.

Close your eyes, Blackbird. Story is happening.

9.

GERRup EVree BOdee AND! Sarah and Natalie fall on the bed laughing, high-pitched and still hugging as the song begins to fade, a *bumpbumpbump* on the door as Sarah's dad tells the girls to TURN IT DOWN PLEASE IT'S TOO BLOODY EARLY FOR THIS! The girls now laughing harder, faces an inch apart as the next track of this disco compilation tape handclaps a beginning, and *bumpbumpbump* goes the door again, SARAH!

Eyes meet, hands across mouths stifling laughter. YES, DAD o-KAY! The girls now sitting up and letting go of each other, Sarah tottering across her bedroom carpet in bright purple platform wedges three-inch deep as the kick drum *bumpf-bumpf-bumpfs* ... SARAH!

Eyes meet, grins. YES, DAD O-KAY! The volume on the hi-fi slid from 8 to 3.

THANK YOU SARAH! The sound of footsteps going down the stairs.

Miserable sod. Sarah looks down to her shoes. Chuffin'

hell, I'm gonna kill meself in these tonight.

Natalie is laid out across the bed again, looking at the cassette cover. Deadpan: Weren't even fuckin' born when this stuff were out.

Sarah is still looking at her shoes. Good though, innit.

Deadpan: Suppose.

Sarah kicks her shoes off, goes and stands in front of the mirror. What d'yer reckon then, Nat? 1979 or what?

Natalie looks up. Deadpan: That, or an explosion in a prozzer factory.

Aw, thanks.

Anytime, darl.

Sarah looks at herself in the purple blouse, eyes the shoulder pads, turns her arm and watches the sparkles sparkle in the morning sunlight, the silk sleeve hanging wide like the sleeve of some fairy princess thing, now looking down to her cleavage, wishing her boobs were bigger, again, looks to her friend's reflection in the mirror. Trying yours on?

Natalie shrugs, sits up, stands and walks the short distance to the door where a black sparkly silk blouse with big puffy sleeves is hanging see-through on a coat-hanger, a pair of red Lycra leggings half-hiding behind. And in what looks like one movement in the dressing table mirror, the clothes are flung onto the bed and Natalie's Beastie Boys t-shirt is off and onto the floor. Sarah draws eyeliner across her eye, her best friend in soft focus as she slides her jeans down her legs, steps out of them.

Natalie eyes the clothes on the bed. When we meeting Tom?

Sarah blinks. Looks up to the ceiling. Blinks again. He's comin' over about half-eleven.

Natalie slips the leggings off the hanger, tugs her knickers out of herself. Got your uni application in yet?

Sarah works on the other eye. Blinks. Nope.

Good. Me neither.

Natalie, in black bra and knickers, holds the leggings at arm's length. Deadpan: Gonna feel a reyt twat in these.

Sarah looks at her in the mirror, turns around grinning, her left eye watering, just. Ah come on, Nat … DISCO! She leans across and slides the volume up to 7.

GOOD … TIMES! THESE, are, THE … Natalie rolls her eyes, pulls a slow Travolta, arm raised, pointy finger a reluctant jab as from down the stairs SAAAARAH!

Sarah pulls an uh-oh face and turns it back down to 3.

O-kay DAD! Eyes meet, grin. Miserable sod.

Sarah fishes for her mascara on the cluttered dressing table. She looks up into the mirror, and Natalie is stood behind her, a look of mock-horror cartooned on her face. Deadpan: Fu-cking hell … camel-toe or what?

The girls laugh, high-pitched and stabby, like for like as Sarah stands up, lifting her blouse up to her chin, revealing black spandex leggings and bare belly. Snap! More laughter. Natalie points to the reflection. Mr goodygoody Goodman's gonna love that, Sare … woof woof.

Sarah blinks. Pulls a sarky face. Says, Shut up, idiot.

Natalie punches her on the arm. The mascara bottle is on the floor. A knock on the door. The door opens halfway. Sarah's father.

Just off to do that fencing for the Beresfords, Sare.

Sarah stops rubbing her arm, lets go of her blouse. Natalie quick-wraps an arm around her chest, half-turns her back to Sarah's father. DAD! we're GETTING CHANGED!

Eyes downward, exit Paul Alcock. Soz.

Dad? Goin' to the carnival?

The door is still ajar three inches.

No. Got this job on, then stayin' in tonight.

The door clicks shut.

10.

Paul Alcock locks the front door behind him, adjusts his headphones, clicks start on his Walkman, picks his toolbox up, *hiss* ... feeeeedback guitar angry down the path past a rusty red car on bricks, open the gate onto Virgin Lane turning right towards Eden Street, eyes downward as the voice in his ears spikes for a lover not got WHAT DO I GET? stupid bloody carnival no I'm not bloody goin' what a bag of shite, oh great, wave to Mrs bloody Owen yes yes put your dustbin lid down luv I've waved back, god what's she mouthing now?

Press stop.

SAY AGAIN MRS OWEN ... COULDN'T HEAR YER ... NO, NOT GOIN', MRS OWEN. TOO MUCH ON ... YEH WILL DO. HAVE A GOOD UN, LUV.

Press start, guitaaarrr ... what do I get? bakin' competitions, dogs doing tricks, stupid marchin' bands, ooh look my cucumber's bigger than yours all topped off with three hours of bloody disco crap ... *twats* ... let's pretend it's 1979. Well no it's not luv it's 1999 and some of us don't want to play stupid fancy dress games and listen to puffy bummer music that were shit then, still fuckin' is ... Oh Jesus fuck, will you look at Eden Street ... least I'll be in Beresford's back garden when that fuckarsed parade goes arse-trumpetin' its fuckarsed way round. Wonder if Childlove's is still open this afternoon? Need some tinnies for tonight. Garage'll be open if not ... Yes, luv, excuse me, middle-aged fart coming through listening to music eighty thousand times better than that Boyzone shite you listen to, yes, watch my bloody toolbox ... Thank Christ they only do this once a year ... Oh great ... Jim Romney and his herd of bloody majorettes. Cross over? Nah, head down. Nice arse, lass ... No Jim, not taking me headphones off ... EY JIM, Y'ALREYT? ... HANG ON, CAN'T HEAR YER. Press stop. Put toolbox down. Take headphones off.

Say again, Jim?

Jim grins, says Gettin' vibed up for the disco tonight, pal? nodding to Paul's Walkman.

Girls in pale-blue mini-skirted uniforms twirling batons swarm past like cattle into milking. Paul looks to his Walkman. Nah, this is Buzzcocks, mate. None o' that disco shi ... Paul stops himself, glances left and right, smirks. Paul and Jim laugh. The majorettes continue to swarm past.

Should be a good un, though, Jim says, looking up to the blue cloudless sky. Comin' down for a pint or six?

Paul looks to his toolbox. Nah, got too much on, Jim. I'll be knackered. A few tinnies and ... A majorette nudges Paul's toolbox as she goes by.

Soz, Mr Alcock. Grin.

Glancing over his shoulder, Paul smiles at her. Y'alreyt, Lyndsey?

Lyndsey is walking backwards twirling her baton. She's still smiling. Paul glances at her legs, then corrects himself.

Yes Mr Alcock. Is your Sarah comin' down?

Paul gives her the thumbs up and she does a little wave, turns around and walks on with the last of the majorettes.

Yer need to get yersen dahn, Paul. Get some bevvies on.

Paul shrugs. We'll see.

Jim pats him on the shoulder. Anyrowd ... best get me girls sorted. He nods up the road to where the majorettes are headed. Hope to see yer later, pal.

Jim heads off after his girls. Paul puts his headphones back on, picks his toolbox up, presses play and walks on, guitar a wasp staccato repeat, leading him unwitting back to Sarah and Natalie by the mirror, Sarah's face red around the cheeks, Natalie with a look on her face that he can't quite determine. Is she smirking? And now he sees that Sarah's grown so quick he can't remember it all, where did nineteen years go? He sees her stood on the kitchen table, she's five, maybe four. She's angry at him. He has the scissors in his hand and he's just cut her fringe. He's telling her he needs to try and straighten it again because it's still wonky but she's had enough, and anyway, it's already too short. Paul feels himself smile. He sees her by the dresser again. She's holding the bottom of her blouse in her hand and her hand is under her chin. He sees her belly, the button hid by the black leggings she's wearing. She lets go of the blouse and shouts. She looks angry. She looks so much like her mother ... And the song is done, another begun, and now the voice in his ears is dirt and he's hurt ... Best. Song. Ever. FALLEN IN ... look at *fu-ckin' that* ...

Paul stands stock-still looking down Eden Street towards Forgiveness Green. Red, white and blue. People. Too many, too much. The marquee. The tents. The stalls. The rides. People. Too many, too much. His toolbox feels heavy in his hand, his insides even heavier. And he doesn't want to think about her but he does. Twenty years ago. Her. Him. The whole fucking mess of it. And he wants to go back. To change some things. To make some things different. And he hates himself. He closes his eyes for a second and he sees her again. She's crying, shouting, holding her head in her hands, shouting, crying, and he wants to cry too but he can't because he's too fucking angry at her, and this year he *will not* do that fucking stupid anniversary arse bollock thing, he will *not* open the old Christmas biscuit tin he keeps hidden in the wardrobe, reading the letter he knows off by heart, the letter that Sarah knows nothing of and never will, *Paul, I've gone, and I need to tell you why, don't look for me, I'm not coming back* ... turn right onto Salvation Close, broken fence, claw hammer, three-inch nails, four-inch, pliers, saw, number 111, number 110, Sarah looks so much like her ... stop, number 109, *knock knock, knock knock.*

11.

Funny how some people get stuck in a time, isn't it Blackbird. Like goat in a field. Maybe goat could jump wall, but it won't. Is it happy with this grass? Or does it think this grass is only grass? Paul's gone inside now, look ... Mrs Beresford shouts her husband, and down his stairs he comes, all shaved wiping face on towel, Eyup Paul, come through, I'll show yer me fence ... chuffin' wind, rattled it cock-eyed, buggered, Barbara, stick kettle on, and on it goes. Are you still with me, Blackbird? It's easy to get mixed up with all this people move. Look up road onto Eden Street. More people. Colours, electric between, and ... tell you what ... let's have a minute. Come stand by wall.

You are looking over a waist-high limestone wall. You watch the river, and it is beautiful. The sun is behind you, and the wall has a shadow that carries over the lip of the bank and onto the water. You watch the line between dark and light, one side a blackened grey, the other a light brown movement of silver glints. The shadow line looks like it's moving, but the more you watch, the more you see it doesn't. The water changes the shape of it, even though …

It's a trick, Blackbird. Line is moving. Sun doesn't stop, moon slow never turning, chasing after world like tortoise after hare, does it sleep? Sun torch lighting world face, arse, everything turning, turning … wheels, on and on. Jeremiah made Edendale when people life was changing. Big mills some said were devil houses. Said walls squaring fields were devils too. A wicked foot-stop of greedy. Mine, mine. And before clockwork told, people would sleep in dark and wake at light. Spring Summer Autumn Winter, changing, changing, but everyone in time with. A dance, to heaven turning … After that, prison happened. Wake when clock says, not Mr Sun. Sleep when clock says, not Mrs Moon. The quick brown fox jumps over the lazy dog. They found her in river. Her face wasn't like it anymore. Turn around, Blackbird. That woman coming out through a door is Dee Dee. She's been here thirty and three years all her time. She was Rose's friend, back when before. Today she needs milk and bread and we need to follow. Line is moving.

Come, Blackbird. She goes.

12.

11:07. That gives me fifty-three minutes until the service. Eight minutes to get to Childlove's, perhaps four minutes to buy the bread and milk, eight minutes back. This is twenty minutes in total.

Dee Dee stops at the end of Salvation Close and looks first at the church, and then down to Forgiveness Green. People, everywhere. The sound of something being hammered. Snatches of trumpet. A golden star appears against the backdrop of hills, hoisted up on a pole. She makes out the word BAR across it in red dots that look like light-bulbs. The star suddenly falls, a stuttering arc onto the roof of the beer-tent. Three men are frantically tugging at the pole. The star rises back into the air. Dee Dee, head down, moves quickstep across Judgement Walk, refusing the shadow of the terrace, keeping over to the light.

11:09. One minute lost, that means twenty plus one which means home by near half-past. About thirty minutes before the service. This means ten minutes to make tea and toast, five minutes to eat it, leaving fifteen minutes.

Dee Dee says hello to Mrs Greenway who is arranging pamphlets on a table by the church back gate. Mrs Greenway smiles, says hello back. Dee Dee doesn't stop. She hears Mrs Greenway call out Nice day for it! and Dee Dee turns to look behind herself without actually looking, sings Isn't it! and on she goes, turning left up Grace Street.

11:10 ... 11. On schedule. And when I get to the service I shall have a handkerchief in my hand. And I will say everything with a sad smile when Mr and Mrs King speak to me. And I will dab my eyes every now and then but not too much. And I will tell them that Rose is gone but not forgotten. Wait. I said that last year. No. I will say Rose will always be with us. That's better. And I will thank Reverend Haywire for the service. And smile sadly.

Dee Dee looks up as a voice calls her name. In the school playground is Mrs Fletcher. She is stood by a flat trailer decorated with crepe paper and bales of straw. There are children dressed as pirates running around waving swords and shouting YAARRR. Dee Dee smiles and waves. Mrs Fletcher does the same, as Dee Dee quicksteps on.

11:13. And then I will make my apologies and say I have to go because I'm needed to help out at the jumble sale. I can't let Margery and Teresa do all the setting up. They'd make a right pig's ear of it. And if anyone asks I'll say the same as always. A tragedy. Such a terrible thing to happen. Such a lovely girl. My best friend. They should have strung Johnny bloody Bender from the chuffin' church tower, accident my ... Here.

Dee Dee opens the door to Childlove's shop, the doorbell ringing a single ring as she glances behind her down onto Gospel Road, where flat-back trucks and tractors with trailers stand decorated for parade, people in bright colours and fancy dress milling around the vehicles for as far as the road stretches, twenty years, bread and milk, close the door.

13.

I'm sorry, Blackbird. Don't step away. Story needs to tell. Nothing like a god came to help me. It let them call me bad things. One threw a brick and it crashed my window, glass over my bed. I wanted Mother to tell them stop but she was under a stone. I wanted Father to say it but he was gone for bread and never back. Before, when Mother was getting thinner, she stayed in her room. She went to sleep holding my hand. I'd gotten a chair from kitchen and put it by her bed. I slept too, and it was cold that going night, her hand like it was holding a cup of water in morning time, but it wasn't cup of water it was my hand, no blink, looking marble eyes at ceiling light. Father came in, said No good now, and pulled sheet over her head. Told me to let her go but I couldn't. He picked me and chair up in one, and we all went backwards. Mother came half to us, Father on bottom, chair on top of Father, me on chair, Mother staring upside down mouth saying oh without an oh half out from under bed sheets. Father laughed. Said There's one for yer family photo book. I didn't understand, because we didn't have a family photo book. Then some people came and closed her eyes, took her away. Gone. After brick, people all talked in a big room. Said Rose was an accident happen, that she fell dizzy into river. Trippety-trip. After that, it stopped more glass on my bed but still swears were said at me. Back and forth, brown fox bites lazy dog, carries blood away on teeth. Will you stay, Blackbird? Please ...

You watch Dee Dee close the shop door behind her as she leaves. A sign on a little chain rattles on the door window. From this side, it reads CLOSED.

You are inside Mr Childlove's shop, which is open for business, and business, today, is:

14.

B-loody murder Debbie, it's been non-stop bloody go since I opened up, but like Harold Shipman said, where there's a will there's a b-loody way!

Alan Childlove slaps the counter, then turns to the tobacco rack, pulls twenty Rothmans from a shelf, turns back to Debbie who is pulling a face that says *too far*, throws the Rothmans onto the counter. Oh come on, Debbie, I'm givin' yer my best material here.

Debbie picks the Rothmans up, slips them into the mouth of her shoulder-bag. Smiles. Shakes her head. You can be an inappropriate bugger sometimes, Alan.

Alan frowns. Then makes a face with a silent oh mouth when he gets it. He looks to the floor. Oh yeh ... Poor Dee Dee ...

Rose ... Mr and Mrs King ...

Yeh ... Rose ... Mr and Mrs King ... Bad business. Bad bad business. Alan shrugs, sighs. Owt else, Debbie?

Debbie looks to the ceiling for a second, narrows her

eyes, then says No, that's it, ta.

Rightee-o then. Alan stabs the till with a stiff forefinger. *Ping*. That's three-sixty then, luv.

Debbie hands him a fiver, glances out the window. Grand day for it.

Alan says Luv-lee, sticks the fiver under the clip, *clack*, slides a pound coin from the drawer, one, two, three, four ten-pence-pieces, drops the change into Debbie's hand, smiling. Sorted yer outfit then, Debs?

Debbie laughs, puts the change into her purse, drops the purse into the mouth of her shoulder-bag. God yeh. An old dress I wore in me heyday. Amazed it still fits.

Alan laughs. Give-over lass, yer a bloody rake.

Debbie frowns for a second.

I mean ... you look as good now as yer did back then, luv.

Debbie looks down at herself, smiles. Runs in the family, Al. Me mother were skinny, me gran ...

They were good-lookin' women for sure, says Alan. Tha from good stock, lass.

Debbie laughs. Says thank you. Asks Alan what time he's closing up. Alan turns, looks to the little clock behind him that says eleven forty above the cigarettes. Ooh, about twelve, I reckon. Then get sussed for parade, then off to me sarnie tent at the carnival, then beer, lots of lovely beer.

You dressin' up, Alan?

Damn right. Still got me gear from the first un. Shirt's got a collar on it like a bloody Harrier Jump-jet. One gust and I'm up over that marquee I tell yer.

Debbie retrieves her cigarettes from her bag, unwraps the cellophane. Alan holds a hand out, takes the wrapper from her, drops it into the bin under the counter.

Debbie says Jesus. How time flies. Doesn't seem two minutes since the first one.

Alan shakes his head. Agrees. Laughs. Remember Bert Hardcastle's Mickey Mouse head fallin' off at the parade and gettin' run over by the W.I. float?

Debbie guffaws, says yeh through pig-like snorts.

And then he tried to put it back on and it'd only fit sideways! Alan slaps the counter, wheezing with a laugh that sounds like a broken accordion.

Debbie leans on the counter, snorting, now going *ah-ah* and dabbing her left eye then right with her little finger, checking the fingerprint to see if she's run.

Alan slaps the counter again, the accordion in, out. And old Haywire ... that dance ...

Debbie frowns as though searching through her mind's eye, and then she finds it, raises a fist into the air, snorts.

Alan does a little jog around the counter, punching his fists into the air one after the other and wiggling his backside as Debbie joins in, her shoulder bag slipping into the crook of her elbow as the shop doorbell rings. Alan puts a hand onto her shoulder. They stop. Look at each other. Grin. And then in chorus both yelp: PUNCHIN' MRS FERGUSON in the FACE! Now they are both face down on the counter, gasping for breath. Debbie now going *ah-ah* God she was an old cow anyway. Alan slap-slap-slapping the polished wood.

A voice behind them says Alright there?

Alan and Debbie stand up straight, turn, see Michael Goodman stood behind them with a can of Fanta, smiling. Alan play slaps him on the arm. Debbie looks to her bag hung in the crook of her elbow, pulling the strap back over her shoulder, the unlit cigarette still in her hand, saying nothing as she looks into her bag for her lighter.

Alan grins at Michael. Just on about Reverend Haywire's dance moves, lad. Alan punches the air. Michael smiles, says Ah yeh, nods.

Debbie shuffles past them, calls See you later then, Alan.

Alan returns to his place behind the counter as Michael puts the Fanta down by the little green Polo dispenser.

Owt else, lad? asks Alan, poking the price of the pop into the till.

Michael follows the line of the spirits shelf to the cubby-hole that houses a microwave. Got any cheese pasties in, Al?

Alan points to the aisle behind Michael. The finest cheese pasties in Derbyshire, lad. Nay, the universe.

Michael turns and walks the short distance to the bread and pasty shelves. Alan looks him up and down, realising Michael is wearing green nylon flares, a purple wide-collared nylon shirt, and looking down to Michael's feet, a pair of brown leather boots with two-inch heels. He laughs. Michael, cheese pasty in hand, turns back to the counter to see Alan waving a finger up and down in elaborate strokes in his direction as the shop-door bell rings.

I see I've got me some stiff competition, lad.

Michael puts the pasty on the counter. Looks down at

himself. Smiles, nods.

Alan waits a moment for Michael to ask him what he's wearing for the carnival but Michael doesn't. He just stares at the pasty.

Want it heatin' up, lad?

Please, Alan.

Alan puts the pasty into the microwave, says something about the wonders of modern technology, how in ten years you'll be able to get hot sausage rolls and women from a computer, asks Michael if he's going to be strutting his stuff tonight.

Michael doesn't reply. Michael is looking to the sound of the voices coming from the back of the shop.

Alan prods the price of the pasty into the till. That it, lad?

Michael twitches. Turns back to the counter. Says yeh, looks at the total lit in little green lights on the till window, places the pocket-fished two pound coins into the outstretched palm of Alan Childlove.

Alan drops the coins into the till drawer, mildly irritated that Michael doesn't appreciate his jokes.

Michael watches the coins drop, very irritated that Childlove insists on calling him lad even though he's thirty-fucking-nine years old, irritated by the slow hum of the microwave, irritated by the wasp of right things to say that buzzes round his head and won't stay still long enough for him to find the right things to be said, because if that fucking pasty doesn't hurry up he's going to have to … MR GOODMAN!

Michael turns in seeming surprise even though he already knows who it is. Natalie Grant. Tom Watkins. Sarah. The wasp pops into a sparkly puff of dust.

Natalie grins, says Nice gear, Mr Goodman. Tom nods, half-smiles. Sarah just looks at him, her face expressionless, a straighter than straight hello returning when Michael says Oh hello you three.

The puff of wasp drops to the lino in a slow brown dust.

Michael tells them they all look great, their outfits very '79 … great … Natalie getting an up and down. Wow, yeh. Tom getting a Nice shirt I used to have one like that, to which Tom says he pinched from his dad ha-ha, *cunt*, and Sarah, who looks so beautiful, so …

And he could take her face in his hands and kiss her here and now, to tell her she was wrong to call it done, and to hell with that promise of keeping it all in. And to hell with everyone, with himself and every last thing he's ever known, because nothing of anything matters other than this. And she blinks, not replying to his bumble of Nice blouse, him now leaving with a handful of too-hot cheese pasty that burns his palm. And he wants it to keep burning, the shop-door closing with the ring of a bell that says *you forgot your Fanta, you forgot but you ain't going back*, the dust of exploded wasp now reborn as a phoenix swarm of belly fire, sent out to sting that bastard face of that bastard Tom, a nothing of a boy that has everything and doesn't even know it. But the wasps don't send, they stay, buzzing and burning in his gut, the cheese pasty chucked in the bin on Grace Street as home now he goes, a poem to finish, a poem to say it all, to tell her. And there was a time when you saw your life as a straight line, this flat avenue lined with tall trees, its cobbled walkway glinting from a low sun, minutes after the soft rains have ceased, alone, and happy to be so, this magnetic north arrowed perfect, and this concrete mathematics perfect, everything mapped out in tangentless easy. And then you took a left under a glass roof, sheltering hothouse palms that will soon disintegrate, casting particles of green life and glass, this million smithereens, exploding out into an uncaptured sky, the sun some dark eye eclipsed, watching, as all birdsong stops in a moment's tumble, a playground game faltering as a red ball hangs unfathomable in the peppered air. Until all you can see, is her, and the seashell flecks in her eyes, and the ink drops that blot soft, her lips that part slow, imperceptible, beautiful, as the whole stage-set melts into the floor, and a clock calls the time unseen, as you fall into each other helpless, unmade, the maps burning under your bare feet as she pulls away, closer ... please, come closer.

15.

No, Blackbird. Don't follow Michael. Poem's not ready yet. You need to wait here. Story is about to tangle like muddy hair on belly of sheepdog.

Watch.

16.

They leave Childlove's shop with a big bottle of Woodpecker each, out into the sun, out onto Grace Street, an intention of drink walk talking a crooked U around the village until parade. Natalie is laughing, Tom not saying much because sandwiched between Natalie and Sarah he is always the bit-part player, and Natalie now pops with C'mon SARAH! WHAT'S with YOU and MR GOODY-GOODMAN? And Sarah says Nothing, giving Natalie a frown that turns into a straight-line smile, a tiny shake of the head, her blonde ringlets holding sunlight as they shiver around her blush-pink cheeks, the words Why, what do you *mean*? travelling to her lips but not coming out, because. And Natalie singing back *Nuh*-thing ... *Nuh*-thing ... then: Why so *weird* with him then LITTLE MISS teacher's PET? Tom looking down, watching where he walks, a flat back-hand to Sarah's hip to warn of the dog-shit approaching, Sarah feeling it, that slight twist of a tightened gut, that same feeling she feels every time he touches her, now, kisses her, now, tells her he loves her after they've fucked, or fingered, or ...

I wasn't *be*-ing weird, she tells the pavement and Natalie, dampening the indignation to something like a pretend amusement of what the fuck you on about? Now turning the focus of all this towards the school playground where the pirates have boarded the ship, where the tinfoil and cardboard cutlasses flash and spar with yells of YAR! the three watching as a bearded seven-year old is yanked from two-steps up on the rope-laddered mast by Mrs Fletcher, Sarah now feeling the relief of diversion, thankful that all three of them are glued by their days with this school and old Mrs Fletcher, as through Sarah's head another diversion coils of ha! remember when? But Natalie will not leave it, C'mon Sare, what's with you and Goody-Goodman? You were WELL WEIRD with him ... c'*mon* ... reaching across Tom to poke Sarah in the ribs, Natalie finding gap between bottom rib and next, Sarah feeling it, a different kind of feeling it, flinch, and Sarah knows this won't be left alone, so she tells it, straight out, these words that stop this slow procession towards Forgiveness Green, Natalie open-mouthed, shrieking a laugh that hits a cloudless sky and spreads over tor and moors, into the heather and down, down into rabbit holes where small mammals curl.

OH! my! GOD! I knew it! I KNEW IT! and now Tom: You're FU-cking KI-dding ME ... Sarah's eyes still to the pavement as from far away the waft of a brass band brings a marching tune, a sound of soldiers stiff and brave and English, and Natalie hops in front of her friend, STOP! TELL ME AGAIN! and Sarah will confirm it with an eyes down repeat of the same words in the very same order, a steady emphasis to underline each fragment of truth, these sounds made in the air from tongue and lips and breath, as the brass band dissolves after a one chorus refrain: I said, he came onto me after class a few weeks ago and I don't want to talk about it, *okay*?

17.

Let them go, Blackbird. We need to rest a while by bones. Come on. Let's go sit on grass. Two more stones in a field of stones. What a beautiful day it is. Parade will begin soon, and we can watch if you like. I don't very much like parades though. It's a pretend. If it wasn't hiding things it would be something better. Have you ever dressed up as something else, Blackbird? School once made it a book day, and everyone had to dress as their favourite book person. I told Father and he laughed and asked me what books have I ever read. I told him we read books at school, and my best one was Tiger Who Came To Tea, a tiger who ate all food from cupboards, drank all water from tap, and Father said it sounded stupid, and I said it wasn't stupid, and Father said all books were stupid because they made things up that weren't real, and it made people think there were better things in world when there wasn't. He hit me on my head. But after I thought he felt bad about it. Because then when it was book day he said he'd help me be tiger by drawing tiger lines across my face with a pen. Father hadn't been so near my face for so long a time before and I watched his eyes as he made me tiger. They kept going thin, like he was watching tiger lines carefully as they came out of pen. Sometimes, I watched his mouth, and end of his tongue popped out a little bit like it was watching tiger lines too. Then he said done, and stood back. I think he smiled. Off you go, he said, and I did. All way to school I practised my tiger who ate all food and drank all water. I stood on playground and got in class line. Everyone looked at me without saying anything. They were all dressed as book people in clothes and paint. I didn't know what everyone was but it didn't matter because I was tiger, and tigers are brave. Teacher walked down line quick and she looked at me too. Her face said something that I didn't understand, then her mouth said GO *and* WASH THAT OFF ... NOW! *and I said but Miss I'm tiger and her mouth said it even louder,* GO! NOW! *and I ran to toilets but didn't cry because I wanted to keep my tiger lines for longer and I thought cry wet would wash tiger lines away, and then when I got in toilets I looked in mirror. It wasn't tiger lines on my face but words. But words like that sign we looked at from behind and you couldn't read it saying backwards, remember? And then I remembered what Mr Curtis said in class about reflections like a pencil in glass of water, so I took mirror off little book and turned around backwards so I could see my face in two mirrors, and it felt like I was here and there and here, and here said words not right but there it said them right but it wasn't right because words said*

I
KILLD
MUM.

Cry was wet but words seemed to stay ... People at school didn't laugh or fun at me anymore after. It was like I had a bad cold, and they all moved away when I was near them. Whispers behind hands and eyes flick flick like snaky tongues ... flick flick ... Forgive me if cry is wet now, Blackbird. I didn't want to tell it but I had to. Fib words are October and November, leaves from trees that look over Went, drop drop drop into river, carried on and on from here to everywhere, and true words are July and August, green, on branch where they are born, known only to tree and birds who live there ... sorry, Blackbird ... leave me for a little tick-tock ... go walk around stones a minute ... sorry.

You walk, leave Johnny to himself, and as you walk around the gravestones you realise that your feet are bare. Have they always been this way? The grass is warm cool beneath you. This stone is leaning. *In loving memory of John Potter, son of Robert and Mary Potter, died aged 13, August 19th 1794*. You walk on. The river is a long breath, a sigh from the belly of everything, and *Here lies Charles Mullery, son of Arthur and Joan Mullery, who died at Edendale Mill to be with God and angels, aged 15, January 9th 1797*. Behind you the breeze brings a murmur of life, of things about to happen in this place, a music in music, and you cannot feel the grass anymore, and *Rest in peace George Chambers, died aged 31, November 23rd 1811, beloved son of Jack and Nelly Chambers, brother to Daisy Chambers, gone and never returned, together in Heaven soon*, and something is coming back, like the sound of crow over fields from woods, and Johnny is calling you, and the grass is warm cool beneath you, and you walk.

You're starting to see things now, aren't you, Blackbird. I know what it's like for you. Like being in cloud, like being here but not. We can watch, we can hear, but we have no mouth. Like when Mother and Father would shout, and I might say stop, but they couldn't hear me. Sit down, Blackbird. Pluck that dandelion clock from grass. Find your breath and blow. There. Close your eyes. What time is it, Blackbird?

> *He sits in a chair by the fire. It is a big chair. Like a throne. The fire is too hot. This place has no breath. He is without his wig. It sits on his lap. He looks older. The fire is too hot. You feel faint. You feel sick. He stares at you, drinks from the glass... smiles?*
>
> *Sit down, he mouths.*
>
> *You are crying. You are sitting down. The chair is too close to the fire. You feel you are burning. He stares at the flames. His teeth are grey, his lips wet, he is laughing as he throws his wig onto the fire, and now the fire burns hotter, the hair crackling and spitting, the flames*

shivering the throat of the chimney. He stares at you. A clock chimes.

You are a careless girl, he says.

Open your eyes, Blackbird. Come back for now. For now is today and time is parade. Look, it comes.

18.

And out of the old mill grounds comes the first float, Mr and Mrs King smiling aboard the flat-back truck from Gobden's Animal Feeds, the bunting shivering above their heads as the Castletor Cavaliers behind them a rattle of snare, horns lift and swing, *oh when the saints, go marching in, oh when the saints go* ... and he's telling her remember to wave darling, and smile, a pat-pat on the back, and her saying yes, yes of course *dar*-ling (I'm not. A *fu*-cking. Dog.) and up Grace Street they go, the Kings waving at the people, the brass band step-step shoulders left, shoulders right, and behind them comes the pale blue majorettes, twirling and grinning, knees up girls, knees up keep smiling, and Mr King now telling her she was a lioness at the service, brave, brave as a tiger, and she's smiling at the watchers by the church hall, wave-wave, well done Sandra well done (*shut up!*), and Dave on first clarinet hits a flat one, *oh when the* fuck *oh when the* fuck, *oh when the* Low Peaks Kennel Club secretary's Highland terrier takes a snap at Mrs Johnstone's labbie, *be*-hayyve Wensley! a dozen over-pruned dogs and middle-aged women, rigid and sexless and pristine ahead of the Castletor girl guides, Mrs Frengle's fat arse and calves juddering on point, leading a charge of arm-swinging pink-faced smiley girls, and Jenny telling Cheryl she hopes Steve isn't watching or she'll just die, and behind the guides comes a fire engine, and on the back of the fire engine are two firemen pointing a waterless hose, pretending to put out a fire behind them, a fire of dancing Frank and Carl dressed in cardboard flames, and Carl saying to Frank are you sure this is funny? Because, like, I've seen people on fire and it isn't, like, funny ... and behind the dancing flames march the toddlers club, pushchaired and wriggling, three across, six deep, with Jackie Henderson up front pushing James, wheelchaired and nine not really a toddler, Helen Fricker still fuming two rows behind pushing Teresa aged three, last week's slap-down still stinging, Helen's ambitions of leading the group with new ideas and fresh fun things denied by that bitch and her mong who isn't a bleedin' toddler and it's time she fucked off we all agree, and Here Comes the Sun, the Jamaica Five of Freddie/Jaz/Trevor/Jimmy/Lee, the token blackie steel band as Alan Childlove puts it in select company, although Lee is white, dreadlocked, says mon and all fruits ripe far too often, to the annoyance of Freddie/Jaz/Trevor/Jimmy, who only put up with the skinny hippy jancro because he's the only bass pan player they could find this side of Derby, and Lee feels cool when they call him dutty gal, thinking it means something cool when in fact they're likening him to a tin of mackerel, a reference to his smell after ten minutes of jamming.

Way up front now the parade begins to curl onto Gospel Road, the pavements fuller, the village fuller, and Mrs King is empty, except that hard red ball in her gut, and yes she would call it hate, for now, for him, for making her do this when all she wants to do is go back to bed but there's no way out, and nothing in the last twenty years has filled the hole left by Rose ... Rose, you were everything ... all of it ... and by now I might have been a grandmother, and the joy would have kept coming, and coming, oh Rose ... and she feels his hip bump against hers as now he starts doing some stupid fucking come on dear let's dance ha-ha (fuck *off*) and meanwhile behind the Jamaica Five, Eric Kips the scoutmaster keeps sniffing the air, what's that god-awful smell? Bloody blackies need a bath, stinky bloody ... a clatter, a glance over his shoulder as Giles Randcliffe picks the scout flag back up, scowl, the boys laughing, Eric half-shouting C'MON BOYS, ORDER then correcting himself into a pretend laugh, but Jason Tinsley isn't laughing at the back, because last night his dad called him a puff, and he's not a puff, he isn't, just because his dad came into his room and saw him and Richard Clark wrestling on his Spiderman duvet, and behind Jason comes the banner held by Alan Childlove and the Reverend Peter Haywire, *EDENDALE CARNIVAL 1979 – 1999*, and of course the Reverend is thinking of his adopted daughter Maggie who he hasn't spoken to in nineteen years, who lives god knows where, who's doing god knows what, a girl who he makes up stories about (a successful entrepreneur in Australia, a mother to two beautiful boys, a god-fearing husband the boss of a soap company, a good clean man for a good clean woman) and I'm so proud of her, a difficult child, yes, but with God's help she found happiness, despite Gloria passing away, despite ... eyup Peter, what do you call a deer with no eyes? and the Reverend looks across to the grinning idiot, I don't know Alan, the Reverend tight-smiling with the patience of a saint, no idea says Alan, no I've not says the Reverend, no that's the joke says Alan (what?) *no i*-dea says Alan, the Reverend shaking his head mute and confused as Alan rolls his eyes upward to heaven, good god, man.

And behind the banner comes the fancy-dress swathes, twenty-three villagers dressed as a Saturday Night Fever and the DJ of course is Disco Dennis, whose float *bumpbumpbumps* behind the white suits and the flares, behind the leggings and the sparkly see-through blouses, the high harmonies telling everyone to listen, that something's going to happen, they can FEEL IT, and to this onward stomp of shrill warning Disco Dennis is doing the Travolta, this accusing finger that points at the people, and some are laughing and some are doing it back, and some, like Paul Alcock, aren't, as he hammers the last nail into Mr and Mrs Beresford's fence even harder to drown out that fucking Bee Gees shite wafting over the houses, and yet his daughter is amongst it, smack-bang in front of the disco float with Natalie and Tom, and Tom is still a little numb with what Sarah said an hour ago, and Goodman's a teacher for fuck's sake, can't he get arrested for that? And Natalie is laughing, and Natalie is dancing, the Woodpecker doing its job, and

Sarah is dancing too having done nearly half of Tom's as well, and she's already made a promise to herself that she's not going to think about it today, that she's going to have a good time, and that while ever Natalie is with her everything is okay because Natalie is her magic girl (where's Michael?), a girl that refuses to believe there is any such thing as sadness or anxiety, that Sarah should just cheer the fuck up, that it could be worse, that she could have fell into the Went and drowned like Rose *ha-ha*, and so what if the pervy old bastard came on to you, it's good to be come on to, it's better than being ignored for fuck's sake, and is it me or is the bloody carnival queen a bit ugly this year, Natalie saying this as she jab-jabs a thumb over her shoulder, to where the queen's throne seats her above and behind Disco Dennis's pretend DJ booth, complete with its tinfoil mirror-ball, and now they all laugh because the crowned fourteen-year-old Kim Price is ginger and tubby and blind, the 1999 Rose Queen as the title now rings in memory of, and do you think she believes she's fit seeing as she can't see how dog she is says Sarah's magic girl *ha-ha*, and Tom gets grabbed by the wrist his arm lifted and jig-jiggled, C'MON TOM cries Sarah, this chorus now demanding a little dance, a little love, a cartoon wink as the parade snakes left onto Eden Street, get DOWN TONIGHT, down onto Forgiveness Green as the people cheer and the carnival begins.

19.

From her gravestone perch, a blackbird unnoticed takes to the air, the yellow sun to her left, the grey tor behind. Below, the houses and streets, cupped by the glinting river, comes the drifting sound of a peopled happening, a jigsaw music of call and bustle, this boundless sky a blue movement that swirls a turning world, dips over the tor and lifts from the valley an up-draught that takes her higher, this instinct of brown feather now a swoop towards the swarming green below, into a hubbub rising, a warmer air lifting from the soiled earth becoming an easy slipstream, this blackbird unnoticed. Except for that one child looking up, his lips parted with a breath not a word, seeing this flight curve into the near sky, landing stop-still on a barkless tree-trunk pole that rises up through a red tent by the river, the child tugged by his mother from the vision as the blackbird tilts her head to look, down through the roped gap between pole and canvas, into where the light changes into a darker hue of movement and thrum, to where a man called Michael sits alone on a bench by a long table, by a plastic glass of beer, a notebook, the pencilled words, and all you now know is this: the song of all history unmaking itself, recasting into thin shards that dance in the light of this new moon dancing over a midnight sea, the seen momentary, the unseen deeper than you will ever know, unless, you listen not to the howls of the wind, that chair spinning out through a doorway flung wide, the shouted calls of retreat to the storm cellar, because the known world must correct itself, reform into what it was before: safe, and predictable, and oh, come closer, please.

And Michael is hurting as he reads what he's written, seeing her face in that greenhouse light of Castletor Gardens, that walk from the café where they'd sat and talked around her poems, about Sylvia Plath and her sheep, about a sadness too hard to talk about in straight lines, him feeling her foot near-rest upon his under the white-clothed table, not moving away, beneath the empty pot of tea and the empty cups, and he knew it, the kiss a black mass paused in the air between them, hanging minutes pregnant all the way from the table to the garden, and then it happened, and he sees her face an inch from his, drink, drink from the plastic glass. For now, there is a dying heavier than death, for she still walks and breathes, and the sound of her as he puts himself inside, fuckin' hell Sarah, I don't know what else to say, and he's on the college steps again, her, one step above, the sun blinking over the art department roof, Sarah's face there, gone, there, and she says she's made her mind up, that she's sorry, that ...

MI-key BOY!

Michael jolts. Turns his notebook over face down. Hey Den, looking sharp mate.

Dennis laughs, points to Michael's collar, then his own. We got wings, baby. And glancing under the table: SHIT-hot TREWS, PAL!

Michael grins, turns on the bench and stretches a green-flared leg out, wiggles a brown leather boot with a two-inch heel, says Oh yeh.

Dennis puts his pint down opposite Michael and sits, drinks, dull clacks his plastic glass against Michael's, Here's to it.

Cheers, Den.

Dint fancy the parade then?

Nah.

They both glance around the beer-tent. The bar has a dozen people waiting for drinks, the tent thirty or forty people full, with more coming in, as outside the sound of a microphoned voice introduces the first round of the sheepdog trials, *and here's Fly with his owner Eric Stales ...*

Dennis puts his pint down. Looks at Michael. So, Mikey. What's the plan?

Michael shrugs, slips his notebook and pencil into his back pocket, points to his pint. This?

Dennis nods. Reyt enough.

You all set up then, Den?

Yep. Brought it all down earlier. Used an old tape-deck through a shitty mixer for the parade. An half-decent deck sussed in the band tent for this afto. Me top gear set up in the marquee for tonight. Sounds well good. Bottom end'll sound even better wi' some bodies in theer. Got some proper killers lined up.

Grin. Drinks.

Michael nods. Drinks. What you thinkin'?

Well, can't play owt from after '79, but that's mighty fuckin' fine. Kingy were bendin' me ear sayin' disco this disco that, anniversary blah blah, but he knows nowt ... daft cunt even asked me if I could play some Village fuckin' People ... *like fuck* ... wunt know proper disco if it jumped on his dial an' fucked him in his gob ... daft twat ... anyrowd, gonna slip some old school stompers in theer. That owd cunt'll not know fuckin' difference.

Michael and Dennis laugh, dull clack their half-finished pints. Michael feels good for Dennis's company. He tilts his head to one side, fixes Dennis with a mock interrogation glare. Temptations?

Dennis smirks. Maybe.

Velvelettes?

Dennis runs a coy finger around the rim of his pint. *Per*haps...

Four Tops?

Of *course*, says Dennis with no filter on his sarcasm.

Michael looks up to the roof of the tent. Game on. O-kay ... At The Discotheque, Chubby Checker?

Dennis winces.

Michael punches the air, laughs. Get in.

Dennis drinks, a slow smugness creeping over his face as he puts his pint back down. Although ... I've bought all me vinyl down, so perchance I go off on one ... it'll be in theer, sunshine ... *boom* ... but then again ... Dennis shrugs, fights a grin, and Michael can see it.

What?

What do you mean, what?

What you grinning at?

Dennis puts his pint down on the table, puts his hands together like church, like steeple, then flexes his hands, his knuckles making a soft crack. Let's just say ... I have something up my sleeve, Mikey boy ... something that will blow your fu-cking mind, my friend ... Let's just say ... Dennis looks up to the red ceiling of the beer tent, taps two fingers on his lips. Hmmm ... let's just say, I have invented a *time machine* ... and I'm going to transport us all back ... back ... in a groovy ball of fuck ... *so groovy* in fact, that you lot'll not know what fuckin' day it is, so convincing will be my selection of tunes ... and time ... time, my friend ... will have no ... meaning ... at all ... Dennis quick-tilts his head to stare wide-eyed at Michael, now singing a *ningle-nangle-ningle-nangle* Twilight Zone, now wiggling his fingers at Michael's face like a pissed hypnotist.

Michael feels good for Dennis's company. This is the first time he's laughed in days. He's already decided that he'll get the next ones in. He wants to keep Dennis here for a little longer. Dennis is shaking his head. Fuck, Mikey. Where did twenty years go, ey? Only seems ten minutes since that first un.

Michael nods, looks to the table. Dunno.

Dennis leans into the table, says in a half-whisper: And

yeh, it were a bad job wi' Rose an' all, but I hope Kingy don't get all heavy wi' it tonight … you know? Shit happens, and it's over, done, and I don't think I'm bein' a cunt saying we all just want a good time tonight, yeh?

Michael finishes his drink in one. Nods. Nah, you're not being a cunt, Den … I heartily concur. Michael points to Dennis's near-empty pint pot. Another?

Dennis looks at his watch, drinks the last of it, nods, says first spot in the band tent in twenty, takes Michael's pint pot off him. I'll get these, Mikey boy. Milky Bars are on me.

Michael watches Dennis head to the bar, then looks to the table as the weight in his gut returns. He is thinking again of what she told him on the college steps, that it wouldn't work, that it was too complicated, that her dad, her friends, *everyone*, would turn away from her if she went with him. He thinks again of what he said to her, of how it *would* work because they loved each other, of how when he told everyone what he felt for her they'd all understand. So what if I'm thirty-nine and you're nineteen? What does it matter? Love is love is love.

She shakes her head. Says I can't. Says I'm sorry. Her hand now on his arm, stop, his hands flat-palm together in some desperate unthinking reflex, to beg her in front of the whole fucking world, *please, I love you* … and now she tells him that she loves him too, that the time they've had together has been wonderful, amazing, better than anything before, but no, she can't carry this on anymore, it's done, it's over, and she's sorry, she's … SUH-um TAAARMS ah FEEEL ARRRV got TUH! pints down on the table, Dennis thumps the kick-drum wood twice, *BUMPF BUMPF* ... arms wide waiting for Michael to join in ... shrugs.

Cheer up, arse-face, might never ‘appen.

Michael forces a smile. Soz, Den. Miles away.

Ey, says Dennis, laughing at a joke that Michael is yet to hear, the sound of applause drifting in from outside. Remember when Paul’s bird turned up wi’ a spliff and we all went ‘n’ sat over on bank thinkin’ we were Bob Marley ‘n’ fuckin’ Wailers?

Dennis sits. Michael is still looking up to where Dennis’s face was and now isn’t, to where the barkless tree-trunk tent-pole juts through the canvas way up, to where a dark shape flickers across the gap between wood and canvas.

Gone.

20.

Paul, seventeen and leather jacketed despite the heat, arse flat on the bank but head getting the lifting tickles, passes the spliff to Sally, sixteen and dog-collared, Doc-Martined and tartan skirted, who smiles at Paul, says thanks in that breathy voice that gives Paul the horn. Michael and Dennis, both nineteen and Fred Perryed, are playing it cool, pretending not to glance left at the holiest of holies as Sally puts it to her lips, inhales, suppresses a cough because who wants to look like they can't take it, this home-grown bounty slipped from her dad's tin last night while he slept on the sofa, cool.

Sally, of course, won't tell Paul, Michael and Dennis, that it took her five goes to roll it. Nor will she say this is only her second go on one, the first on her sixteenth birthday, passed grinning by her dad, her mum catching them, saying Robert! She's not old enough! Sally's hippy dad shaking his head saying: Jill, we could all die tomorrow, chill baby.

Dennis takes the spliff from Sally. Fights the grin and just says Cool.

In front of them, across the Went, is Forgiveness Green. The sound on the bank is the sound of Dennis inhaling, a treble of *pffft* over the badly-tuned radio mishmash drifting over the river from the carnival. Dennis can't help it. The coughing fit takes him onto his side as he passes the spliff to Michael. Wooo! says Dennis, the four of them now laughing the laugh they've kept in a box for the last three minutes. Where d'you get this shit? says Dennis, now laid on his back, cloud-watching.

Oh … I know a man, says Sally.

Paul watches her lips when she speaks. He wants to kiss her but he doesn't want to look a soft-arse in front of the lads.

Sally senses him watching, turns, leans across and kisses him, soft and soundless, a single pressure that fills Paul with sunlight.

Saw you, says Dennis.

Sally puts her hands over her face in mock horror.

Paul jabs Dennis in the ribs with a forefinger. Shut up, *fool.*

Michael is miles away, somewhere else but not.

Down by the bridge, Maggie Haywire, carnival queen and adopted daughter of the vicar, is stepping down the portaloo steps, Rose King following. Michael watches as Rose says something to Maggie, who stops as Rose adjusts the sash around Maggie's shoulder and body.

When you're ready, drug hog.

Michael twitches. Paul holds a hand out, leaning over Sally and Dennis's legs from the end of the line. Michael passes the spliff. Dennis is soft-singing the lines from Kim Weston's Helpless, underlining his mind is in confusion but Michael isn't listening, he's watching Maggie tell Rose something, and off she walks leaving Rose on her own, who watches Maggie walk away in the direction of the music tent, and Michael is thinking how Rose is thirteen or fourteen yet her mum and dad seem to dress her like a seven year-old, white socks up to her knee, shiny black shoes, a yellow dress that shows white knickers as Rose bends to redo the buckle on her left shoe, looking up as something calls for her attention, Dee Dee Gamble, pushing through a clutter of flat-cap farmers and pork-fattened wives, the two girls now talking, excited arms accentuating the words that Michael cannot hear, Dee Dee hooking a right hand through the air as she takes two steps from Rose, *c'mon* it seems to say, and off they run, swallowed by the movement and colours of Edendale carnival, the tor behind so big and grey and big and we are nothing but small insects, dust, nothing, something ...

You're up, bro. Dennis passes the spliff to Michael.

Sally and Paul are stood up. Going for grub. Catch yer later.

Dennis and Michael snigger as the couple leave earshot. Reckon he's in theer, says Dennis.

21.

Sally would like Paul to hold her hand as they cross the bridge, but this, their third date of a two-week thing, seems to be showing Paul as either shy or not the touchy-feely type. Sally, is hoping it's the former. She wants a boyfriend who holds her hand, because. And no, she refuses herself to be the stereotypical young girl romantic type, more like a sassy savvy girl who knows what she wants, like Melanie Daniels in that Hitchcock film her and Paul watched on their second date, Sally thinking Paul would like it seeing as he told her he likes horror films, his comment when the birds chased the kids down the hill that he wanted eyes pecked out, *you know, some proper gore*, leaving Sally punctured for a few minutes because this was one of her favourite films ever and she wanted Paul to love it too.

Still, Paul is punk, the real deal, that spikey metal ball of cynicism that seems to rattle around inside him kinda sexy, a sexy she imagines becoming softer when she thinks of them making love, a doorway into a velvet Paul that opens only for her.

Someone needs to say something, she thinks. Nothing has been said in the two hundred yards from the bank to here, as her and Paul stand by the hook-a-duck stall, Paul looking for what she assumes is a place to get some food.

What you fancy? she says trying to catch his glance, his face turning left then right. I'm here, she wants to tell him. She brushes her fingers against the back of his hand, a hand that is half-hidden in his jeans pocket. He twitches. Looks at her. A pink hue seems to colour the top of his cheeks, a pink that is at once endearing and disappointing. She asks him again: What do you fancy?

He takes his hands from his pockets and pats his belly. Looks left and right again. Sally wants him to say You, to kiss her, here, now, in the middle of this hot swarm of bodies, amongst the stink of July grass and candy-floss, amongst the hubbub of strangers' voices and the too cheerful organ puke of that merry-go-round, but Paul doesn't, he just turns his back to her, a bleach-blonde head of little spikes, a blackhead in the middle of his neck, his ears a bit sticky out, her finger now tapping between his shoulder-blades.

He turns to face her. His forehead is damp, his nose a little too shiny, the spots on his chin too red, his lips, curving into a smile. Well? she says.

How about a sarnie? He jerks his head sideways in the direction of a small blue tent between and beyond the merry-go-round and a shooting gallery.

Okay, she says, making a slow grab for his hand. Too

late. But walking through the bustle, two steps behind him, avoiding a dropped ice-cream that sits yellow on the grass, she tells herself no, that *he* should make the first move on such things, that if she keeps trying she's gonna look a right slag, a desperate girl in a kiss-me-quick-and-fuck-me hat.

Melanie Daniels wouldn't behave like this. Get a grip, Sally. Be cool.

Paul stops dead in his tracks ten feet from the sandwich tent, turns quick to Sally, says Look! An arm now hooked around her shoulders and side-by-side they look.

By the entrance is a tall wire bin. Beside it are two blackbirds, one black, one brown, hopping around the remains of a toffee apple. The birds stop and regard Paul and Sally, heads tilting. Paul laughs. Wouldn't it be great if they suddenly swooped on them kids and took their eyes out? Sally wants to say No Paul, that'd be horrible, but something else takes over. It's a light that fills her, a light that spreads from the fingers she feels upon her shoulder, down to her belly and back again. He thought about the film at the same time I did.

A sign.

She wraps an arm around his waist and squeezes just enough for the light to pour from her skin and into him. They step slow towards the tent, not letting go, watching the blackbirds, who are watching them, so close now that Sally can see the sun reflect off their tiny black eyes.

22.

Alan Childlove looks up from his slab of ham. He thinks Rose and Dee Dee look cute in their aprons that reach to their feet. He also thinks it's cute how they both stand with their hands on the makeshift counter, a trestle table covered in two white tablecloths, the two girls ready to serve, adopting an air of grown-upness that Alan finds charming.

He has showed them how to work the till, carefully underlining the importance of checking the change, although he will, of course, keep an eye on each transaction as he slices the meat, as he lays the slices upon the bread, adding mustard or horseradish or mayonnaise as required.

He runs the knife quick around a slice of ham, removing the fat with a precision that only comes with practise, sliding the line of fat across the marble chopping board to join the other lines of fat. He likes the smell. The glisten. The moisture that collects on the blade. He looks up as the girls both say in perfect unison: What would you like? Giggle.

At the counter stands Paul Alcock and a girl he doesn't

know (is she wearing a dog collar?) The girl is smiling at Rose and then Dee Dee. Paul is looking across to Alan, his arm letting go of the girl, the girl letting go of Paul. Alreyt, Al?

Not bad, Paul. Good day for it.

Paul nods. Says it is.

Rose and Dee Dee stand patiently to attention, awaiting their orders. Sally asks Rose if she has any pork. Rose glances to Alan who nods. Rose tells Sally that she does. Sally smiles, says One pork sandwich, please. Rose turns to Alan and says with clear pronunciation, One pork sandwich, please, to which Alan says Certainly madam. Alan opens the bread cob as Dee Dee asks Paul what he would like. Alan lays the slices of pork onto the buttered bread, then says with back still turned, Would you like stuffin' lass?

Rose and Dee Dee don't quite understand why Paul and Alan are laughing, or why Sally rolls her eyes and says dryly: No thank you.

Paul opts for ham and mustard, Alan noticing the glance that Sally gives Paul when he hands Rose a fiver to pay for both sandwiches. First the sarnies, then the mortgage, lad, sings Alan over Rose's head as she presses the till keys five zero dot five zero, total, *ching*. He doesn't gauge Paul and Sally's reaction to his quip because Rose and Dee Dee are heads together snorting and giggling and … oops.

Y-es … says Alan, looking at the till window, That'll be fifty pounds and fifty pence please … tell me, will you be paying by cheque or firstborn? Alan closes the till drawer, presses cancel, takes Rose's hand, holds her finger between his thumb and forefinger, puppets her to press dot fifty plus dot fifty, total, *ching*. Dee Dee, stood at the other side of the drawer looks to the till window to check, slides four pound notes from the drawer, and places them one, two, three, four, into Paul's open palm.

Alan, Rose and Dee Dee watch as the couple leave the tent, stopping for a moment at the entrance to look left, saying something they can't hear, then turning right, gone. The three stand in silence for a moment. Through the opening in the tent they watch a clown walk by, a balloon sausage dog in his hand, stop, wave the sausage dog at a passing mother and her pushchaired daughter, who recoils back into the pushchair, the mother smiling a smile at the clown that says *not now thank you*, the clown exiting stage left, the mother and her daughter stage right. Alan remarks on how busy it is as half a dozen blue-uniformed men enter the tent, a splinter of the Castletor Cavaliers, Alan telling the girls to run off and have some fun, that one day they'll make excellent housewives, or shopkeepers, or con-artists, the random erection in his trousers unwanted in front of six uniformed men who are discussing ham and beef and pork, the girls chorusing Thank you Mr Childlove as they remove their aprons, the shop-keeper picking up his knife to slice a thigh that once belonged to a pig, telling the girls ta for their help, to come back if they want to help again, and Oh, take ten bob each from the till for ice-cream, Thank you Mr Childlove, total, *ching*, his back to the counter willing all things to soften as the girls exit and the men decide on their meat.

23.

The girls run through the huddle by the doughnut stall, dip/turn/shoulders first, under and between, around and out, into the green hot space by the music tent where the music pours out, stop, the line broke, the monkey got choked, and they all went to heaven in a little row boat but, oops, Dee Dee misses so Rose's right hand flaps thin air, funny, as now palms meet out of time but it doesn't matter, fancy a 99? And off they run again, past the fortune teller's tent between boy scouts past the dark-haired Norman Standish who Rose has a crush on and Dee Dee knows this hand on mouth, giggle, stop it, clap pat, crab-walk by the hammer bell test your strength where a dad tells his son to give it some, c'mon lad, show us what you're made of, and ... there, the queue snaking one two three four five long, breathe, breathe.

Your cheeks are red, Rose tells Dee Dee, putting a soft back hand to her friend's face.

Yours too, says Dee Dee, mirroring. And then: So, Rosie Posie, are you going to marry gorgeous Norman then?

Rose squeaks behind hands that cover eyes nose and mouth ... Shut up! But Dee Dee doesn't, she sings Rose and Norman sitting in a tree, kay eye ess ess eye en gee ... Shut up! Rose now hands on hips, fixes Dee Dee with a scowl that lasts less than a second before both girls are laughing, play-pushing each other until: Queue's moved, lasses. Rose looks up into the sun to see the dark shape of a thin man she doesn't know. Dee Dee tugs Rose's sleeve, crab-walking three-feet sideways-forward to glue back to the end of the queue. To their left, a microphoned voice calls their attention to the roped-off square, and to *give it up for The Highlights, who are Rachel fourteen, Kirsty thirteen and Gary fifteen!* and clap ... clap ... clap c-clapclapclap go the hands of the people in time to the Rose Royce intro, as the red spandexed Highlights turn, spin, reach in unison with bright yellow sponges as giggling Dee Dee pokes Rose in the ribs, look, Gary taking point in front of Rachel and Kirsty to work that invisible carwash, Dee Dee now flapping a limp hand as Rose says What? and Dee Dee mouths *bum-mer* but Gary doesn't care he's doing what he wants to thinks Rose, but she doesn't say this to Dee Dee who's still watching Gary and grinning, as are most of the faces around the roped-off square, nudge-nudge, wink-wink, and Rose is looking but not, because she's seeing herself in a white wedding dress in an empty church, and now she puts people in it, and now they're all smiling at her, and she's walking slow-step ... step ... down the aisle to where a boy waits for her with his back turned, turning, but Rose will never see him because Dee Dee tugs her sleeve, says Two 99s with strawberry sauce please Mr Wilmot, who smiles at the girls, asks them if they're having fun, Rose and Dee Dee chorusing Yes Mr Wilmot, who now tells Rose she'll be the next queen for sure, and Dee Dee nods, says Yes she will everybody says so, but something like a worm wriggles in her belly, and Dee Dee thinks the worm is a little bit angry, or something, Mr Wilmot now reaching down with a 99 from the van window, the red syrup dripping off the lip of the cone and onto Rose's fingers as she walks away with it, *lick, suck*, and the sight of Maggie Haywire head down walking quick with her stepfather Reverend past the fortune teller is blurred by the flake stuck into it, *lick, suck,* and No Maggie, an ice-cream is messy and would drip on your sash, your dress, your shoes/God, Dad I'm not a chuffin' doll/No need to use His name in vain Maggie, and no, you're not a doll because dollies aren't fat/Sod off I'm not fat/Maggie! watch your language or people will think you a potty-mouth one-hit wonder with nothing else to give beyond this and I'll tell you what girl, you *will be fat* if you keep eating idiot food like ice-cream and I'll tell you something else girl, you *won't be winning* next year if you look like a pig, for those who live by the flesh will die by the flesh, *the quick brown fox jumps over the lazy dog, now close your eyes Blackbird,*

> *the wig a fast crackle of white fire burning, and the fire is in his eyes ... you silly, silly cunt of a girl,*

listen, it's river turning back, don't be frightened Blackbird.

24.

The fire is too hot. You want to move, to stand up and move away from the fire.

After all I have done for you, he says, the glass dropped from his hand onto the floor, the thin stem between cup and bottom snapped, the sherry that was undrunk a little puddle on the floorboards, and you are scared.

The fire dances on his face, a face that won't look at you, and you are burning. You slide an inch or three across the soft-hard cushion of the chair, away from the fire and into the arm, the horsehair and wire a creak of small notes between the crack and spit of fire and the sound of his breath.

Stay where you are, you silly, silly cunt of a girl.

The wig has burned up, the heat is falling, Jeremiah stands in one quick movement, walks across the red rug of his study to the dark brown cabinet that seats the decanters and the unbroken glasses, and still he hasn't looked at you. He takes the crystal stopper from a low-bellied bottle, lifts the decanter to his nose, sniffs at it slow and long, pours one glass, then another.

I took you from a shit-pot in the ground.

He puts the stopper back into the neck.

I taught you to read and to write.

He lifts one of the glasses to his mouth, drinks.

I gave you position above the others.

He drinks again. His back turned. He is still not looking at you.

You came to me with your cunt, the only thing you could give in return.

He puts his glass down onto the cabinet. Takes the stopper out of the decanter again. Pours.

And I, like Adam, sinned under your whore's duress.

He turns to look at you. He has a glass in each hand. He walks slow across the red rug, the red of the fire dancing around his black boots, step, step. He hands you a glass.

Drink it.

You drink from the glass. A hot shiver quivers from your belly to your tongue and back again. He stands by your chair. His waistcoated belly too close to your cheek, the brass buttons orange yellow glinting as he tells you to drink again. You feel his hand on the top of your head. Pat-pat.

And you, sweet Blackbird, singer of loom songs, have taken it upon yourself to begat me a bastard.

Your hand tightens around the glass as he pats your

head again. Pat... pat... pat.

He turns, his black boots stepping slow across the orange glow on the red rug, towards his red chair, and now he turns, his dark eyes fixed upon you, his head wigless, an old man, and a devil is what you see, and then, he smiles, and the devil is gone.

The clock ticks.

Miss Daisy Chambers ... sweet ... blackbird ... please forgive me my anger.

His eyes are kind. They look to his glass, then back at you. He smiles again.

God will forgive our sin if we repent, for God is with us and he is a benevolent God.

He drinks. Walks the three steps to kneel at your feet, the fire giving him half a face of light, the other half in shadow as he clasps your hands in his. He closes his eyes. You don't close yours.

Dear Father, we beseech thee to take pity on your daughter, for she now knows of her sins, her bringing of the apple like Eve unto Adam, and we pray for your forgiveness oh Lord, for we are at thy mercy, for thou has blessed us truly, a gift of Eden amongst the dales, and we beseech thee oh Lord to show us the way, to cast us not from thy mercy, for we recognise our wrongdoing, for we have strayed from the path, from the light, from thy holy command in our moment of sinful lust, oh Lord, give us the opportunity to make amends, we ask that you cast us out not, but to show us the way back to the lamb, to the holy cross, to the blessed land of thy service, where we will remain for all days, for all nights, and spurn the temptation of the devil and his ways, for we are in your service oh Lord, and beg of thee to light the light for us again, for we have sinned ... oh Lord ... show us the way, in the name of the Father, the Son, and of the Holy Spirit ... amen.

His eyes open. His face is that of an angel. His hands, on your hands.

Forgive me, Daisy. I beg of you to forgive me my harsh words, my manner of speaking that must have caused you fear. We are but God's children ... fallible, instinctive, and error is our nature.

His hands are on your knees.

And here, sweet Blackbird, is what we shall do. We shall say nothing of this to anyone. We will send you to a place for you to give birth to the bastard, a place where the child will be taken from you to be given to a barren mother and father, who will care and provide for the child, a mother and father who will have the provision that you do not, and you, sweet Blackbird of the loom, will return as you are, unblemished, living in God, the people of Edendale believing you to have been sent by me to another mill of my owning, to aid the loom workers in their understanding of a new machine, a machine designed by me, their benefactor, your benefactor, and no-one will ever know of our bastard, of our sin, for this is between us and our Lord God Almighty, who has taken it upon Himself to forgive us in His infinite mercy.

Jeremiah stands, and you are looking up at him as

the fire spits, one sharp note that cracks the ticking of the clock.

Is that clear, Blackbird?

25.

Open your eyes, Blackbird. You've returned. Sit down on grass. He's gone now. Two minutes down staircase, or two hundred years down river. It's all same. You've been walking a long time haven't you. Question, question, you must have. I could tell you answer, but would it be right? This day of all days in a day we are ears and eyes, never mouth. It's better that way. All these stories come into story and we learn. One day, two days, a day is a day is a day, round and round from start to stop … end. Angels blow trumpets. So many starts, so many ends.

Look at me, Blackbird. We're same. See? Outside from them. Wiped off like doggy poo from shoe. Look across river at carnival people, quick brown foxes grabbing happy like bite on necks of midnight chickens, handing over monies for a minute of nice. Candy floss, toffee apple, ice-cream. Do you think all are happy ever after? People are stubborn made, machinery born in heads with cogs already fixed, turn, turn, turn go wheels, and for most it stays that way. Happy is grab, and then it melts like snow. Michael loves Sarah, but how Sarah feels it we don't know it yet. And if love will be her story for Michael where will they go? Young lady, old man. Buh. Ah. Duh. Are Kings a happy love? If love is how inside eyes look out, then his love is in majesty, and her love a love for Rose. Not there. Gone. Sally won't love Paul on and on, will she? Went away, left him letter of no not, gone. Makes fib of start, she wanted that happy grab back then, didn't she? But without happy grab there'd be no Sarah, and without Sarah what story would we have? Paul sees Sally when he looks on Sarah. He sees happy go unhappy, of what could have been without her no not ... Trapped. Is Maggie happy as queen? Would she rather have ice-cream? Reverend tells himself that he is her looker-after, that with help of his god he will stop her getting fatty pig and keep her a queen. And Rose? River asks no queen, not really.

But ... that's story to come. Dee Dee turns away from it now. Her happy grab is time, time, time. Every minute a list of to do. Looking at next thing. Tick, tock, tick ... She seems big difference from then to now doesn't she, Blackbird? Some people are like that. But then again, sometimes bad things happen that make change. You're same, Blackbird. You have been walking a very long time. Foggy mud of sad. Heavy nothing that never leaves. Things of want that never gets. On and on. A machine born in head like mill-wheel in river ... turn, turn, turn. Everything else going round and round from that one thing. Some say take a hammer to it, stop it turning, stop all other wheels from that one bad stone. Others try and tell it good to themselves over and over until words are medicine to make it right. Michael makes his poem to Sarah, nearly done. Look, down there next to river he sits. All people-hum in front across water, but he doesn't hear it, see it, inside his head a turn, turn, turn. Blind man's bluff. Seeing nothing else but. Do you think her beautiful, Blackbird? I think Michael would kill for. Some love turns wheel so fast a dizzy is made. Like a drunky drunk. Anything can happen when everything is a one thing.

But. I hear me being mouth. Shall we get on with story? Next bit is called Maggie and Debbie smoke cigarettes behind a tent of songs. Two minutes down staircase or twenty years. It's all same. Time to close eyes. Time to have feather. River run back. We take to air.

26.

I FUcking HATE CROWS ... SHOO! yer dirty BLACK FUCKERS.

Debbie laughs as her friend waves her arms and stomps her feet at the two birds sat on the wall by the river, Maggie's sash slipping down into the crook of her arm as she flaps.

They're not crows you divvy, Debbie tells her friend as the pair of blackbirds hop over the wall, and out of sight. Debbie puts Maggie's sash back over her shoulder as she turns to face her, Maggie's face flushed at the spark. Debbie passes her the can of Carlsberg, telling Maggie they were blackbirds, and anyway, one was brown. Maggie drinks, grins.

Black, brown, pakkies, nignogs, no difference, says Maggie, handing the can back to Debbie. Laughter.

The girls are hiding, between the limestone wall that hides the Went and the back of the music tent. Debbie takes a packet of Benson and Hedges from her shoulder bag, opens the gold lid and offers. *Click, click* ... lit ... lit.

Inside the tent the DJ is filling the fifteen minutes between bands. He is still feeling the effect of the spliff that Sally passed around. The intro to Can You Feel The Force? feels particularly good, and when the horns hit, Dennis raises both hands in the air for a second, corrects himself, glances up from the decks to see a near-empty tent, excepting the middle-aged denimed four-piece setting up taking no notice, and three giggling girl scouts looking on.

Outside the tent, between the wall and the tarpaulin, Maggie drinks then rolls her eyes. Surprise, surprise … another shit song from Dennis.

Debbie agrees, says Whose fuckin' idea was it to ask him to DJ anyway?

Maggie curls her lip, her nose tilting, just. My stepdad and Childlove, and lord and lady King. He only got the gig cos he's doing it for nowt.

Debbie blows smoke up into the air in a sharp jet. *Pffft.* That's like sucking a labrador off just cos it's got a cock.

Laughter. Maggie takes the can from Debbie. Speaking of dogs, seen that woofer that Paul's trying to shag?

Debbie takes the cigarette from her mouth, replaces it with two stabby fingers, goes uuuURP, says Yeh … what … a fuckin' … minger.

Maggie nods, says Yep … another Castletor slag.

From inside the tent comes a microphoned voice, *testing testing one two one two*, as The Real Thing ask again if the people can feel the force. Debbie passing Maggie the can, who says No, but I can hear some fuckin' shite.

Laughter … Pause. Debbie asks Maggie what was going on with her stepdad when she walked over to them, the

Reverend telling Maggie in a stroppy voice to make sure she was at the main tent by eight, Maggie seeming pissed off and not really talking until they hid behind the music tent for cigarettes and lager. Maggie drops her fag-end onto the grass, grinds it out with the sole of her silver flat shoes. Oh ... you know ... he's just being a cunt again ... telling me I'm a fat heifer ... usual stuff.

Debbie spits lager onto the ground. What?

Does me head in. Me stepmum never says owt to defend me, just sits there in her wheelchair like a dumb spack, and everyone's all ooh Reverend yer such a good man thanks for helping me wi' me soul blah-blah fuckin' blah, and I mean, fair enough, him and her have been alright and that, and it beats being in that fuckin' shit kids home, but like, *fuck off*, you've only known me four fuckin' years, you don't fuckin' own me.

Debbie doesn't know what to say. She passes the last of the can to Maggie, who takes it, drinks, squashes the can and throws it over the wall as Dennis mixes The Real Thing into Martha Reeves and the Vandellas. Maggie holds her palms out to the heavens, her silver plastic tiara slipping a little as she looks up to the sky.

At fuckin' last. Dennis plays a decent tune! No-WHERE to RUN! to... BAY-bee!

Debbie fishes in her shoulder bag, finds what she's looking for, offers Maggie a Polo, who just sticks her tongue out, closes her eyes. Debbie laughs, places a mint onto the tip of her friend's tongue, who opens her eyes, takes tongue and mint into her mouth, winks.

Mind you, old Rev were still a bit pissed off from last night when I chucked his mongy cat down the stairs cos it pissed in me room.

Laughter.

He were like, Maggie! Maggie! What have you done to Luther? Turns out I'd fucked its shoulder up and poor Rev had to nip it to the vet's.

Laughter.

Fuckin' hate cats.

Laughter.

Debbie pulls a quarter Smirnoff from her bag, waves it in front of Maggie's face, grins.

Shall we, my queen?

Maggie and Debbie high-five. *Testing, one two, one, one...* Debbie unscrews the top off the bottle. Maggie tells her to turn around, quick, look. Thirty yards away, through the slim tunnelled gap between wall and tent, Maggie and Debbie watch Paul, Sally and Michael, who are stood talking. Michael is nodding towards the entrance of the music tent. Paul is prodding a thumb over his shoulder in the opposite direction. Maggie and Debbie make short vomiting noises.

Woofer.

Slag.

The blackbirds are on the wall again. Maggie drinks, screws her face up, corrects her tiara, coughs FUCK, OFF, to the birds who take to the air, *Good afternoon EDENDALE CARNIVAAAL! we are STATUS CROW! and THIS! is ROCKIN'! all O-VER! the WORRRLD!*

27.

Michael is laughing at the look on his friend's face as Dennis makes his way out the music tent, weaving through the gathered friends and family of the denimed four-piece as they LAAR-lar-LAAR-lye-KIT, LAR-lar-LAAR-lye-KIT, Dennis's scowl somewhere between severe constipation and sudden migraine, For fuck's sake take me away from this ... grabbing Michael's arm and tugging him quick-step, Take me to the beer, NOW! we only got twenty minutes before I have to be back ... Paul and Sally gone off to get married then?

Fortune teller, says Michael, side-stepping a half-eaten dropped hotdog.

Dennis laughs, quickening his pace. Hope Madam Zaza tells Paul he's on for a fuck.

He turns to see his friend's reaction but Michael has stopped to talk to Rose King and Dee Dee Gamble. Dennis can't hear what's being said for the warping organ of the merry-go-round. He calls his friend's name, and Michael turns to look. Dennis crooks his arm, points to his watch that says five past four, taps the face, mouths: Time.

Madam Zaza, real name Betty Makeshift from the nearby town of Ramsdale, is doing well today. She thinks she's made around forty quid already. Not bad for two-fifty a customer. She quick-wafts her silk scarf in front of her face, says Hot, to no-one but herself. Something catches her eye from above, the silhouette of a bird, no, two, hopping across the roof of the small red tent.

The door-flap opens, and it's a teenage girl. One of those punky types. Is she wearing a dog collar on her neck? The girl tugs a boy into view by the hand, says C'mon. The boy rolls his eyes, and the couple enter Madam Zaza's little tent.

Betty thinks the girl likes the boy very much. She can tell these things. Betty smiles and says Welcome, come in, take a seat at the table. The boy looks reluctant. But still he approaches the table with the girl, who smiles at Betty and says Thank you. These two are at the beginning of their relationship, thinks Betty. They will stay together, she thinks. It's a matter of instinct and observation. The signs. A pretty girl, who isn't afraid to lead, to show the boy she likes him, sees him as a keeper. Betty smiles as the girl sits, who tells the boy to sit, which he does. Betty makes the same joke she makes at every young courting-couple session.

It is custom to ask you to first cross my palm with silver, but in the modern age we also accept a five pound note.

The girl laughs, pulls a purse from her shoulder-bag, nervously, Betty observes, the way her fingers tremble, just, as she takes a five pound note from the purse and lays it across Betty's outstretched palm.

Betty puts the note into the buttoned pouch sewn onto the side of her kaftan. She looks first to the narrow-eyed boy, and then to the nervous girl.

Right then, first we must light the candles.

Betty pulls the box of matches from her other pocket, takes a match and strikes, looking intently into the flame as it sparks and burns, lighting the left, then the right candle that stand either side of the silk-covered crystal ball. She senses she will have to win over the boy through the girl. Signs. She thinks the boy plain, and despite his seeming reluctance, must be flattered to gain the attention of such a pretty girl. Betty removes the silk handkerchief from the crystal ball, smiles.

Pause ... breathe ... breathe ...

Let us begin ... (breathe ...) ah ... I see a tree ... a branch ... a dark bird ... ah, it is joined by another. This tells me you two haven't known each other for very long ... is this correct?

The girl's eyes are wide. Yes, she says, twitching in her seat, Yes, that's right isn't it Paul?

Paul doesn't say anything, but smiles weakly as the girl glances at him.

Betty waves a hand over the crystal ball.

And now I see a nest ... ah yes ... a sign of things that are made by two ... a relationship ... and ...

Betty soft-claps her hands together, once, chuckles then looks to the girl and then the boy who seems to be softening.

And in the nest, is ... a baby bird.

Betty sees the girl has a pink tinge in her cheeks. A sign. Yes, she is in love with this boy, a boy who is now staring at the crystal ball. Got him. Betty wafts her hand over the table in a fluttery arc.

A future made by two ... two, that are meant to be ... and oh!

Betty chuckles again.

The mother bird has a worm in her mouth ... a worm to feed the baby ... ah, contentment ... happiness ... and oh ... yes, yes ... the male ... now he's flying across the face of the sun, high, high up in the sky ... success ... a bright future ... my, my ... these signs are ...

A candle sputters out.

The fox is running. The bird hanging limp twitch in its mouth. The moon and stars turn red then drip blood onto the black leaves of the forest. A blue-black vision that's as black as coal but as sharp as teeth. Hard shadow of animal. Paw hard on the flapping blackbird.

Rip, rip.

And Betty holds the table between thumbs and forefingers, tells the girl and boy about bells and paper snowflakes, about a garden in full flower as the fox licks a long black tongue along its scarlet-black muzzle, now retching and heaving, a black violence of spasm as a screaming blood-black baby vomits from the fox's cracked-wide jaws, dropping wet and grasping onto the blue-black forest floor among the blue-black feathers and bones, little black fingers clasping at nothing as the fox licks her offspring under a black shaking tree.

28.

Madam Zaza, real name Betty Makeshift from the nearby town of Ramsdale, is doing well today. She thinks she's made around seventy or eighty quid already. Not bad for five quid a customer. She quick-wafts her silk scarf in front of her face, says Hot, to no-one but herself. Something catches her eye from above, the silhouette of a bird hopping across the roof of the small red tent, no, two.

The door-flap opens, and it's a teenage girl, then another, and then a teenage boy. They are dressed in disco clothes, and as Betty smiles a hello she thinks it funny how the girls totter in their too-high shoes, funny how the spotty-faced boy is dressed like an old man puffter, how back in '79 she remembers no-one really dressing like this around here, all these big bright blouses and wide bright ties, sparkle and flash, like history repeating if history was a cartoon, a coloured-in fib of selective memory.

Betty wafts a hand at the chairs at the other side of the small table, tells the teenagers to please sit, telling the dark-haired girl to grab the stool next to the silk-covered packing box that tables Betty's homemade jewellery, runestones and birthstones on leather bootlaces, a recent addition to her services, suggested by her granddaughter. Betty smiles at each face in turn. The girls are long-time friends. Betty can tell this by the way the dark-haired girl gave the blonde one a little shove when they came into the tent. Familiarity. Betty also sees the blonde one's arm is touching the arm of the spotty-faced boy. They are an item. They are comfortable in each other's space. It's a matter of instinct and observation. The signs.

It is custom to ask you to first cross my palm with silver, but in the modern age we also accept three five pound notes.

The dark-haired girl raises her eyebrows, says How much? Looks to the blonde-haired girl, say Fuck that, and standing up: Come find me when you're done.

There is an uncomfortable silence as the dark-haired girl leaves the tent, a Five quid my arse left in her wake, the blonde-haired girl coloured pink in her cheeks, the spotty-faced boy looking to the blonde-haired girl as though waiting to know what to do. Betty chuckles, soft-claps her hands together.

Your friend is a feisty one … am I correct?

The girl looks to her lap, then back up at Betty with a weak smile, says Yeh … sometimes … she's alright though.

The boy is holding a tenner out to Betty. The girl turns her head, just, and smiles at the boy. Betty takes the ten-pound note, says Thank you, and understands that not only are this girl and boy an item, but they have been together a while, it is something established, fixed, and the boy is eager to keep it so. Betty puts the note into the buttoned pouch sewn onto the side of her kaftan. From her other pocket she takes the lighter, and with a *click, click*, she lights the candles that stand either side of the crystal ball.

Right then ... (a smile at the girl, the boy) let us see what the future holds ... And with a softly dramatic sweep, the silk handkerchief is removed from the crystal ball, and placed onto her lap.

Pause ... breathe ... breathe ...

I see ... I see a clock ... (breathe ...) the hands are moving round and round ... this tells me you two have spent a lot of time together ... yes?

The girl nods, smiles at the boy, who smiles at the girl. Betty sees she has them already. She wafts a hand over the crystal ball.

My, my ... two clocks ... the hands go forward, the hands go back, faster, faster, wait ... the clocks are now one clock again ... gone ... I see the moon on water ... a river ... this would tell me of something running on and on ... and now the moon is a clock ... hands go back, back ... the shadow of two birds upon the water ... no ... two lovers who kiss ... but stop ... look ... someone is coming ... for I will remake the world for you, gathered from atoms and planets, shaped from the clay that yields, that if a god loved you as I, he would give, and all this on the thin strand of seven days, and on the first day I will give you me, and on the second I will give myself, and on the third I will give you the heavens, and on the fourth I will give you the birdsong, and on the fifth I will give you the slowing dusk, and on the sixth I will give you a garden of winter, mute and beautiful, held under a glass roof where cold sun bleeds warm, where I will kiss you, and hold you, and bathe you in the waters of Eden, and I will love you Sarah, I will love you, and on the seventh day you will finally know.

Michael thinks the poem is done. He thinks it says what it needs to say.

29.

Boo!

You open your eyes and see Johnny. He is laughing. You're on the riverbank again. You see Michael walking across the bridge, back onto Forgiveness Green. You want to ask Johnny what he is laughing at, and then you hear it.

Why
are you
laughing?

Johnny jumps to his feet. He is dancing a jig. He is pointing a finger at you.

See! See! You have mouth!

And now he is singing, turning, spinning ... *ohhh I am a young maiden, my story is sad! For once I was courted by a brave sailing lad ... He courted me strongly by night and by day ... But now he has left me and sailed far a-way ...*

... and if I was a blackbird I'd whistle and sing ... and I'd follow the vessel my true love sails in ... and on the top rigging I would there build my nest ... and I'd flutter my wings o'er his lily white breast...

Little Billy Slaney scuttles under your loom as you feed in the leader threads. You watch his quick hands collect the dropped snarls, pushing them into his pouch. He glances up and grins, scuttles across the floor towards Mary's loom.

You will not give this baby away. You will tell Jeremiah this tonight. You will give him your word that you will tell no-one who the father is. You will ask him for one more month's work. Time enough before the belly shows. Time enough to prepare. And then you will leave Edendale without telling a soul. You will walk to Castletor in darkness. Take a carriage to Derby. Or Nottingham. Find work. Find lodgings. Tell them the father is dead. Measles. No-one is taking your baby. No-one.

Mary is calling you. You turn your head and look. She is smiling.

Sing us home, Blackbird! The bell's not long for ringin'!

Boo!

Johnny is sat now, cross-legged in front of you. He is holding your hand. He looks sad.

I had to leave too. Window bricks stopped. Swear calling didn't. Every corner, every street. Dirty hate looks.

I was murderer. Kiddy-fiddler. Bad man. I stayed in house. Days and days and days. Couldn't walk, and walking was my time. Now everything was night. So I went to Father's shed. Got rat poison he fed to rats who lived behind our cupboards. Made a boiling pot with it. Put sugar in it, tea-bags. And when it was colded down I drank it, all of it. Dizzy sick dizzy, fall down ... sleep. We're same me and you, Blackbird. And here we sit, over river, away from breathers. Bridge between us and them. Dream, dream, dream. Between wake and sleep. But this bridge is not wooden. No clip-clop sound of feet on cut-down tree wood. Two minutes down staircase or twenty years. Two hundred. No difference ... but is. And story from beginning of all tells us monster is waiting. Makes us scared to cross over. What if monster comes, push us into river? Wet dead forever, meat gobbled by fish then bones break on river rocks. Then where does soul go? Rose was took out all torn. Put in box and burnt up. Put in a jar behind glass. Trip, trip, trippety-trip. But river being river, Rose is here somewhere, at this time not today but then and now, and if I was a blackbird I'd whistle and sing, time to close eyes sweet Daisy, for time flies, and so should we.

30.

Mr King surveys the unpeopled marquee, turning a slow left to right from the very middle of it, scrutinising every detail of this tented lawn strung with bunting, the edges tabled and benched like a Viking hall, a wooden stage trimmed with boxed disco lights, shouldered by two ten-foot stacks of speakers, between which hangs a purple glittery banner declaring the twentieth anniversary of Edendale carnival, below which sits a trestle table where Dennis's record players lay (checks watch ... four thirty-four ...) and smack-bang in the middle of the stage a microphone stand complete with microphone (checked ...) where Mr King will stand and deliver his speech to the people (of which the half-wits had better appreciate his efforts) and finally, directly above Mr King's head, attached to big black box that does the turning (where the fuck is Reg? I said electrics check at half-past) that bloody mirror-ball that'd better be worth the forty-quid hire from that rob-dog arsehole at Marsden's music shop, a grinning hippy prick who thinks he's Elton fucking John just because he played guitar on a record that was in the top forty for five fucking minutes twenty-five years ago, and next year, Mr King has decided that he will go elsewhere for such things, because no fucking way is he going to fund that fat has-been Kenny fucking smug-git Marsden's no doubt maraji-bloody-warna drug habit by hiring rip-off mirror-balls and speakers and spotlights from a no good …

HELL-oo-HOO … MIS-ter KIH-hiiing …

And turning he sees the waving jalopy that is Mrs Price, wobbling towards him with her daughter Kim hanging from her flabby arm, Kim, the blind ginger carnival queen, selected for political reasoning, positive advertising, a flag-wave for equality, although now Mr King has his doubts.

Oh, hello there Mrs Price … and hello to Kim, our beautiful carnival queen!

Mr King claps his hands together, smiles his smile as the jalopy and her offspring approach.

And are you enjoying your day, Kim?

Mrs Price and Kim are face-to-face with him now, the three of them alone in the middle of this will-be dance-floor, and Kim is grinning, nodding, saying Yes Mr King.

Mr King doesn't know where to look when she speaks. Her eyes seem to wander off on their own accord, the left a dark and drunken half-moon aiming over his head half-under the top lid, the right sinking into her bottom eyelid, gazing brown and dumb towards his London-made shoes. Mrs Price corrects the silver tiara on her daughter's head, runs a palm over Kim's tangerine red hair, plumping the curls that dangle around her shoulders.

She's having a wonderful time, aren't you princess?

Kim grins and nods again. For a second Mr King feels something like a glow in his belly.

And what can I do for you two lovely ladies?

Kim's chin lowers to her chest, Mr King's eyes twitching as they stray to the pubescent cleavage that peeks over the sash. Mrs Price clears her throat.

Well, Mr King ... Kim and I were wondering whether you would be kind enough to run her through another rehearsal for tonight?

Mr King feels the right-hand side of his mouth dip into what would become a frustrated scowl if he let it. He diverts the scowl into a soft chuckle of Yes! Yes, of course! No problem at all!

Kim lifts her chin and smiles weakly. Mrs Price pats Mr King's arm.

Oh thank you Mr King! It's just that ... well ... with Kim's ... she's ... well ... nervous about the whole thing ... there being so many people watching and all.

Mr King is thinking what the hell does it matter when she can't even see anything, let alone a whole fucking tentful of people.

No problem, Mrs Price! More than happy to oblige!

He tickles Kim under the chin with his forefinger. Kim jerks back as though pricked with a hot needle. Mr King claps his hands together, once, holds an arm out, tells Kim in a too-loud voice to hold onto him, and in measured steps he takes her to the side of the stage, each third step marked with a *Near*-ly there ... *and* ... stop.

They stand at the bottom of the short wooden steps that lead to the stage. Mr King turns and waves to Mrs Price who stands beneath the mirror-ball, a tissue dab-dabbing under her nose. Right, Kim. Remember what we said? Just before you come up onto the stage, you will be brought over to stand here, and you will hear me doing the part of my speech that refers to you. Remember?

Kim says Yes, that she does remember. Mr King gives her a thumbs up, quickly bends his thumb back into his palm, then says Lovely! looking to the dark and drunk half-moon as for a second it eclipses all together, now clearing his throat, noticing the freckles on her chest, thinking how a girl like this could marry any three-legged swamp-donkey and not know the difference, saying Right Kim ... I'm going to leave you here for a moment, and go stand on the stage.

Kim nods, moves her hand off his arm, breathes out. Up the steps he goes. One, two, three, four. Walks to the mic, waves again at the jalopy who is now dabbing her eyes with the tissue, turns to Kim and tells her he will now do the part of the speech that happens just before he comes and gets her. Okay?

Nod.

Okay ... Twenty years ago today we lost our beautiful daughter, Rose ... and ... through you ... our friends ... our community ... my wife and I have been given such strength ... such hope in the face of such a terrible loss ... that we ... my wife and I ... cannot thank you enough ... (two, three, four ...) but ... Rose's memory lives on ... and will continue to do so while-ever we celebrate this community ... because community is what we are ... and will always be ... (two, three, four ...) And so ... without any further ado ... I'd like to introduce you all to this year's Rose King Carnival Queen ... (two, three, four ...) a girl that has battled with a severe disability since birth, a girl that despite life's cruel taking of her sight, has been an active member of the Castletor girl guides, has been a fund-raiser for the Low Peaks RSPCA, and is the captain of the Woodsworth Special School netball team. Ladies and Gentlemen, it gives me great honour to announce this year's Edendale carnival queen, the very brave, the very beautiful, Miss Kim Price!

Mr King refuses to look at Mrs Price who he can hear blubbing like a pig in labour. He strides across the stage, down the steps, tells Kim to put her hand on his arm, Yes, like that, and here we go ... no rush ... that's it ... yes ... last step ... SORRY I'M LATE MR KING! And Mr King quick-turns to see Reg jogging across the grass dance-floor towards him, the next step not where it should be under his London-made shoe, and with jerk and twist he is on the grass before he can blink, Kim Price dragged down on top of him, her dark eyes now wide and startled staring direct into his, a hot inch between their faces, her breath quick and sweet as it enters his open mouth, and Mr King is caught between the hardening in his London-made trousers and the vision of his daughter, drowning.

31.

Rose stares at the goldfish, her eyes moving across the lines of dangling bags pinned to the board behind Mr Hopkins, ten ... fifteen ... twenty fish housed in knotted plastic bags of water no bigger than bags of crisps. She wants to ask Mr Hopkins how they can breathe inside these horrible little bags, but she understands the difficulty in asking her question. She imagines the look on her mother and Mr Hopkins' faces if she asked it. She doesn't want to appear stupid. Of course fish can breathe in water. She knows this. But such a small bag. And the more she looks, the more she feels sad.

Rose makes herself look away, focussing instead on the sign that stands on the wooden table in front of Mr Hopkins. HIT A BULLSEYE TO WIN A GOLDFISH! She looks to the dartboard that hangs an arm's length from the little plastic bags and wonders on the possible, of how many bullseyes she could hit, of how many fish she could save from their terrible prisons.

Her mother is still gabbing to Mr Hopkins. The book club ... *blah blah*. The meeting next Thursday ... *blah blah*. What the Dickens? A wonderful idea ... *ha ha!*

So, Sandra, are you going to reveal your favourite Dickens to me now or do I have to wait?

Rose doesn't like the way Mr Hopkins says that, nor does she like the way her mother laughs, patting the back of Mr Hopkins' hand and saying Yes Jed, you'll have to wait until Thursday ...

Rose grabs three red plastic-flighted darts from the table, waves them at Mr Hopkins, says Can I have a go, please?

Rose's mother and Mr Hopkins turn as one and look at her. Her mother seems annoyed. Mr Hopkins smiles. That'll be twenty pence then, Madam.

Rose already has her purse in her free hand, the hand holding the darts unzipping it, her forefinger now sifting the change as a rash of maths freckles inside her head.

Her mother and Mr Hopkins continue their conversation. Last month's turn of the century ghost stories ... *blah blah*. Turn of the Screw another great name for the meeting ... *ha ha*. That story by May Sinclair a bit saucy ... *blah blah*. Doing the dirty with a ghost ... *ha ha*. And Rose wishes they'd just shut up a minute while she works it out. She hates maths, hates it. And twenty times ten pence is ... add the nought ... two pounds. And twice that is four pounds. And if she can hit one bullseye in every six throws, that's ... one go equals three throws ... times everything ... by two is ... eight pounds? And in her purse is ... Mother, can I borrow three pounds, please?

Rose's mother stops mid-sentence and glares at her. What on earth for?

The goldfish.

But Mr Hopkins has already told you it's only twenty pence a go.

I want to try and win them all.

Mr Hopkins barks a laugh that makes Rose twitch. Her mother looks to the sky and says something about God and Almighty, then turns to glare at Rose again.

Saying things like that makes you sound a spoilt little girl, Rose. You can't have them all. And I can't believe you would suggest such a thing at your age. You're thirteen not six ... goodness me ... really.

Rose puts the darts back onto the table. She looks to her feet as her mother tells Mr Hopkins they have to go now. Village hall ... *blah blah*. Cake competition ... *blah blah*. Rose tells the grass and her mother that she doesn't want to go to the cake competition. That she wants to go find Dee Dee.

Her mother's hand is on her shoulder. A finger: *tap tap*. Don't you dare show me up, young lady. The controlled yank of her mother's hand around Rose's arm controlled enough for Mr Hopkins to think nothing of it as off they go, a mother and her young daughter squabbling, the mother's arse looking great in that dress, even better without it last Wednesday after the book club committee meeting, a drive up to Mamley Edge in his butcher's van, the back scrubbed out especially for the occasion, the meat hooks jangling above as he does her from behind with her knickers still on, the pushed-aside gusset feeling good as it scratch-rubs against him, and god such a potty mouth for a posh lass, as plop goes a bag onto the grass, the knot undone, the goldfish curling and open-close mouthing in the neck of it, the water gone, fuck it, grind it out like a fag-end, no matter, nineteen left, and that lass Rose is gonna be a reyt cracker when she gets some tits on her.

32.

How lovely Went water feels on feet, Blackbird. I like wiggling my toes in river. Ten little fishes. This is my best place under tree here. Bank like a little seat for playing fish toes. Don't think too much of that butcher man. He's a horrible one. Chop-chop all day. Pigs in a mincer to make sausages. When I look over my shoulder, back to when I was a breather, it makes me sad to see Johnny swallowing sausages. People like butcher man see everything as sausage makes. Happy only in chop-chop. Trees and sheep, chickens and people, just to be a pennies fatty. But you already know that don't you. Do your feet feel nice in water, Blackbird?

You look at your feet. You say it, and you hear it.

Yes.

And you told Jeremiah you were keeping baby, didn't you.

Yes.

Well, I see you have made your mind up, my girl.

Yes. You say it, and you feel strong. Jeremiah's study looks different in daylight. The heavy red curtains open, a view of the trees over the Went, the hills, the sound of the mill-wheel turning in the water beneath the window as now Jeremiah lights his pipe, blowing smoke in a sharp gyre towards the painting on the wall. You move your weight from one foot to the other as he taps the frame with the mouthpiece of his long curling pipe.

My dear father, he says. What a fellow.

In the painting, a man stands erect with dogs at his feet. The dogs look obedient. The white-wigged man doesn't smile, one hand on his waist, the other on the head of his belly-high cane.

Jeremiah looks at you, and you can't tell whether he is angry or not. He takes another puff on his pipe.

My father made his money in tobacco and spices, shipped from the blackies, who knew not the worth of their merchandise.

Jeremiah looks to the picture again.

My father made a fortune on their Godless ignorance.

Through the window, the tree nearest holds a blackbird on its branch. You want to leave this room. Jeremiah turns quick on his heel and glares at you.

Like my father, dear Blackbird, I ... am a man of education amongst the ignorance of cattle. And, like my father, I am also a benevolent man. Do you know what that means, Blackbird?

You feel yourself tighten. You hear your voice say that it means kindness and well-meaning unto others.

My, my, he says through a thin smile. How well I have taught you, Miss Chambers.

Jeremiah turns his back to you, taps his pipe bowl into a silver plate on the sideboard by the window.

Yes, Blackbird. Kindness ... and well-meaning.

He lays his pipe by the silver plate, and turning, walks from the light of the window towards you. You feel your heartbeat quicken. Your hand is now in his hand. He lifts it towards his mouth, and bowing to meet it, kisses the back of it, his lips remaining on your skin as you fight the flinch, his eyes looking up into yours, the dark middles two half-moons, and the ugliness makes you want to run away, from him, this room, this village, and still his lips press against the back of your hand ... how did you fall into giving yourself to this terrible man?

You look away. He lets go of your hand. But now, he strokes your cheek.

I will allow you your wish, Daisy Chambers ... but ...

His finger traces your lips. You feel sick.

... I declare rights to this bastard equal to your own ... which means, I have a say in its future. So, here is what will happen. It will be just as I told you the last time we spoke, but my ... kindness ... as you put it so competently, dear Blackbird, and my ... well-meaning ... will incorporate your wish. Therefore ...

He smiles. A thumb and forefinger holding your chin like a playing card.

... I will pay for your passage to Manchester, where you will supervise that aforementioned new venture of

mine at my Lancashire mill, for which, I will support you and your child with wage and lodgings ... Benevolence. His finger taps your nose. You blink, blink ...

... And the water feels good and cool, like silk ribbons moving around your feet, a something that wasn't there before but now it is, and Johnny is holding your hand, smiling, splashing his feet in and out of the water as across the river comes the music and voices again, and Johnny is laughing, swinging your arm up into the air, singing, *and if I was a blackbird I'd whistle and sing ... and I'd follow the vessel my ...* he stops. He is watching for something over the Went.

Father said that silly is not what a man should do. That it was for little girls and stupid women. He was wrong. Silly is meant for everyone. It stops normal think, stops same same same. Nothing gets found out if not through silly, sometimes mistakes get made. Come, Blackbird. Let's walk to bridge. They won't see us. You understand now, don't you, and this part of story needs feet. Goodbye ten little toe fish.

You both stand. You feel the grass under your feet as you walk, and it feels different to the cool ribbons of water. To your right you hear children laughing. To your left, Johnny is talking.

When you were a breather you kept asking it, didn't you? Why did I give me to him? But you forgot you liked him once, when it was before. You liked that he picked you out and gave you nice. Felt it like a special, didn't you? The quick brown fox jumps over the lazy dog. And I think it that this silly is why you've been walking all this gone time. On, on ... blame on yourself for accident happen. Two minutes down staircase or two hundred years. No difference. But ... this part waits for later. Not now. Come, Blackbird. Let's do a fun. Come over to tree with me ... Here. Look how first branch is like a help hand. Follow me up. One foot on help hand. Next foot on next. That's right. No need for scared. Up. Up. One more. What fine blackbirds we are. Your branch, my branch. Let us not sing it though, because we need to listen. Watch. Look to bridge, Blackbird. Sarah is coming. See? Look how she eyes behind her. Takes shoes off. Do you think her mouse? Maybe she is. And look who comes behind. Is it cat? Or is it Michael? Hush now, Blackbird. They're coming to our tree, to hide behind away from eyes, to say it away from ears.

33.

Sarah stands with her back to the tree. She looks up towards the branches and blinks. The sun is white through the crooked black lines. Everything gets bleached out.

Her eyes close to it.

From over the Went the sound of a twisting violin cuts the birdsong and the running of the river like everything is falling ... the violin now giving way to a *thump-thump* drum, the words a distant waver of sailing away, and she doesn't know this song, or why she nodded yes to his mouthed message through the crowd, the tree, meet me at the ...

Sarah.

She opens her eyes. Michael stands before her. Her heart is beating too fast.

Hello Michael.

He half-steps closer to her, his hands raising waist-high, reaching ...

She holds a flat palm against his chest, says Don't ... please?

Michael steps back. He looks sad. This is not what she wants. He looks to the ground, to the roots of the tree that elbow through the soil, the grass.

She puts a hand on his arm as the chorus wanes a once living thing, terrible, and Michael is looking at her, into her eyes, and now they're hand in hand, and this is not what she wanted, this is not what she wanted at all.

I'm sorry, she hears herself say. I didn't want to hurt you.

His grip tightens, the space between them less, the voice in her head saying please, don't.

Sarah, listen to me ... whatever it is ... whatever ... I can make it right ... it doesn't matter what people think ... we can move away ... anything ... I love you.

The roots of the tree make a V around their feet. The sun makes a dark skeleton of branch on the grass around them. She tells him again that she's sorry.

He lets go of her hands. He is looking to the Went, and he looks older, she thinks, angry. He turns to her.

Why? After everything you said to me? I don't understand ...

She doesn't want to but she pulls him closer, out of view from the carnival, the people. She puts her hands on his arms, tells him again that she's sorry, that she's made her mind up, that she doesn't want to carry it on anymore, and now she's holding him close to her, and she thinks he's near crying, telling her again that he will do anything, give her anything she wants, anything ... and she cannot tell Michael she loves him, or how when she's forty he'll be sixty, how he's certain to die before her, how she's sorry the pillow-talk that time drifted to having kids, but this she knows: kids need a dad, and so does she, and her dad would never speak to her again if she went with him, her, the slag who went with her college tutor, a man twice her age, a man who talks of giving up everything to keep her, but what about how much she'd lose? Her dad, her friends ...

Michael lets go, pulls some folded paper from his trouser pocket, says something about a poem, for her ... but fuckfuckfuck she needs to go now, Nat and Tom thinking she's nipped to the loo, and soon they'll be looking for her. She puts her hand on the folded paper.

Can I read it later? Please? I really need to go.

Michael blinks. Shrugs dumb.

Sarah takes the poem, slips her shoes on, and goes.

34.

Back over the bridge the smell of hotdogs. Push the folded paper into the bottom of her bag under purse scrunch it up. She won't look behind her to see if he's following, hands tighten into fists as she walks onto Forgiveness Green, sharp smell of candy floss. Feet hurt in these shoes. Her hands now together belly-button high, clench prayer of forget it, fingernails dig in, scratch, scratch, pinch left hand, pinch right hand, where will Nat and Tom be? Hot waft of doughnuts try the beer-tent that's where she left them. Buy something for Tom. Take Tom on a ride. Merry-go-round. Hook-a-duck. Stop. Scratch will show, smile at little girl, toffee apple toffee on cheeks. Right thing to do. Stop it. As old as Dad. Scratch. Pinch. Stop it.

Paul looks out the window at his garden. He should cut the grass. He should get that old Vauxhall fixed and sorted. He imagines driving it along Edendale Pass, dark red and polished, engine tuned to perfection, windows open, warm air a purr all around him as the cassette player bangs some class tune out ... Crass, The Damned, Discharge, The Fall ... just him driving to where the fuck he wants to drive to because he can, yeh ... need to get that Vauxhall sorted.

Behind him the TV yack-yacks Yorkshire news, in Rotherham yeh whatever, and today in Sheffield so fuckin' what, and Paul turns from the window and goes to switch it over because this isn't local news and it never is, fuck Yorkshire Television and fuck Yorkshire ... *and in the Peak District today there is a warning for walkers to stay away from the potholes above Castletor, a spokesman for the High Peak Rescue Team says a disused lead mine has collapsed, causing as-yet undetermined damage to a network of tunnels accessed via the Old Mother Blake Cave, with walkers and potholers warned to steer clear until further notice. And in other news, today in Leeds city centre saw the* ... Off.

Paul walks back to the window, looks up over Edendale towards Mamley Edge, imagines a massive hole in the moor, sheep and dogs and people falling into it as the ground twists down, down, like a vast heather whirlpool, a grinding gear of rocks and arms and heads and legs.

Behind him, on the coffee table, is an old Christmas biscuit tin unopened.

In less than one minute's time he will go sit on the sofa and stare at it for a further two and a half minutes. He will then make a noise that will sound like annoyance or frustration or hurt, a noise somewhere between a sigh and the grunt of a stomach pain. He will then lean forward and untie the string that keeps the lid on tight. And then, he will take off the lid, and stare at the surface of contents. He will never call this a keepsake box. Nor will he ever consider it a box of remembering.

But it is, and it does.

Remembering, like that photograph on top of the pile remembers, a Polaroid of colours not true, the orange hue too strong in the top left corner, an orange of sunlight bleeding across the people walking by behind the canvas backdrop, bleeding across the painted sun, the painted hill, the painted sheep, bleeding across his own face underneath that floppy old-fashioned farmer's hat, stem of wheat in his mouth, the grin, the smock, the shepherd's crook, and her by his side held in truer colours, her green eyes narrowing just, her red lips parting just, a split-second before she laughs from under that white cloth bonnet, that white milking dress, her arm through his, a pretend farmer's wife for a pretend farmer.

He will put the lid back on the box, sit back and close his eyes.

Sally looks out of her window at the flats opposite. Hers is four floors up and this makes her happy. She likes this place better than the last, a council house on an estate on the edge of the city. This place is closer to the middle of it all. And if she gets that promotion at Debenhams she might even be able to move closer still. She likes to look, to watch, to guess what people are. She likes the hum of traffic at night, the sound of things happening.

Across at the other flats she is watching a man look out of his window. Third floor. Vest. In his fifties. Picking his nose, wipes his finger on his trousers. Scruffy git. Lives alone?

Four windows across, second floor. A boy presses an Action Man against the glass. Makes the doll climb the curtains. The boy's lips tell her he is making sounds. Perhaps it's gunfire. The boy turns quick to look at something behind him. That'll be his mother. Perhaps telling him his tea is ready. Her and him. No dad?

A siren from below catches Sally's attention. An ambulance blue-flashes towards the city centre, cars and lorries pulling over out of the way. What's happened?

Sally, at age fourteen, watched Alfred Hitchcock's Rear Window with her dad. She wanted to live somewhere where you could watch windows ever since. And now she has it. Here.

Fourth floor, straight across from her. A woman backing into a table, hands gripping the edge. A man in the shadows. Pointing a finger at the woman?

Sally moves away from the window and sits on the chair by the small dinner table. What to do tonight? Pictures? Maybe go rent a video? Chinese take-away? Sunday tomorrow. A lie-in. Lovely. She should turn the radio on. It's too quiet. Maybe she should get a cat. Can you have cats here? She stands up quick, goes over to the mantelpiece and turns the little radio on. Right. She's going to the video shop and she needs her shoes on. The radio plays an old song she knows, a song she used to like, Debbie Harry telling it again she's losing her mind, Sally smiling because she can still remember the words, grabbing her bag, putting her shoes on, closing the door behind her as she leaves, the radio left on for when she gets back, *clip-clop* down the concrete steps because the lift is broke, remembering herself back when, erase, maybe she should get a cat, can you have cats here?

35.

Blondie!

Paul pulls the farmer's smock over his head, smiles at Sally who is doing a little shimmy as she unbuttons the milking dress. Love this song, she says, taking the dress off.

Paul nods, says it must be Dennis over in the band tent, but doesn't say he thinks the song is poppy disco crap and not punk at all. He likes the sight of Sally taking a dress off though.

Here you go, lovelies.

Mrs Kelly the photographer hands Sally the Polaroid picture. Sally and Paul look at it. There is an orange hue to it from where the sun is peeking from behind the canvas. Mrs Kelly can tell that the couple are a little disappointed. She points to the corner where the sun is, tells them it does that when it's too sunny, that she'll knock fifty pence off the price, and anyway, you both look really cute in it. Sally tells Mrs Kelly thank you and smiles at Paul who does the same. Mrs Kelly busies herself putting the props back onto the coat rack as the couple slow walk away.

Paul, still looking at the photograph, tells Sally she looks beautiful, and is surprised to hear the words come from his mouth.

Sally hops in front of Paul, grabs his arms, kisses him full on the lips, pressing so eagerly that he has to take a step back. They both laugh, because it's funny.

Paul holds the Polaroid out to her.

She shakes her head, smiles. It's yours, she says, keep it.

Dennis is pleased with the mix from the arse-end of Heart of Glass into the higher tempo synth intro of Slap and Tickle, and to celebrate, he gives himself a little pat on the thigh.

Nice work, Den-machine, nice work.

The music tent is filling up for the last band, a middle-of-the-road club covers band from Castletor called Hot Potato.

This lot ain't gonna like this track, he thinks, smiling to himself, scanning the crowd for a response. Nothing. Natter natter, stare into space, blah blah, sup sup, nothing. Dead fuckers. All the music out there, all the good shit yer could listen to, and this lot choose to come see a band that play Hi-Ho Silver fuckin' Linin' ... twats.

Dennis squats down by his record boxes as the singer of Hot Potato brushes past him to get to the stage, knocking Dennis onto one knee. Dennis mutters shit-arse fuck-face, but then thinks he may have said it louder than he thinks he did due to the headphones over his ears. The singer, pale blue-suited, permed, dicky-bowed, moustached, spins on his stack heel, one step up onto the stage, fixes Dennis with narrowed eyes, gestures for Dennis to take the headphones off, sneers: You what, mate?

Dennis smiles, gives the Hot Potato singer a thumbs up, says, I said, ace aftershave, mate ... what sort is it?

The singer looks confused, starts to say something, stops, rubs a smoothing thumb and forefinger over his moustache. Erm, just Brut, he says, still confused.

Dennis gives him another thumbs up.

Suits yer mate. Proper cock-strong. ROCK ON!

Dennis turns the thumbs up into a Black Power salute, the singer of Hot Potato doing a hesitant likewise, a confused look still on his perm-framed face, a single uncertain nod before stepping onto the stage to join the rest of Hot Potato to get sorted.

Dennis is still laughing to himself as quick-slides the Blockheads from his singles box, pulls the vinyl from the cover, places it on the turntable, swift-cutting Slap and Tickle into Sex and Drugs and Rock and Roll. Turn it up. Annoy the corpses.

There you go, pal.

Dennis looks up from his decks to see Michael holding a plastic pint of lovely frothy beer.

Bless you, my child, he says, shaping a forefinger crucifix from his forehead to his Fred Perryed chest, belly.

The two drink for a moment and survey the crowd, both of them turning to glance at the stage as the guitarist plays the riff to Tiger Feet, tweaks his amp, turns and grins at the singer as feedback rings, the guitarist pouting, shaking his perm, Dennis and Michael looking at each other and laughing, Dennis quick-wafting a wank hand between them, turning Ian Dury up one more notch.

Hey Mikey-Boy, yer missed yer song a minute ago.

Michael drinks, frowns. Dennis grins, finger on chin in mock reflection.

Summat about 'er bein' frigid 'til she gorra boyfriend called Michael …

Squeeze, says Michael nodding, pretending not to smell the piss-take. Heard it from the beer tent. Tune.

Not that you'd know owt about shaggin' of course, says Dennis, pretending a matter of fact.

Fuck off, says Michael, pulling a sarky grin.

Oh sorry, says Dennis, taking another drink, forgot you fingered Claire Dibner in the graveyard that time … Mister Luvver.

Michael play-thumps Dennis on the shoulder, beer slopping out of his pint onto the decks, the needle hop skip jumping over the piano solo, Hot Potato sneering from the stage, the crowd's chatter halting as everyone stares at Dennis and Michael.

Do you have Friends Electric? *Or what?*

In front of the decks, stand Maggie Haywire, carnival queen, and her friend Debbie Foxglove.

Well?

Dennis stutters yes to the queen, yes he does, who tells him in no uncertain terms to put it fucking on then, and to stop playing *shite* if him and his mate want two fit girls to talk to them for the few minutes and whatever seconds that the song lasts for, that is, if you have the *twelve inch fucking single* and not the weeny little *seven inch*.

Maggie curls her little finger in front of Dennis's face, who stuttering says, yes, yes he has the twelve inch, Debbie trying not to laugh as Dennis quick-squats behind the decks, rifling through his record cases, glancing up at the nervy-looking Michael, trying not to panic, *fuckin' hell*, he mouths, heart quickening like a jazz snare as he glances between his quick-fingered twelve inch singles and the girl's legs from under the trestle table.

In the marquee, Mr King checks his watch. Six twenty-two.

The Reverend Haywire clears his throat.

Mrs King scratches her leg under the table, the sound of fingernail on nylon causing Mr King to glance furrowed at his wife, who stops scratching, clasps her hands together on her lap.

Sorry I'm late! sings Alan Childlove, a half-jog across the soon-to-be dance-floor grass, sliding himself onto the bench next to Mrs King, who smiles patiently as Alan elbows her in the left breast, Alreyt lass? followed by a nod to the mirror-ball that dangles slow-turning strung above the dance-floor.

I bet thee King Kong dint 'ave a ball *that* chuffin' big, eh?

Right, let's get started shall we? says Mr King clapping his hands together.

The schedule, please Reverend, if you will.

Michael, quick-back from the bar, hands Maggie and Debbie their drinks, the girls offering quick tight smiles as a thank you.

Debbie is shoulder-to-shoulder with Dennis behind the decks, busy asking him what this knob does, what that knob does, a game where she pretend reaches to turn it, then Dennis stops her by putting a hand in front of hers, saying bass, pan, reverb, *don't*.

Maggie stands facing Michael a few feet away from Dennis and Debbie, leaning on the tree-trunk pole that supports the corner of the music tent. Without breaking her eye-contact with Michael, who stands nervously sipping his beer, Maggie shouts Debbie, tells her to ask Dennis if he has Rock Lobster or Gangsters.

Still with her eyes fixed on Michael, Maggie sings *waiting, waiting* ... the call now coming from Debbie that Disco Dennis has both, Maggie now shouting BOTH THEN ... B-52S FIRST ... NOW! Grin.

Maggie prods Michael in the chest, who twitches, smiles stiffly at Maggie.

Talk to me, she says.

About what? says Michael.

Do. You. Like. Girls? says Maggie, as though trying to communicate with the dead. Michael can't help but laugh. Maggie laughs too, softens. Michael thinks the scary girl not so scary, her face seeming different now. He meets her eyes for a moment.

Yeh, he says, feeling more confident. Why wouldn't I?

And so ... just to reiterate, says Mr King, left eyebrow raised as he looks to each of the three committee members in turn: the final lights and sound check will be undertaken by Reg at 7pm, doors open at 7:30, the disco to start at 8, my speech at 9:30, the fireworks to begin at 11:45pm. Any questions?

The Reverend clears his throat. And the queen?

Yes, Reverend, my apologies, says Mr King. The queen shall be presented just after 9:30 during my speech, like we just discussed ... no more than five minutes ago.

Mr King regrets the epilogue as soon as it leaves his lips. Mrs King closes her eyes. Alan Childlove can't help but grin. The Reverend's lips are pursed, his fingers tap a quick drum-roll on the trestle table.

There's *every reason* to ask *such a thing*, spits the Reverend, I thought the presentation of the queen was an *important part of the proceedings*, Mr King.

Well, yes it ...

And just because the queen is my daughter I see no reason *not* to ask such a question ...

Reverend, I ...

Because I would have asked the same if it was *your* daughter, *Alan's* daughter, *any*body's *blinkblooming* daughter! And now ... now you've made me swear!

GENTLEMEN!

Mrs King is on her feet.

It's been a busy day for all of us, and I think it quite natural that we are all a little frayed.

Mrs King, hands on hips, glares at her husband.

Jeremy. Apologise to the Reverend.

Mr King, tight-lipped, folds his arms across his chest.

Jeremy!

Mr King twitches. Alan Childlove passes wind. They all turn and glare at him. He wafts a hand over his lap, smiles sheepishly, says sorry, cheese pasty, Mrs King grabbing her bag from the bench, quick-exiting stage-left under the mirror-ball.

So what's it like being the queen, then Maggie?

Maggie wafts a hand in front of her mouth, says Yawn. Then: Is that the best you got?

Michael blinks, moving his hand from the tree-trunk pole that Maggie leans against, a hand that was flat-palm above Maggie's shoulder, a move he'd seen in a film to show a girl you like her, but this girl is harsh.

He lights a cigarette, plastic pint-pot in hand, doing his best not to look ruffled. Dennis is playing The Specials, him and Debbie laughing at something Michael can't hear, Hot Potato's lead singer: *one two, one two*, telling Kenny from Marsden's Music that he wants more reverb. Kenny, near the back of the packed tent with his mixing desk, sticks a thumb up in the air.

Do I get one? says Maggie, holding two-fingers up, minus cigarette.

Michael doesn't see this. He's watching Paul and Sally snake through the crowd towards them.

Mrs King would like a drink. Head down, she quick-step manoeuvres around a huddle of old ladies eating ice-creams, glances up towards the beer tent entrance where the dark hubbub of bodies makes her stop. She needs space.

A break. She decides to head home for a while, the thought of a couple of quiet gin and tonics very appealing. She turns on her heel, hoping for clear passage, the sound of the merry-go-round's warped organ, the voices, the shouting, the laughing, the applause, the ... *idiot, what on earth was I thinking with Jed Hopkins?* She tells herself to shut up, that he's married too, that he has as much to lose as she does, he'll say nothing, just let it cool off slowly, no dramatics, a quiet word next Thursday, *where's Rose?*

So ... Sally ... is there a hidden *meaning* in wearing that DOG collar?

Sally narrows her eyes at Maggie, feels a burning in her belly that rises hard and heavy, feeling the heat in her cheeks, the only response to this tart-bitch cow-bitch that pushes against her gritted teeth a *fuck* and *off*, stopped only by this cow-bitch slag-bitch raising her arms in the air, a sudden bozzy-eyed jag squawk of ADDYADDYADDYADDYA, Lene Lovich's Lucky Number the only other song in Dennis's singles collection that the queen would let him play, Paul slipping an arm around Sally's waist, whispering into her ear to ignore the daft bitch, you look ace, Michael at once repulsed and strangely turned on by this show-stopping act as Maggie now starts to dance in a clockwork mechanics of something like mad marionette, Debbie now laughing as Maggie screech-yelps AH-OOH AH-OOH towards a back-stepping Paul as the chorus turns, half the crowd watching on bemused when: *POP!* a flash-pod goes off on the little stage, a cough of smoke, Dennis killing the tune as Hot

Potato kick into T-Rex's Jeepster, Dennis turning to Michael shouting TIME TO GET PACKED UP 'N' FUCK OFF THE ONLY WAY IS DOWN, Paul saying him and Sally are OFF FOR A BEER CATCH YER LATER, Debbie telling Maggie she's GONNA HELP DENNIS PACK HIS RECORDS AWAY MEET YOU IN THE MARQUEE, leaving Michael shrugging at Maggie, him still turned on by something he can't quite figure out: FANCY A WALK?

What ... are *you doing*, Rose?

Mrs King stands before her daughter in the hall at the bottom of the stairs, Dee Dee stood beside Rose looking red-faced, and Mrs King knows something is afoot, she can tell.

Needed the toilet, says Rose, smiling. The ones on the Green are smelly.

Mrs King watches her daughter and Dee Dee walk towards the front door, somehow looking too normal, too not right, and Mrs King knows something is afoot, she can tell.

Rose opens the door, half-turns towards her mother.

See you inabit, Mum.

Rose?

Rose, the door half-closed, looks at her mother, but doesn't. Yes, Mum?

Don't go wandering off tonight.

Rose frowns. Looks to the doorstep. I won't.

Dee Dee, over Rose's shoulder, waves to Mrs King as the door closes.

Walking the bridge with Maggie Haywire, Michael feels the difference of less people, no people, except this loud, sexily unself-aware girl dressed in the red dress of a devil's bride, this sometimes scary girl who seems to be growing softer by the minute, now leaning against the wooden rail, watching the water, Michael watching her big brown eyes watch the movement of light, his hand lightly on her back as he leans on the rail next to her, her now humming a song he doesn't recognise, Maggie now turning to look at him, a finger on his mouth in an unsaid shush, the finger now parting his lips, Let me look at your teeth, she says.

How much did you get? Dee Dee asks Rose as they skip past the tombola stall, the early evening grass of Forgiveness Green littered and flattened.

Fourteen pounds and sixty pence, says Rose gathering pace.

You have shit teeth, Maggie tells Michael.

She turns and steps slow towards the other end of the bridge, stops one foot on the grass, looks over her shoulder at Michael who isn't quite sure what ...

Are you comin' then?

Michael isn't looking at Maggie, or listening to her.

He is looking toward the trees, where Johnny Bender sits at the foot of an ash tree, cross-legged, watching, mouthing something like he's talking to someone but no-one is there.

Crazy Johnny Bender, mad as a bag of rats.

Who is he talking to? What is he saying? The shapes he

makes with his mouth …

the
quick
brown
fox
the
quick
brown
fox

… and Maggie has her hands on her hips, saying Well? What? Cat got your tongue?

36.

Ah Blackbird. That was best bit yet. I like that I'm in story now … Johnny breather. Around village, across bridge, onto moors up there where heather and sheep live. Sometimes I'd get lost in time of things here on bridge. Watch water, fish. You know this bridge don't you, Blackbird. Coming back is different though, isn't it? All things change but some things don't. Like these hills, but trees get chopped. Same, different. And sometimes fog can last so long you almost forget, like mice hiding behind cupboard till cat goes sleep but never does. There is no time here, Blackbird. Only on, and on, and on, and on. When we cross bridge we carry only what we carry in hands of nothing, and all we carry is remembering until we forget. Foggy morning that takes longer to leave than our breather days, a longer with no end, and only thing that carries with us in our nothing hands is thing we sad about, remembering longer longer than all happy, over and over the quick brown fox the quick brown fox …

... the door opens to a room pushed by Jeremiah's hand. You have heard each step, up, up, and he is smiling at you but there's something else, something else you know is there but you don't know what.

Your mother was so proud when you told her, a lie to the one who gave you life, your mother saying over and over how grateful you must be to this great man who deems you singular ... you, the one to take a new knowledge to the workers of a Manchester mill ... and her helping you to pack your bag, the tears, the words of caution telling of men and the city, and your heart is a sound in your ears as you follow Jeremiah into this room.

Prepare thyself Blackbird ... for a true wonder!

And there stands a thing bigger than twenty looms, a thing of chains and wheels, of iron and spikes, and your heart is a sound in your ears and he is laughing, now taking the sword-length lever into his grip.

Hail! The Devil!

Jeremiah brings the lever down with a jolt, the wheels crunching and groaning, the room juddering as the drum turns, the spikes biting into the raw cotton, turning, and tearing, and your heart is a sound in your ears as he beckons you closer, takes your bag from you and puts it to the floor, his arm now around your shoulders.

See, Blackbird, see how it breaks the bale! What was, is now not! For I have dragged the next century back here by its coat-tails! Look Daisy Chambers! Look upon my GLORY! You WORTHless! CUNT! of a SLUT!

And the first spike is through your right hand.
And the second is through your arm.
And the third is in your neck.
And the fourth is the end.
And the fifth will smash your ribs.
And the sixth will break your spine, iron shaft that nails your unborn child to the never will. And on the seventh you will walk the bridge, fog, the sound of a crow, ever winter the black bones of a tree.

37.

From the bridge, Michael stares at the water. Sometimes, the only sense of movement is in a leaf floating by, so smooth is the flow. Today, he cannot hear the water, or the birds, or the sheep on the moor. Just the sound of a carnival, an empty noise of people, a celebration of less than nothing.

He shouldn't be here. He should go before he makes a fool of himself. No-one knows. He promised her, didn't he. Is it over? Is that it?

Three and a half months.

He can't remember what things were like before. Like everything started then. Waking up. Different. Full. He didn't even know he was missing out on anything before. And now? Too easy to say his guts feel ripped out. Too easy to say he feels lesser than he can measure. Too easy to say he cannot see anything ahead of him, except, that pair of blackbirds hopping across the bank, stop, tilting their heads as though to scrutinise him.

He feels everything is watching. Him.

Small.

Empty.

Losing.

The blackbirds look on. He hears the words *What can I do?* empty themselves from his mouth. The blackbirds take flight, turn in the air above the ash trees, curving over the river. Michael watches as they circle, landing on the marquee. If given one chance at something so beautiful, how can he accept he has lost? She lost her nerve. That's all. She needs to be shown this can work. She's never known a love like this and she doesn't understand. Time. Tonight he will show her. Michael leaves the bridge and heads to the beer tent.

Maggie leans against the ash tree, tells Michael she has to go soon to meet her stepdad, so if he wants to kiss her, or something, he'd better get on with it.

He takes one step forward, a hand on her hip, presses his lips against her lips, a warm still pause, break, his face now a few inches from her face, looking into her eyes, waiting.

She pops with a high-pitched laugh, a yelp: Are you twelve, *or what?*

Michael feels himself shrinking. What do you mean?

Call that a kiss?

Sarah pulls her leggings and knickers down in one, checks the toilet seat again, lifts her blouse, sits down. The place smells of chemicals. A dull drum of feet from the men's portaloo next door. She lets her bladder open, and is at once conscious of the sound of her pee hitting the plastic. She leans forward as the sound tapers, stops. She reaches into her bag, fingers feeling for the paper.

There.

She winces at the sound of the poem being uncrumpled, imagining the man next door not just hearing, but seeing. Quietly, her hand smooths the papers torn from a notebook that lay upon her bare thigh.

Deep breath.

Michael tugs Maggie by the arm, presses her against the tree. This time he kisses her hard, open-mouthed, tongue as deep as he can push it into this harsh girl's gob.

He opens his left eye, just, to try and gauge if she ... her eyes are wide open, he feels her lips tighten into a smile, her teeth against his lips as she laughs that high-pitched laugh, her breath still hot in his mouth as he takes a step back.

She grabs his left wrist, pressing his hand hard against her right breast.

Is *this* what you're after, Mr Dirty Bugger?

Michael looks to his hand that hides 1979 on Maggie's sash.

Maggie pushes Michael in the chest, walks towards the path down the bank, still laughing.

Sarah closes the portaloo door behind her, walks the three wooden steps careful, these wedges a chuffin' pain, but she likes how tall she feels, her stride the movement of a woman, not a child.

Her period is late. Three weeks now. And she wishes the carnival had a big wheel. That'd be wonderful.

And the first spike is through your right hand.

She stops dead in her tracks, looks up to the tor, a slow eye-line across the ridge, the dip by the left hand shoulder down to where a cardigan of trees dress the neckline, the white sun stretching long shadows across the grey throat, and some things are so beautiful they make her cry.

38.

And this is where everything changes.

Dennis pulls another seven inch single from the box, and underlines the words Love Train, O'Jays, then taps the date: 1974.

Debbie pulls a face that says And?

So, says Dennis, smiling, if you take a line from summat like this ... He quick-glances down to another singles box, a dry sound of fingernail across the cardboard covers, there, quick-slides another single out, a thumb under the words Detroit Emeralds, Feel The Need In Me, a forefinger tapping the date, 1971 ... You can hear it, see? The journey to disco ... from this to that and onto ...

Debbie laughs because Dennis seems a fizzy mixture of seriousness and excitement and cute, but now, Dennis looks hurt. She puts a hand on his arm. Makes her face go as serious as she can, says How so?

Dennis puts the singles back into the boxes: one, two, says a half-hearted Well...

Debbie pulls at his arm, turns Dennis to face her as the lights above the turntables flicker for a second, a man in overalls crawling out from under the stage to their left, shouts Sorted. Tell me, says Debbie.

Dennis slides the singles out again. Holds the Detroit Emeralds up by his shoulder, says This is soul wi' funk, *well* fuckin' dancey, but his lyrics are sad, wantin' summat he can't have, which is soul lyrics full stop. Yeh?

Debbie nods.

Now this, says Dennis, holding the O'Jays single up to his other shoulder, this is 1974, a couple o' years before disco kicks off big style, but the thing is, it's already happenin', you know? It's just that we're not gettin' it yet cos it's in New York 'n' stuff, yeh?

Debbie nods, says Yeh.

But. It's in the lyrics, Debs.

Debbie smiles, but hopes he doesn't keep calling her that. What do you mean? she says, tilting her head to one side to underline her interest.

Dennis eclipses the two singles together in front of his face, comes out from behind, grinning.

The O'Jays is well fuckin' dancey, but the lyrics are about stuff you *can have*, yer know, love 'n' stuff, like, soul was all boo hoo can't have her, and disco ... Dennis quick-turns, puts the singles onto the mixer, stoops and fingers the twelve inch box, slides out another record, stands up, holds it next to his big grin face, and Debbie can't help but laugh, and this is alright because now Dennis is laughing too.

Nineteen-seventy-fuckin-six ... just three years ago,

Debs ... You + Me = Love, The Undisputed Truth, an' she's tellin' him they're gonna gerrit on ... right here, *right now*, cos yesterday don't matter an' tomorrow don't mean shit, so yeh, let's gerrit on cos now is now is NOW! And THAT, ladies and gentlemen ... is ... DISCO!

Dennis hands Debbie the record, bows, Debbie clapping her hands and flapping the record, Dennis now soft-grabbing her hand, taking The Undisputed Truth from her.

Careful lass, big tune that ... hard to find.

All set up there, Dennis?

Dennis and Debbie turn as one to see Mr King stood in front of the stage, rubbing his hands together, now palms out like a cheesy Jesus.

Yeh, says Dennis, as Mr King nods, gives Dennis a wink and a thumbs-up, turns and walks across the grass dance-floor towards the entrance.

Dennis looks at You + Me = Love, says It's gonna happen tonight (Debbie thinking What is?) Dennis now sliding the vinyl out of the sleeve, blowing a speck of dust out of the groove: Goin' down big style ... bang.

Michael opens the flap to the marquee and sees Dennis on the stage behind his decks. He watches for a moment as his friend holds the headphones to one ear, presses something, puts the headphones onto the trestle table. Dennis looks up, squints, waves his friend on.

Alreyt Mikey-Boy.

Michael raises an arm, walks across the grass dance-floor towards the stage.

How's it goin' Den?

Alreyt. Proper lookin' forward to this. Nothin' beyond 1979 … it's like the world ended, Mikey … Brilliant.

Michael stops, looks down at his trousers, shoes, says Yeh, mumbles something about partying like it's nineteen …

A-ah, says Dennis, jumping off the stage onto the grass. That's Prince from '82. Verboten.

Dennis waggles a finger in front of Michael's face. Tonight, my friend … we are entering the Twilight Zone … The year is 1979, and you and I shall drink beer an' wiggle our arses like two nineteen-year-old love-stud disco gods … Okay?

Dennis puts an arm around Michael's shoulder, turning him around to face the exit.

Whatever yer think yer know, forget it. Back is now forward, the past is present, and the prize is beer 'n' fanny, or death. Now go fetch me the first of them requirements, my dear, the other two we can suss out later. Reyt. I'm gonna play some music. Fetch.

39.

Listen, Blackbird. Church clock sings for half gone seven. A sound not heard by most on Forgiveness Green, but if you were that blackbird up there, up, up, as high as tor, you might have heard this sound of bell louder than all other sounds. Time. And look … look how sun begins to leave. Remember? Hides behind tor bringing night too soon quick like someone blew bed candle out. We have met all people that matter to story now, and I told you what I know, so maybe you'll remember. Seems a long time long from morning, doesn't it Blackbird. One day, twenty years, two-hundred years, it's all same. Like you, I've been walking. And when no-one speaks to you, all you can do is listen, watch. Do you think me a fib because I told you I never was mouth? It was trick meant well, so you'd learn watch and listen. In fog you walked alone. On and on. Only yourself to hear, words, words, words, that aren't words but things inside, said in head like church bell sing in tower but never ding-dongs outside. Song needs mouth to get out. How can anyone hear sing if behind brick it stops? Can't. People always believe themselves to be truth-telling to themselves because why would they fib to themselves? It makes truth like a bee in jam-jar. Here is bee, buzzy buzz real, look ... but bee isn't living in jam-jar. It lives in meadow with flower and hive and other bees. A bee in jam-jar is not truth. It is death. Like me drinking Father's rat-poison. Like Father writing bad words on my face and telling me tiger-stripes. Like you telling you that spikes were your fault, that making baby was your fault, that baby not being born is your fault, like them saying I ...

Sorry, Blackbird. That isn't what needs here. We have other things to see and hear before any of that sings ... Once upon a time there was a village called Edendale, and some people were good and some people were bad and some people were inbetween. Do we know who is what yet? I don't think we do. I have been walking long time, and what I see is people are like those Christmas crackers Mother once brought home. She said each one has something different inside, and our game was surprise. Snap, snap. Snap, snap. Snap. This one a little red car, this one a spinning top, this one a needle and thread, this one a quick brown fox, this one a drowning girl, this one a little red car. That means they're not all different, I told her. Yes, she said. Sometimes things happen again, she said. Snap, snap. Snap. Remember when I told about a mirror to see words read right in another mirror? Remember, Blackbird?

You think it, and then you hear it.

Yes.

Johnny touches your cheek, smiles.

In front and backward ran a river of me, and me myself, there in middle. And it felt like I was there and here and there and ... I was happening over and over and over and only when I looked away did it stop. Time ... But. That's like bee in jam-jar. I say it in story so I see it again, but really it isn't here. See? Snap. Snap ...

Oh Blackbird. What a puzzle all this sings. Maybe we shouldn't think too hard about it. Maybe we should just sit and watch now like it's a sing-song show. Would you like that?

Here, take my hand, Daisy. Close eyes. Our story is short, village falling into shadow too soon, but way to midnight a dance happen until clock stops, tick-tock, and some people will dance it and some people will not, and sky will light up with fire and dying will happen, this one a little red car, this one a spinning top, this one a needle and thread. Watch. Four angels are coming. A mouse, a cat. And our game, sweet Blackbird, is surprise.

40.

Into a funk of love song teach and repeat, Michael, a plastic pint in each hand, enters the sparsely-populated marquee filled with the fuzz guitar of Jackson Five, glancing to his right where Maggie is stood with the Reverend, along with a grinning Alan Childlove and a sombre-looking Mr King, Maggie now seeing Michael looking, the chorus of child telling how simple a boy plus girl should be, ABC, easy as Maggie now raising her left eyebrow as though to say: Well?

Michael turns his gaze to the stage, not too sure what the situation is with this girl, the pair of them walking back from over the bridge only a short while ago, her scornful laughter still ringing even though she'd then become that softer version on their minutes-long journey towards the marquee, holding his hand, Come see me in a bit, yeh? that warm kiss on his cheek the surprise b-side to an iffy hit single.

Michael side-steps Rose and Dee Dee with a wink, the only two people daring to dance just one record in, Rose giving Michael a little wave, Michael mirroring, Dee Dee stopping her wiggle-hop dance to lean forward, hand cupping her mouth as she says something only Rose can hear, nod, Michael now mounting the stage having steered both him and the pint-pots through a huddle of majorettes, realising as he hands Dennis his beer that he hasn't got Debbie one in, but Debbie doesn't seem to mind, giving Michael a smile and a cute finger wave as Dennis hands Debbie his drink and slips the headphones on, finds the kick-in point of the next track, both Michael and Debbie watching as Dennis rolls the light-catching vinyl back then forward with a single finger ... *there* ... starts it turning, switching the faders one up/one down, the sudden stab of trumpets a *one* ... *one two* ... *threeee* ... punching through the fading angel yelps of the Jackson Five as the Harlem Shuffle's belly of bass and reverb-fat kettle-drum *ba-hooms* out the stacks and into the mirror-balled marquee, the outdoor light slow-quickening to a deeper dark as the last of the sun begins to slip behind the tor, the inside blink of red/green/yellow/blue blanching more obvious as a galaxy of white stars turn, freckling the marquee walls like a universe captured, bagged up by some unseen inquisitive god, an almighty decree to see just what would happen if all things were put together into one small space, forced to confront each other with all secrets exposed, and Michael and Dennis and Debbie a slap-mute-clatter of high-fives, Michael shout-telling Dennis that THAT ... was FU-cking ... ACE!

Rose and Dee Dee exchange frowns. They don't know this

one. Dee Dee slows, arms still angled out like a marionette dangling. Rose is feeling the bass in the bottom of her belly, and it feels like an invisible hand is pulling her under. The girls stop to a hesitant pause as a dozen majorettes surround them, making the right moves, laughing as shoulders, hips, feet, swing and step-step bang on the beat. Dee Dee shrugs. Rose glances behind her and sees her mother stood talking to her father and Mr Childlove, the Reverend and Maggie Haywire, who nods at something Rose can't hear.

Maggie sees her looking, blobs her tongue out, winks.

Rose pulls Dee Dee's arm and they head for the exit, dodging the bodies coming in as out they go, the lights of the stalls and merry-go-round flickering in Edendale's premature nightfall. The air is cooler out here. They walk, not speaking for a minute, each playing a game of look normal, look normal, now stopping on a patch of open grass between the hotdog van and the Castletor Animal Rescue tombola stall as the excitement of criminal plot rises. The girls face each other. Grin. Rose grabs both of Dee Dee's hands.

Fourteen pounds and sixty pence, Rose whispers.

Dee Dee nods excitedly.

Ready? Rose says, looking hard into Dee Dee's eyes.

Yes, says Dee Dee. And off they run.

Into a funk of love song teach and repeat, Michael, a plastic pint in each hand, approaches the marquee entrance, that fuzz guitar cajoling, but seeing Debbie Foxglove amongst a clutter of people at the entrance he decides to pause, letting the small group go inside, ABC, easy as because he doesn't want a repeat of that fuck-awkwardness in Childlove's shop earlier.

He takes a sip of his beer, watches as Debbie disappears into the marquee chatting with some scruffy white gadge in dreadlocks.

Okay, go.

Inside, Michael pauses again, smiles as he sees Dennis onstage behind the decks doing a robot half-dance to the Jackson Five. The mirror-ball turns, casting a movement of starlight around the marquee, onto the walls of the tent, onto the benches and tables, onto the grass dance-floor, the canvas ceiling, onto the few dozen people already in here. Sarah's not. He knows this, seeing her in the bar ten minutes ago with Natalie and that boy. Time. Eyes fixed ahead of him, Michael walks across the grass dance-floor, under the mirror-ball towards the stage as a *one ... one two ... threeee* of horns punch Bob and Earl through the fading Jackson Five, and for a moment, just, he feels a rush of certainty, an assured walk towards an unstoppable fate fuck-begging to become, a happening birthed from strut and iron.

Killer.

Fucking.

Track.

Debbie watches Michael over Lee's shoulder. Lee is saying something about water signs and their compatibility with earth signs but she isn't really listening him. She watches

Michael climb the steps up onto the stage, handing a drink to Dennis.

Do you wanna dance, baby?

Debbie twitches in her seat, refocuses on Lee across the table. Sorry?

I said, do you wanna dance?

Debbie is regretting this date already. It's only half an hour in and the hours ahead seem to stretch out forever, just like that hike up Kinder Scout with that bearded veggie bore Liam last summer. Why does she always end up with middle-aged fuckarse hippies?

No, Lee. Not yet. Later perhaps?

Lee strokes one of his blonde dreadlocks, smiles, nods, says Sure … easy baby.

Debbie knows she won't survive this unless she says something.

Lee?

Yeh, baby.

Can you not call me baby, please?

A flicker of tittering skits around the long wooden table, the rest of the Jamaica Five and their wives and girlfriends all listening in. Lee casually strokes his goatee, tells her Sure, easy, all fruits ripe, then asks Debbie what star sign she is. The wave of laughter almost shakes the table. Debbie stands up saying she needs the loo, pulls a tight smile at the Jamaica Five entourage, turns and walks towards the entrance, telling herself over and over *be nice be nice don't be racist be nice* … side-stepping Paul Alcock's daughter and her friends, Hey Sarah … yer dad comin' down?

Sarah shrugs, the bagged goldfish in her left hand tilting, the half-drunk plastic pint of cider doing likewise in her right.

Don't know, Debbie ... probably not.

Debbie quick-smiles at Tom and Natalie as the bodies entering the tent give her an excuse to move on and out the way.

Sarah, Tom and Natalie, walk into the starlight, glancing around to suss a table, the marquee a third full and filling, the crackle of happening palpable. Natalie elbows Sarah, says There! pointing to a bench halfway down the right-hand side, and off she leads, Tom following, Sarah not so sure, the sight of Michael on the stage too close, the song singing its end with a fading insistence to shake, as now these firm-struck keys open up into another song, a punch-groove of telling off, him telling her that she shouldn't give it to that other boy, she shouldn't, Sarah's eyes now fixed on the goldfish dangling ahead of her in its little plastic bag, a sudden jerk as her right shoe tilts on a bump in the grass, *fuckfuckfuck* keep calm nothing's happened keep walking, keep walking ...

Michael sees her, there, and for a moment the world tilts again as Tom now drapes an arm around her, now kisses her on the cheek as she sits down, smiles, holds a bagged goldfish to the boy's face, and BAY-BEE! LUV! really URTS! wi-OUT! you-HOOO! Michael now flinching from Dennis's yelled chorus into his ear, Dennis pulling a sad fat bottom lip baby face because Michael isn't joining in.

What's up, Mikey boy?

Nowt.

Hey, Mikey.

What?

Notice anything about the tracks I've played so far?

Michael drinks, shrugs.

Like … ring any bells?

Michael frowns. You've lost me, Den.

Dennis pulls a tatty notebook out from under the decks. Flaps it in front of Michael's face. Michael flinches as though attacked by a blackbird.

Be-HOLD! THIS … is me SET-LIST from NINETEEN-SEVENTY fuckin' NINE! AND … WHAT YOU'VE been LISTENIN' TO … is … EX-ACTLY what I PLAYED … that FIRST … FUCKIN' … GIG! Dennis freezes open-mouthed and wide-eyed, jazz hands now making a disco-lit red and green minstrel as the notebook blackbird attacks again: IT'S a FUCKIN' TIME maCHINE, LAD! and Michael cannot help but laugh as they chink pint-pots, Dennis now putting his drink down, glancing at the notebook, squatting down and fingering through one of his record cases, shout-speaking something about SLIPPIN' SUMMAT DIFF'RENT IN IF NEEDED … JUST IN CASE WE NEED A LEFT-TURN, these last words lost on Michael as now he watches Sarah who's caught his look, feeling something she doesn't quite know what, a something that she doesn't want to know what, and on stage Dennis slips his headphones to one side and tells Michael it's time to get these fuckers dancing, the mirror-ball stars turning, turning, turning upon the dark walls of the marquee, and Sarah is telling Natalie and Tom that she isn't happy how the goldfish sits in its bag, that it's not fair, that she's gonna nip it up home and she'll be back in ten, waving the *we'll come with yer* away as she stands and starts to leave, back soon, you two stay here, a swirl of strings, a hit of snare and falling bass notes as she walks away and it all kicks in, dark bodies moving from the edges and onto the dance-floor like they're all closing in on her, her now closing her eyes as she walks, BURN baby BURN ... And Dennis is the god almighty of groove, telling Michael he already has them in the palm of his fuckin' hand, look ... and Michael looks as the dance-floor becomes a lit-flicker of insect life, Sarah bumping blind into Alan Childlove, Alan laughing as he does something like the Watusi, thrusting his loins towards the girl carrying a goldfish who nearly falls over, Alan grabbing her by the waist, still thrusting, Sarah pretending to laugh but wanting to punch the cunt in his fat fucking mouth, DISCO IN-fer-NO ... quick-step through the bodies pushing past the boy scouts and out, out into the Edendale night-shadow of tor, quick right heading towards home the goldfish staring.

Under the red and green string of lights, Rose takes careful aim, one eye closed, the other eye looking straight along the dart shaft and onto the bullseye, her crooked arm now moving back and forth slow, slow, as she prepares to let fly, Mr Hopkins smiling as the twelve remaining goldfish stare out from their bags, the pouch tied around his waist holding three pounds already from Rose King, who bites her lip, jerks her arm forward as the red dart takes flight, landing dull-thump into the narrow green of seventeen a finger-width from the outer bull, the girls both letting out sad sounds as one, Mr Hopkins saying Ooh nearly, holding back the grin of another three darts done and no win, knowing as he does that this little rich girl will play again, just like her mother will next Thursday night.

Fancy a go on the goldfish, Sal?

Sally stops and watches for a moment, hand in hand with Paul, the sound of the disco tugging at her insides, the thought of dancing with him a sparkler in her belly, if, that is, she can get him to dance. Did he just call her Sal? Smile.

They watch as Rose hands some money to Mr Hopkins the butcher, who hands Rose the red darts.

Nah, says Sally, squeezing Paul's hand. Let's go to the disco, yeh?

Sally is feeling more confident with Paul now. She feels it, like the hand she places on his hip as she turns to stand face to face with him, the single kiss she places full on his lips, soft and sure, pulling slow back to see the smile, that look in his eyes.

Sure, he says. But if you're gonna make me dance to shite can we at least grab another beer or three?

Sally is about to laugh, to tell Paul how that sounds a very good idea, but something catches her eye behind the goldfish stall.

Who's that? she asks Paul, nodding over his shoulder.

Paul turns to look, says it's Rose and her friend Dee Dee

… Mr Hopkins the butcher … but Sally tells him no, not them, behind … that bloke by the ice cream van.

Paul squints through the shimmer of the red and green lights around the goldfish stall, to where a figure stands watching Rose, stock-still as a mannequin, eyes unblinking as Rose throws again.

Johnny Bender, says Paul. The village weirdo.

Sally tightens her fingers around Paul's, just.

Gives me the creeps, she says as a dozen or so of the Castletor Cavaliers troop behind the goldfish stall, blocking her view of the village weirdo, who now, as the blue suits pass, isn't there.

Fuckin' hell, breathes Sally. Horror film *or what*.

They both laugh, turning to walk in the direction of the bar as suddenly a girl screams.

Dee Dee is pointing behind Mr Hopkins, who, spinning around is shouting *What? What?* as Rose hops onto the wooden trestle table, kneels leaning forward and sticks a dart into the bullseye, a crafty act not quick enough as Mr Hopkins glances left and sees her, shaking his head and saying Rose King! What *would* your mother think? Paul and Sally laughing even more now, heading off to the bar, and Sally thinks this might be the night.

Covenant Bend, Moderation Alley, Divinity Way, Grace Street, the graveyard. Sarah feels strange being away from the noise. She stops a moment by the wall, looks across the tombstones to where a movement catches her eye. Two blackbirds, male and female, flickering between stones in the dim light, this early nightfall she's known all her life, the sky above the tor a dimming red-blue-gold, the space around her grey, the street, this village, waiting as always for the streetlamp glow to hail their darkness for real, but until then ...

These are the sounds she hears as the two birds twitch, change stones: a muffle-bump of music to her right, the Went's wordless song in front behind the trees, and to her left the main road, Edendale Pass, that comma, comma, wool-dull hum of passing cars that tell her she's nearly home.

She holds the plastic bag out at arm's length, the goldfish open-closing its mouth as it dangles over the wall. Through the bag, everything distorts, blurs, as Sarah closes one eye.

This is the sound she hears: her own voice saying fish, blackbird, bones under soil.

Both eyes closed, she whispers a prayer that the blood will come.

The streetlamp above her flickers on. I'll call you Colin, she tells the fish.

Behind the beer tent, Sally's mouth is full of Paul's tongue. She pushes hers against it, gaining middle-ground, not wanting to stop this to say no, not like that, like this, softer, calm down, make it sexy, yes, like that, better. And now his right hand is on her left boob. She feels herself push against this too, tingles, little hot weight, stop, stop, wait ...

Paul.

Hand upon his chest, she can feel his heart beating through

his t-shirt. She feels her breath heavy. His too. Nothing said in the small space between their faces. Someone needs to speak, and it needs to be her.

Let's go get that drink, *yeh?*

She kisses him again, no tongue, just a soft-firm truce.

Yeh, he says.

Sarah? Is that you?

Sarah is already in the kitchen, opening the cupboard under the sink, there, the big glass vase that never gets used.

Yeh Dad, she calls. Just popped home to change me shoes.

And now quick-foot down the hall, up the stairs and into the bathroom. Rinse the vase out under the bath-tap. Fill it up with cold water. Fuck, no food for it. Try the shop tomorrow.

In her room, she tears the neck of the plastic bag open with her teeth, and with shaking hands, she pours the goldfish into the vase. *Plop.* Colin drifts to the narrow bottom, tries turning, drifts up to the fatter middle, floats, still and staring.

Sarah is being pressed down into the floor. Under the house. Under the cold soil. Down, down, down. Behind the goldfish is her dressing table mirror. In the mirror is an ugly girl. A slag. A bad person who tells lies. The goldfish floats to the top of the vase, dimples the surface of the water as it opens its little mouth to take in air. Sarah opens her dresser drawer and the water shakes. Behind her lipstick, blusher, foundation, eyeliner, tampons, moisturiser, nail varnish pink, nail varnish blue, lies that little tin box at the back, a box that once held Easter present toffee but now holds a razor blade stolen from her dad eight months ago, six cotton balls, a small bottle of antiseptic, four sticking plasters, as now she sits down on the edge of the bed, her blouse pulled up, her leggings pulled down, the pinch of soft inner-thigh a hand-width from her gusset, teeth clenched as the razor blade makes a silent tiny mouth that bleeds.

41.

Paul,
I've gone, and I need to tell you why, don't look for me, I'm not coming back. Me and you were never meant for each other, it got wrong, and I can't forget it. Please don't show Sarah this letter. She must never know why I left you. It wasn't right to bring her into this world. I know that now. I made a mistake, and I will never forgive myself. Every time I look at her I feel it, and it's so deep I can't change this. I can never be her mother. Please be a good father to her. It's all I ask. I can't turn back time. What happened has happened, and it can't be changed. I am going away. Tell Sarah whatever you want. It doesn't matter anyway. Just don't hurt her. It's not her fault.
Sally

42.

And this song is disgusting with its disgusting words of getting together and baby baby, and Mrs Frengle certainly *does not* like how her girls are behaving with Mr Kips' boy scouts on the dance-floor, which she now tells him in italicised frump gathering her bosom under folded arms, her blue guide-leader shirt swelling an angry comma comma of sewn-on patches, *fire safety*, *crime prevention*, *knots*, Mr Kips seeing nothing more than his boys dancing in a line facing the girls, the girls laughing, the boys laughing, a trend spreading on the chorus hook-line of hands on hips, a little shimmy, the hint of a thrust as the song suggests making a little love. Mrs Frengle shivers again. Well... REA-LLY! and Mr Kips can't help but laugh.

Mrs Frengle, her large frame unmoving, snaps her head ninety degrees to glare at him.

Mr Kips! I really don't see what's *funny* about our young charges behaving like *rampant little animals!* YOU might not care that your boys are imitating acts of copulation in front of *the whole village*, but I ... WILL NOT ... have my girls acting like *French harbour sluts* THANK YOU VERY MUCH!

She takes a determined half-step towards the dancing teens from where her and Mr Kips are standing on the outskirts of the grass dance-floor. Mr Kips quick-lurches forward, placing a hand on her shoulder. Mrs Frengle stops, spins around to face him, glaring as Mr Kips retracts his outstretched arm in a slow careful movement.

Now, Betty, says Mr Kips holding both hands out in a half-surrender, my sincerest apologies for seeming a little, erm ... dismissive of your concerns, but they're only young ... barely teenagers ... and really, what do they know of such things at their age?

Mrs Frengle stiffens.

ONLY WHAT THIS LEWD NEGRO MUSIC is TEACHING THEM!

Mr Kips winces.

Behind Mrs Frengle, back-lit by the flashing colours from the stage, front-lit by the travelling stars of the mirror-ball, is a large black shape, a shape that now taps Mrs Frengle on the shoulder. She twitches, turns.

Excuse me, madam.

Freddie, the smiling dreadlocked member of the Jamaica Five, holds a single finger paused and pointing to the marquee roof, eyes looking upwards for dramatic effect.

I think, madam ... you'll find that this song is by KC, and his Sunshine Band ... a band who are fronted by KC himself, a singer who is startlingly white ... whiter than a

Mr Softee ice cream ... whiter, than the fleece of a new-born lamb ... whiter ...

Freddie stops, opens his eyes wide, stares straight-faced at the open-mouthed Mrs Frengle.

... *than a nun's bed-sheets* ... Now ... if you'll excuse me ... I hear the strains of some proper Negro music that is urging me to go impregnate some white girls with my dancing blackness ... Have a pleasant evening, madam.

And this song is disgusting with its disgusting words of making a love train, Mrs Frengle needs some fresh air and she tells Mr Kips so.

Sarah moves quickly down the stairs, her movements smoother in these flatter shoes, humming a tune she knows not what, a single little hop onto the hall rug, turning right to push the living room door open, her mouth half-open with the beginnings of Hey, Dad ... but Dad isn't there.

She pauses, cocking her head to one side like a blackbird listening. She hears the sound of the fridge door being closed, of something hard being placed on the kitchen worktop, the *clack-hiss* of a beer-can being opened. In front of her, on the coffee table, is a Christmas biscuit tin, the lid slid part to one side like the just-discovered tomb of a pharaoh. From the kitchen she hears the familiar sound of the toaster knobs being clunked down. She steps towards the coffee table, the biscuit tin, the peeking faces from the half-shadowed photograph too loud to ignore. In silence, she takes the lid off the tin, placing it careful on the red-tiled surface of the coffee table.

She picks up the photograph.

A Polaroid of colours not true, the orange hue too strong in the top left corner, an orange of sunlight bleeding across the people walking by behind the canvas backdrop, bleeding across the painted sun, the painted hill, the painted sheep, bleeding across her father's face underneath that floppy old-fashioned farmer's hat, stem of wheat in his mouth, the grin, the smock, the shepherd's crook, and that girl by his side, a girl who looks just like her, held in truer colours, her green eyes narrowing just, her red lips parting just, a split-second before she laughs from under that white cloth bonnet, that white milking dress, her arm through his, a pretend farmer's wife for a pretend farmer.

And now she sees the letter.

But THIS SONG is ABOUT a LOVE TRAIN, TOM ... A ... LOVE ... TRAIN ... But Tom tells Natalie he's not dancing because he wants to wait until Sarah gets back, and anyway, he doesn't feel like dancing. Natalie picks his drink up, waves it in front of his face, reaches out and tickles Tom under the chin, says C'mon Tomikins, drink up ... Sare'll be back in a minute, and Tommy be a happy boy then ...

Tom takes his drink from Natalie and places it back on the table. He isn't looking at Natalie. He is looking towards the stage, to where Michael stands behind the flashing lights, behind the decks with Disco Dennis. *Cunt.*

Natalie turns, bobs her head from side to side finding a moment's parting through the dancing bodies, sees Michael, laughing, clinking pints with the DJ. She turns to face the glum-looking Tom, who chin rested on cupped hand, slow raps the knuckles of his other hand on the table. *Cunt.*

Natalie leans in closer, pats Tom on the shoulder, says Oh c'mon, yer don't think Sarah'd be interested in some farty old twat like that d'yer?

Tom shrugs.

Oh Tom-Tom, says Natalie pressing Tom's nose like a doorbell. Look at him for fuck's sake, he's as old as her dad. Imagine that! Fuckin' yer dad!

Tom doesn't like the image that now flickers in his head, of Mr Goodman and Sarah fucking. He scowls. Drinks.

Tell yer what, says Natalie. Just imagine his bush. Riddled wi' grey fuckin' pubes. Be like suckin' on a vicar's head. Like, no fuckin' way is ANY girl gonna touch *that*.

Natalie jabs her fingers in her mouth, makes loud vomiting sounds, pretend wipes her fingers on Tom's shirt sleeve, and now Tom is grinning.

Know worra mean?

Natalie downs her cider, tells Tom C'mon, let's go get another ... and maybe a round of shots too for when Sarah gets back ... c'mon.

Tom looks at his watch. Says, She's been ages.

Natalie stands up, grabs Tom's arm, yanks him to his feet.

Ah, yer know Sarah ... she'll be yakkin' to her dad ... c'mon.

Paul takes the letter from Sarah, puts it face down on the coffee table, quietly asks Sarah to sit down.

Sarah sits blinking on the sofa, feels numb, feels she is stuck to the ceiling like a squashed bluebottle, looking down at all this, not here … there … somewhere else.

I would have told you one day, her dad says, sitting down opposite in his armchair, picking at a little rip in his work jeans.

Sarah hears herself say it. You lied.

I couldn't tell you the truth, Sarah.

Why?

Because …

Why?

I had to wait …

Why?

Sarah feels her nails dig in above her knee. Everything flexes. Shrinks. Tightens.

Your mother weren't well, Sare. She had problems. He taps his head with a forefinger. Here …

Paul picks at the little rip in his jeans again. Sarah looks down at her blouse, her leggings, her bright coloured nails, each one a different shade, and she feels ridiculous.

Tell me now, she says, not looking at her father.

Paul sighs. The uneaten toast sits cold on the coffee table. He clears his throat again.

We'd not been together long when she got pregnant. We weren't even, like, seeing each other all the time … yer know … were at first, and then … well, guess it just got like an on-off thing. She were unpredictable, just … never knew where I were wi' her … and then, one day she told me she were pregnant, and the baby … I mean you … were mine.

Paul glances up at Sarah. Sarah is staring at her hands, blink.

We got a place together ... a flat in one of them blocks behind Sheff train station ... got a job ... bin-man ...

Paul makes a sound like the start of a laugh. Sarah is still staring at her nails.

Anyway ... she had you, and that's when things got worse ...

Sarah tenses, looks up quick and narrow-eyed to her dad as though ...

No, Sare ... I mean ... *her* ... Sally ... I didn't know how to deal wi' her. She just went ... like ... proper not reyt ... Wouldn't pick you up, yer know, when you were cryin' ... Wouldn't change yer ... feed yer ... I had to do it all ... had to pack me job in, cos ...

Sarah can't help herself. The tears come as yelps. Paul stands, comes over and kneels at her feet, lifts her chin, strokes her hair.

It's not your fault, Sare. It's not ... That's the only thing in her letter that makes any sense. She weren't well, Sarah ... I mean, proper sick ... She used to lay in bed curled up for hours, not asleep, just laid there, eyes scrunched up ... or just starin' not seein' ... not here, somewhere else ... she used to scratch herself ... bad ... it were awful ... scary ... couldn't leave her alone wi' yer because ... cos I were scared what she might ...

And now Paul holds his daughter, her head against his chest, the yelps rising, falling.

C'mon Sare ... it's nobody's fault ... not yours, mine ...

or yer mother's ... she were sick ... couldn't get better ... finished.

Sarah pulls away, looks red-eyed at her father, her mascara black-trailing down her cheeks.

What happened to her?

Paul strokes her cheek. A thumb smudging the black.

She went away ... because she had to.

And now Sarah's father is crying, and Sarah is holding him, telling her father over and over that she loves him, she loves him, and him saying he loves her too, and now standing up, soft-pulling his daughter to her feet, c'mon ... wiping his eyes with his shirt-sleeve ... c'mon ... you need to get back to yer mates ... and now Sarah telling him she can't leave him here alone, and her father is smiling, a smile that says everything she needs to know as he says Okay then, gimme ten minutes, suppose I best get dressed for a fuckarsed disco then? and Sarah hops, grabs her dad's arms, kisses him full on the lips, pressing so eagerly that he has to take a step back, both of them laughing because it's funny.

Paul picks the Polaroid up from the coffee table, holds it out to her.

It's yours, he says, keep it.

There's a GHOST in my house... and Sally can't help herself, Paul turning to look as she does a little hop-squeal as they enter the marquee, the constellations moving across her as wide-eyed she watches the dancing bodies, a hundred dark shapes flicker-lit red green orange, red green blue, and there's a GHOST in my house... and Paul nearly coughs up his just-drunk mouthful of Woodpecker as he sees Dennis slip-scramble back up onto the stage as the song starts to fade, headphones on quick, and just in time the *Daaah! dah! Dah!* Tears of a Clown piccolo lifts through the fade, now a 2-2-3 snare, a cymbal crash, OH yeh, YEH yeah... and this dance keeps dancing as Paul shrugs at Sally, nodding towards stage right, down the front to where he sees Dennis jump off the stage back into the bodies, daft twat, and as him and Sally weave through the dancing villagers all Paul can think is that he just can't dance to this shit, and how Sally is gonna be disappointed with him, but hey if she's real punk she won't wanna dance to what's not punk, and this ain't fuckin' punk, but watching her walk ahead through a tunnel of old farts wriggling like they've just shit their britches, there she is, turning to look back over her shoulder at him, grinning, doing something with her shoulders that looks like dancing, fuck, and now up ahead Paul can see Michael and Dennis and Debbie dancing like fuckarsed clowns near the corner of the stage, and behind them, Maggie, the snarky-bitch carnival queen, leant against that tree-trunk pole holding the tent up, looking bored to fuck, not dancing, drinking, looking somehow a bit punky despite her red dress, sash and tiara, and as him and Sally get closer, Maggie sees Sally, Maggie's lip raising just, the casual snarl of a pissed-off Sid Vicious with tits, now staring at Paul ... wink.

Oh, she's been no trouble at all, Margaret ... have you, Dee Dee.

Dee Dee smiles an angelic smile at Mrs King and her

aunty in turn, Rose looking down to her feet, a little side-step, side-step in time to the song, feeling that heavy glint of guilt stab in her belly, now doing that thing she does, making a voice in her head, telling herself that Mr Hopkins will say nothing to her mother about the cheating trick as she hears Dee Dee's aunty say her name.

Rose looks up to the long thin face of Margaret Banford. Blink.

Sorry Mrs Banford, what did you say?

Margaret Banford, tall and stiff, bends down towards Rose, her breath minty yet somehow sour as she over-pronounces Have, You, Had, A, Good, Day, Rose?

She waits for Rose's answer the way she waits for all answers from people, no matter how soon they reply, the pursed lips, the right eye widening, intense, as though everything depended on the right answer.

Yes thank you, Mrs Banford.

Dee Dee glances at Rose, Rose's lips slow-kissing shapes of oh yeh bay-bee as the song begins to fade, hearing her mother tell Mrs Banford again how the girls have been no trouble, no trouble at all, and the voice in Rose's head saying people are cruel, selfish, keeping goldfish in a bag when goldfish should be free to swim where they please, and she doesn't care what her mother might say if Mr Hopkins does say something, because she's going to do everything she can to rescue the poor sad ... *DURRRdumDUMDUM* ... Dee Dee squeals. Grabs Rose's arm. SISTER SLEDGE! And Mrs King gracefully waves the girls off to dance, smiling knowingly at the respected aunt as the dance-floor swells,

WE're LOST in MU-zic ... the aunt remarking how next year the pretty Rose is sure to be queen, her words caught somewhere in the song's trap, no turning back as Mrs King responds with Well, it could be your niece, Margaret, she's a lovely girl is Dee Dee, and No, the aunt says, not a chance ... too plain.

Michael is dancing. Dennis has turned it up. Tweaked the bottom end. Jumped down off the stage, fell flat on his arse. Got laughed at, laughed himself. Pleased to fuck how when he stands up he can feel the bass so much fucking more ... sorted ... Nice work, Den-machine, nice work.

Debbie is dancing too, and with what started out as a game hatched by her and Maggie, she is now fancying Dennis just a little, despite the initial plot of piss-take, WE're LOST in MU-zic ... And Sally is dancing, laughing as Michael raises both arms into the air, mouthing the singer's UH-uhh to Dennis who mirrors back because yeh, nine to five can get to fuck, and when Michael sings he looks a bit girly Sally thinks, but ... And Maggie still isn't dancing, and Paul still isn't dancing, the two of them leaning against the tree-trunk pole that holds their corner of the tent up, drinking, Paul on the left watching Sally look at Michael, Maggie on the right watching Michael look at Sally, Maggie now looking at Debbie who's doing this stupid-fuck dance with Dennis where Dennis has a hand on her hip and Debbie holds his other hand like some daft-twat tango or summat ... Maggie turns, pokes Paul in the chest with her forefinger. Paul twitches, looks into the glare of Maggie Haywire.

I ... am the QUEEN ... TAKE ME to the BAR ... while THESE FOOLS dance ... to SHITE.

Paul looks to the pint-pot in his hand. Shrugs. Drinks the three-inch of Woodpecker down in one, nods, follows the queen around the wriggle-step-arms-in-the-air stupidity of the fools, catches Sally's eye and waves his pint-pot, and Sally nods, understanding, dancing, WE're LOST in MU-zic ... Maggie now stopping her defiant stride, Paul bumping into her back, seeing over her shoulder as the queen points to the dancing Rose, OFF WITH HER FUCKIN' 'EAD! Laugh. Blow Rose a kiss. Walk on. No turning back.

43.

Let's rest a while, Blackbird. Like they do at a picture house between films. I know this because I went one time with Mother. Did I tell that story? No? Well, maybe I'll tell it another time. Don't feel like it now. Anyway, that story has ice-cream in it, so let's not talk about it. I liked ice cream ... Do you know what a picture house is, Blackbird? Course you don't. Silly Johnny. Well, I suppose it's a bit like what we're doing today. Watching people things happen. Oh ... Did you ever see a people play?

You think about it, and you hear yourself say it.

Yes.

Christmas.

Baby

Jesus ...

I'm

Mary ...

Village

hall ...

Wonderful! So you know what I'm meaning to! Course you do! The quick brown fox jumps over the lazy ... Oh, wait ... nearly forget ... something is needed to see here ... look.

You are on the hill behind the Went. You see the carnival before you. The dark mill to your right. The bridge to your left. And up, up ahead, the mass black shape of the tor, the sky seeming blacker, the stars seeming brighter, and there, way up high, that white eye above Edendale, the moon ... full, and watching.

Night is here, Blackbird. See how sky is coal. Let us close our eyes and pretend we're seeing back inside big tent ... with people, and lights, and music noise. Let us pretend song has finished, a new one begun, and Rose and Dee Dee skip-skip-skippety-skip back to Mrs King who is talk-talk with Mr King and Mr Childlove. Let us pretend that Mr Childlove is telling Mr King how Rose and Dee Dee are good little girls, how they helped him with pig and cow sandwich sell, chop chop. And now let's pretend Mr Childlove gives Rose and Dee Dee more wages money to go feed themselves a sausage in a bun, and how he laughs slavvery at word of sausage. Now pretend Mrs King doesn't like that, and she doesn't like Mr Childlove because she thinks him rude and dirty like a bad man is, but look ... look how Rose and Dee Dee say thank you, and now off they go, skip-skip-skippety-skip to outside of tent. And now pretend this ... they skip-skip bumpety-bump right into me, Johnny ... bad man, kiddy-fiddler, because look, I'm right there ... holding out that goldfish in a bag, bending down close, closer, into Rose King's pretty-pretty face and saying it ... little girl ... little girl ... fish belong in a river.

Night is dark. It is here.

44.

Johnny Bender is a scary creepo and you *should not* have taken that fish from him!

Rose ignores Dee Dee, turning around to walk slow backwards across the bridge. She holds the plastic bag out at arm's length, the goldfish open-closing its mouth as it dangles over the wooden rail. Through the bag, the lights of the carnival distort, blur, as Rose closes one eye.

This is the sound she hears: her feet on the wooden bridge below, a *thump-thump* of drum from the marquee in front, her own voice saying fish, river, breathe under water, the scream of a fox somewhere far off behind as she stumbles, trips, the arms of her friend now around her waist.

Have you gone daft *or what?*

Rose and Dee Dee laugh because it's funny.

I'll call you Sarah, Rose tells the fish.

Sarah and her father walk hand-in-hand down Grace Street, past the place where dead things are buried, turning right onto Divinity Way past the cenotaph, *For those who fell*, and she has listened to her father talk of some things never meaning to be, of moving on from bad times, of a gone weight of heavy anchors left behind, of how he wanted to forget, because some things never come back no matter how much you want them to, of why he never told her the everything about it, because, it would have done no good to tell her all these things when she was so young, and he's sorry he fibbed, bluffed it, wrong to tell her her mum ran off with another fella way back when, and now they're both laughing because it's the most obvious fib to tell, Paul saying at least I didn't say it were the milkman, Sarah letting go of his hand to play-slap him on the arse as they turn left down Moderation Alley, past the lit-up church, past the Fiddler's Rest, the past now past and Sarah now seeing joy in the carnival ahead, in the lights, the music, her friends and the dancing to come, understanding, accepting why her father had to do what he had to do, as hand in hand again they walk, and her now seeing that she did what she had to do too, that Dad is right, that some things are not meant to be, and if part of Michael is still inside her she'll stop it, *and on the first day I will give you me, and on the second I will give myself, and on the third I will give you the heavens, and the fourth is the end, and the fifth will smash your ribs, and on the sixth I will give you a garden of winter, iron shaft that nails your unborn child to the never will, and I will love you Sarah, I will love you, and on the seventh day you will finally know …*

Rose King, under trees by the bottom right elbow of the Went, hearing the mill-wheel turning under stars and moon, the wooden paddles pushed ever-on by the always flow of water, a soft constant singing of *plosh, plosh,* leans over the bank and tilts the plastic bag.

Plop.

White moonlight, a reflection slow-dancing as the rings ripple outward, outward ... gone.

Bye-bye Sarah, says Rose, waving at the water. Hope you're happy in the river.

Dee Dee shivers. C'mon, she says, let's go back. It's dark here.

What's up Mikey? Yer look like you've seen a ghost.

Here, inbetween the marquee and the beer tent, stands Michael, Paul, and Sarah. Michael opens his mouth to speak but nothing comes out. He is looking at the girl, who is looking at the grass. Even in this half-light, between here and there, the black horns of black Cleopatra eye are the eyes of someone else, not her. The black lips, a devil mouth, a mouth he has kissed so many times ... The hair, flat scraped back, tight to her head, pig-tailed in black ribbon ... And the dog collar around the neck, the black t-shirt, black jeans, black plimsolls ... And all Michael can say to Paul's question is: Wow ... didn't recognise you, Sarah.

Paul wraps an arm around his daughter, says something about them deciding to punk it up a bit, that 1979 weren't all about that disco shite yer know, but Michael isn't really listening, he is watching Sarah bite her lip, her teeth white against the black.

A hand hard-pats his arm.

Reyt. Off to grab me a beer.

Michael twitches. Looks at Paul for the first time properly. Seeing the greying spiked hair, the Buzzcocks t-shirt ... Paul turns to his daughter. See yer in there, Sare. Want a beer bringin'?

Sarah smiles the smile of a nervous actress, her lips closed tight, now her teeth white against the black as stage-fright grinning she says Cider please, Dad. And now Paul walks towards the beer tent, turning once to half-call See yer later, Mikey, Michael saying Alright Paul, yeh, and between here and there now stands him and the girl, the father going, gone, a midge-cloud of something to come waxing between the once upon a time lovers, Michael's finger now under her chin, a suggestion of look at me, but no, she steps back, says Don't ... but now, she looks.

Nothing is said as some people pass by, heading for the marquee. Nothing is said as someone shouts come win a goldfish, only a few left, only fifty-pee a go. Nothing is said as Sarah looks at Michael, as Michael looks at Sarah, as the gramophone unwound of merry-go-round soups into the bass of a marquee disco. She half-turns, takes a half-step away, I should go.

Michael puts his hand on her shoulder. No ... *please* ... wait.

Sarah's eyes narrow as she focusses in on him, as she starts to tell him she's...

Did you read the poem, Sarah?

She feels his hand on her arm. How long as it been there? She wants to tell him the truth. That she read it quick in the toilet. That she couldn't take it all in. That she needs time. That today she is in half, and one half is under water.

Yes, she says. It's beautiful.

She feels his other hand on her other arm. How long as it been there?

Does it make you understand? he says. Does it make you feel what I feel? That I'd do anything for you? *Anything* ... That it doesn't matter what anyone else thinks? I can make you happy, Sarah. *I can* ...

She sees the grass at her feet. The flicker of red green orange from lights somewhere else, not here. She tells him again that the poem is beautiful, because ... because she doesn't know what else to say. And now they are kissing. And now, they are kissing. And now ... She pulls away. She is in half, and one half is drowning. She steps back once, twice, as behind him she sees the shapes of Natalie and Tom, and they're getting closer. She looks at Michael. Tells him to wipe his mouth. Tells him her lipstick is on his mouth. That someone is coming. *Quick*.

Michael drags his sleeve across his lips. Sees the black of her on his purple shirt.

Dennis jumps down from the stage, lands two-footed in front of Debbie, who laughing can't make her mind up if Dennis is pissed or just a bit fucking radged, this running up the stage steps as each song nears the end, changing the record, then jumping off the stage to dance with her is all getting a bit fucking weird, and not what she imagines her ideal man behaving like, Dennis now grinning at her, punch-punch-punching the air in time to the kick-drum, Michael leaning across Debbie to shout-tell Dennis FUcking TUNE! and Debbie doesn't know this song, but still, she moves, and now turning her head she sees the grass dance-floor thinning, yet the words a soft-plea of come closer, a sex promise dressed as a need to dance, and what the fuck is this? Dennis leaning into her, kissing her once on the cheek, shout-speaking REMEMBER THAT SONG I TOLD YER ABOUT? THIS IS IT, DEBS ... THE FU-CKING SEX! (kiss) and now the chorus is coming, and she feels it, rising with horns and strings, with quickening bass and push of snare, Dennis now looking blind-eyed to the marquee roof as it hits, YOU! PLUS! ME! and now Sally leans into Michael, shout-speaking into his ear asking what the song is, COS THIS is ACE! Michael turning his face to shout-speak back as hips touch, as his moves are her moves are his, that this is the UN-dis-PUTED TRUTH! his cheek now brushing hers and she's feeling it, and he's feeling it, ONE of the BEST TUNES EVER! and she's smiling, feeling his excitement as her own, his hands now in hers, rising up in the air as the cum-voice cum-squeals she can FEEL IT in her BONES, and Dennis has an arm around Debbie, and Debbie has an arm around Michael, and Michael has an arm around Sally, all of them, jumping, laughing, jumping, now open your eyes ... because here it comes again ... YOU! PLUS! ME! a sudden letting go as hips twist and arms raise, and now is now is now as the bridge drops to a single whispered BAYbeee ... a single heartbeat of kick-kick-kick-drum, and now Dennis has Debbie, and now Michael has Sally, and Sally feels the heat in her rise, feels Michael's hands on her waist, feels her hands on his chest, so ... GIVVIT tuh me GIVVIT tuh me GIVVIT tuh me GIVVIT TUH ME GIVVIT TUH ME ...

So ... what d'yer see in that Sally girl then, Mr Punky Alcock?

Paul takes a drink from his pint, rests his elbow on the bar, dares himself to look into the eyes of Maggie Haywire. In his head there is a feeling of water being swirled in a glass.

Oh ... he says, feeling the warm swell-press of an erection coming, she's alright is Sally ... yer know ... we've just been out a coupla times is all.

45.

The Derbyshire Times 31st July, 1966

REMAINS FOUND AT EDENDALE MILL

A human skeleton has been found at Edendale Mill during renovation. The remains – said to be that of a young woman – are reported to be around two-hundred years old. The skeleton was found within a recess under the mill wheel during work carried out by the Low Peaks council. A spokesman for the council, Mr George Flaw, stated the bones of the right arm to be missing, with significant damage to the skull, rib-cage and spine. Police say no foul play is suspected. This is confirmed by local historian, Harriet Jones, who stated, "The skeleton's discovery will forever be a mystery, but the mill having such a history of accidents in times gone by, will remain the factor most likely." The remains will be buried within the grounds of Edendale church, after a brief service, this coming Sunday, at 1pm.

46.

Pop ... pop ... POP muZIK ... And Tom tells Nat to give him and Sarah a minute for fuck's sake, Nat tilting her head sarking a breezeblock snarl, turning and striding into the dance-floor bodies as Tom pulls Sarah to the corner of the marquee, people glancing, pretending not to, majorette Lyndsey and her gaggle eeking oh my god what the fuck is Sarah dressed as? and in the half-dark behind tables and turning heads Tom has both hands on Sarah's shoulders, WHAT the fuck is GOING ON? WHAT'S that pervy bastard SAYIN' TO YER, SARAH?

Pop ... pop ... POP muZIK ... And Sarah grabs his arms, pulling his hands off her shoulders, saying Calm down, Tom, calm down me dad'll be here in a minute, and Tom now saying he don't GIVE. A. FUCK ... tell me, tell me WHAT THE FUCK'S GOING ON?

NOTHING! HE WAS JUST asking me about UNI IS ALL! STOP BEING SUCH AN IDIOT!

SHOOBEEDOOBEEdoowop ... And Tom is staring into

Sarah's eyes and Sarah is staring into Tom's eyes and Tom is burning, burning … BOPBOPshoowop … And now Sarah has her arms around him and her head is on his shoulder, and he hears her say I love you I love you please don't be mad, why would I give a toss about someone like that when I have you please don't be mad you'll spoil things.

I'm gonna kill that cunt if he comes near yer again.

Pop … pop … POP muZIK … And now Sarah is kissing him, on the cheek, on the lips, her mouth opening, her tongue against his tongue, her arms around him tighter, tighter …

DIR-TY BUGGERS … Natalie is back, because, her arms now around them both, her mouth going *numnumnumnum* into their ears and now they are laughing, of sorts, Tom's lips sticky from the black lipsticked kiss, and now Nat squawks, FUCKIN' HELL TOM, your bird looks a REYT FUCKIN' PSYCHO.

The barmaid places a pint of Woodpecker in front of Paul. Michael watches her hand leave the plastic pint, sees the prints where her fingers were, hears Paul say And a pint of Carling please, Jackie. Then: What's it like in theer? Michael looks at Paul, feels the folded fiver between his fingers, feels himself tap it soundlessly against the waist-high trestle table, feels someone bump soft into him behind, hears the hubbub around, hears himself saying Not bad, pretty full. Paul is watching Jackie the barmaid open the Carling.

Wannit leavin' in, Paul?

Nah, stick it into a pint-pot please Jackie.

Michael hears himself ask Paul what he's been up to. Paul watches Jackie pour the Carling, says Oh, usual shite, yer know.

Jackie puts the lager in front of Paul. Michael doesn't think Paul will offer to buy him one.

Paul and Maggie stand in the entrance of the marquee, looking. They see people dancing. They see lights flashing. They see the mirror-ball stars moving across the walls of the tent, the people, the roof, the people ... ITCHI-GITCHI-yahyah DAH-DAH ... Maggie turns to Paul.

Fuckin' hate this song. Foreign wank.

Paul isn't listening to Maggie Haywire. He is looking for a way through this, through the packed grass dance-floor to where he imagines Sally still dancing with Michael. He feels like he is in half, and one half is burning. His drink spills as Maggie tugs him into the bodies, drags him left, right, through the dance, through the heat, through the stars and stench of happy people, QUEEN COMING THROUGH, that's right, MAKE WAY FOR THE QUEEN.

The marquee shrinks to a black tunnel of metal and fire.

Sally is still dancing with Michael. Sally ... *is still dancing ... with Michael.*

Paul is in half, and one half is burning.

The walk between the beer-tent and the marquee is short.

Paul stops, takes a drink, looks up at the moon.

In the beer-tent, Michael drinks from his drink.

If she kissed me, she still wants me.

He picks Dennis's pint up from the trestle table.

So what if Paul's here? Nothing changes. It's tonight. Or never.

ITCHI-GITCHI-yah-yah DAH-DAH ... Maggie stands hands on hips in front of Dennis. Dennis knows this song will finish in less than two minutes time and he has a dance-floor full of people dancing right now and if he doesn't sort the next song out very very soon he's going to look a right twat.

YOU, DJ DICKHEAD, will OBEY the QUEEN ... and YOU, Mr Disco Dennis DJ DICKHEAD, will play ... the FU-CKING STRANGLERS NEXT ... or I ... MR DISCO DJ DENNIS DICKHEAD ... will CHOP ... your FUCKING ... BALLS OFF!

But ... I don't have any Stranglers ...

Maggie looks to the roof of the marquee. DAMNED?

Er ... yeh ... I think ...

RIGHT! THE DAMNED! NOW!

Dennis looks to Debbie, to Michael, to Sally. They are not dancing anymore. They are all watching Dennis, who shrugs, turns, and jogs up the steps onto the stage.

Paul is laughing. Maggie high-fives him. Paul looks at Sally. Sally looks at Paul. Paul looks at Michael. Michael looks at Maggie. Maggie looks at Sally. Sally looks at Michael. Michael looks at Paul.

Dennis, slipping the headphones off, pulls the notebook from under the mixer.

M – POP MUZIK
LABELLE – LADY MARMALADE
THE DAMNED – NEW ROSE

He can't help but laugh at the memory. Not a fucking chance. No way. He bends down starts fingering through the twelve-inchers. C'mon, Mikey. Where's me beer?

And these drums are a FUCK OFF of hobnail boots kicking out the speakers ... and this guitar is a FUCK OFF of broken glass razz spitting out shards onto the bemused dancers, who now stop, turning as one to look towards Dennis who is pretending not to look as the people shrug, frown at the stage, at the DJ, who is now squatting behind the decks, unable to watch as The Damned spike gnarl and barb, faster, faster, as a hundred and forty-six people leave the grass dance-floor, seeking their drinks, seeking something, anything ... *what the hell is* ... all conversation stops.

There, on the dance-floor, on her own, under the turning mirror-ball, is Maggie Haywire, carnival queen. She throws her shoes off. She pulls the tiara from her head. She jumps into the air, arms tight by her side, jumping again, again, twitching like she's been hit by ten-thousand volts of fuck you. She spits onto the red-lit grass in front of her. She spins, arms outstretched with both hands flapping stiff-fingered v-signs at the open-mouthed audience. She throws her tiara over her shoulder. Jumps. Falls over. Laughs as the song yelps a warning not to get too close or ... Paul Alcock grabs her arm, wrenches the queen to her feet, and now they are both jumping, jumping, arms tight by sides, a pogo protest against a get to fuck disco of shite.

Dennis peers over the decks. Mr King, fifty yards to his left, is glaring at him. Dennis blinks, taking in the mass curve of the peopled marquee, and there could be a man and a goat having sex on the dance-floor, here, right now, and the looks on the people's faces wouldn't be any less slack-jaw dumbstruck than what he sees, as breaking through the hymen of villagers by the marquee entrance comes the Reverend Haywire, pushing his frowning wife in her wheelchair.

Mr King strides across the dance-floor, past the pogoing Maggie and Paul, towards Dennis to get this sorted, *now*, but Dennis is already on it, fader up, drops the needle hop-skip (wince) into Chic, his first impulse of how to drag this terrifying scene out of the dirty noise shit-hole that was and GOOD TIMES ... THESE, are, THE, Mr King stopping dead in his tracks six feet from the stage, raising his eyebrows at the grinning Dennis who gives Mr King a thumbs up, wiggles a pretend finger-dance, to this, thank fuck, one of the safest floor-fillers he knows, but hey, he is the DJ Dennis, and in two tracks flat he'll have everyone back into groove-world, but for now, he needs to sit down on his northern soul box and breathe, breathe ...

Outside, under full moon and blue-black sky of stars, the Reverend tells his stepdaughter that she is a disgrace.

The stepdaughter tells the stepfather to fuck off, walks barefoot back into the marquee, the stepfather telling the wheelchaired wife, SEE ... SEE ... SHE'S of the DEVIL, the wheelchaired wife telling him to SHUT UP, just ... SHUT UP.

Inside her little tent, in fairy-light and candle glow, Madam Zaza is stooped, slow packing her things away. She folds the silk scarf carefully, places it in the little wooden box made by her carpenter husband all those years ago, this supportive gift made and given after she'd nervously declared her intent to venture out and tell fortunes. She picks up her crystal ball in both hands, palms cupping the underside, careful not to place fingertips onto the crystal, fairy-light and candle reflecting soft from the glass.

Something like a flashbulb in her head. Hard shadow of animal. Blackbird hanging limp twitch in its mouth. Moon, stars, turn red. Blood raining down onto black leaves of a forest. Paw hard on flapping blackbird. Rip, rip. Retching and heaving. A screaming blood-black baby vomiting from a fox's cracked-wide jaws, dropping wet and grasping onto a blue-black forest floor, among the blue-black feathers and bones, little black fingers clasping at nothing as the fox licks her offspring under a black shaking tree.

The crystal ball falls to the table. Rolls to the edge. Drops soundless to the grass.

47.

Maggie Haywire doesn't hear the music. She grabs the laughing Debbie by the wrist, yanks her from the laughing Paul, away from the confused Michael, the unsure Sally, pulling the now bewildered Debbie through a tunnel of backstepping people, head down, push, push, her sash thrown to the floor, fuck it, pushing past bodies to get to the entrance, a harder tug on the trailing Debbie who calls out What? What? as outside they go, out under the Edendale blue-black sky, the moon eye watching, the stars watching, Mr King, the Reverend, his wheelchaired wife, a tut-tut clutter by the marquee entrance, watching, Debbie turning to look as the queen pulls her harder past the hook-a-duck, past the dumb paused horses of the merry-go-round, beyond earshot of Mr King's reassurances to the head-shaking vicar who declares his shame over and over, It's alright Reverend, give her a little while to calm down, she'll be fine for the presentation, you'll see, the wheelchaired wife interjecting but ignored, Go apologise to her William, that'd be a start!

Where we goin'? says Debbie, jerking her arm from the grip of the queen.

Maggie stops, arms by her side, head still downward, not turning to face her friend, a slight shake of the shoulders as she begins to cry, then off she goes again, striding fast past the hotdog van, past the ice-cream van, past the tombola stall, past ... THE FUCK OUT OF HERE!

Debbie quickens her pace. By the time Maggie reaches the bridge, her friend has caught up with her, is holding her tight as she sobs.

Hate that bastard. Hate him. HATE HIM.

But, you KEEEP me HAAAN-gin' ON... Paul feels the heat of the marquee on his face as he walks pretend cocky through the draped entrance, stops, drinks, looks left to right, slow.

The place is packed.

Twenty ... fuckin' ... years.

And now Paul is laughing because he can't help it. Because Dennis is dancing like a dick onstage. Because life is fucking ridiculous. Because shit happens and you've just gotta move on. Because some things never change. Because this is Diana fuckarsed Ross and the shit fucking Supremes. Because Dennis is still playing shite like he always has. Because right there, smack bang in the middle of this is Sarah, dancing, laughing. Because it's sorted, finally. Because tonight ...

PAUL!

Debbie Foxglove.

On the bridge, Debbie holds a lit cigarette lighter in front of Maggie's face as Maggie holds a pocket-mirror in one hand, sorting her make-up out with the other. The moonlight isn't quite enough to attend to detail, and anyway, Debbie feels that her friend needs her, and she is willing to do whatever it takes to get her there, back to happy, Debbie not telling her friend that she's never seen her this way before, because that won't help, won't make things better. Beneath them, the black Went glitters. To their right, the black moors rise, and the trees are whispering. To their left, the muffle of Supremes and people noise. Maggie, with eyeliner pencil paused, blinks. Left eye done.

So ... what's happening with you and Dennis then?

Debbie grins, says He's okay, bit of a div, but okay.

Maggie drags the nib of the pencil across her right bottom eyelid, blinks. Debbie's turn: So ... what's happening with you and Michael or Paul then?

Both girls laugh, high-pitched, like for like as Debbie now squeals, her right thumb a sudden too-hot-heat as the lighter goes out, falls to the bridge, hard bounces once, falls between the wooden planks, *plop*. Maggie hugs Debbie tight. Debbie is thinking this is not like Maggie, this is not like Maggie at all. Maggie's words feel warm in Debbie's ear, a warm that reaches the bottom of her belly, lower.

Listen Debbie. Let me tell you a secret. I don't like men. They're cunts. All of 'em. Learnt that when I were a kid. Watching my dad punch my mum in the belly so hard she'd piss herself.

Beneath them, the black Went glitters.

Paul shrugs at Debbie's question, the Supremes demanding he be a man about it, says Just thought I'd have a mooch down, yer know ... see what's goin' off.

Drink.

They both look to the dark mass of dancing bodies, the red green blue lights that on/off to the beat, the mirror-ball stars turning, turning, as somewhere somebody howls like a dog and somebody else echoes it back ... laughter.

Drink.

So ... how yer doin' then, Debs?

Drink.

Debbie looks to her feet, a grin curling, turns back to face Paul.

Better now I've escaped from the clutches of a stinky hippy.

Oh aye?

Yep. Surprise, surprise. Me gettin' latched to a total fuckin' loser.

Debbie makes a gun from her hand, points it to her head, her eyes going bozzy, says bang, then twitches as though remembering something important, says wide-eyed and quick to the laughing Paul: That's not aimed at you by the way.

Debbie likes the feeling of Maggie's hand holding hers. She also likes the sound of the trees, a comma of lush shivers, soft blown by a warm breath. And then, there's the river. This side of the Went, everything else seems secondary, the dull hum-bump of carnival disco not here but over there, after, beyond, and now Maggie's hand is gone, the arm now around Debbie's waist, the hand now flat against the front of her hip, Debbie's heart a *bump-bump* of blood travel, the river a sound of blue-black push, push, as Debbie follows, her arm around the slender waist of a queen, hip, to hip, to here, under this ash tree whose roots reach gnarled fingers across their path, and Look, says Maggie Haywire, slow-turning her friend to face the movement of water, Maggie's palm a gentle pressure, each fingertip, a passage of soft electric into the small of Debbie's belly, a current that travels from valley to neck, from scalp to valley, Look Debbie, look at the moon in the water.

The moon is whole, then broken. Whole, then broken. Gone, as the girls turn to face each other, kiss.

What ... the ... fuck?

Debbie can't help but laugh, and neither can Paul. From where they stand just inside the entrance of the marquee, their view of the stage over the heads of the dance-floor bodies is near-perfect, and with a hand on Paul's shoulder to gain tiptoe leverage, Debbie punches the air, shouts GUW-ON DENNIS! as the Edendale carnival DJ takes centre-stage, the sound of an angel's harp shimmer-filling the star-lit marquee, the DJ squatting on half-bent legs, arms slow-waving up in the air as side-to-side the grinning Dennis moves like ... HE LOOKS LIKE a FOUR-legged FUCKIN' OCTOPUS havin' a SHIT laughs Paul handing Debbie the pint of cider he bought for Sarah ... Ta Paul, grin.

Booo-GEEE NIGHTS... WOH-oh-OHHH... And bang

on the beat Dennis leaps into the air as it all kicks in, the arm waving crowd following, cheering, dancing, jumping, cheering, because life is fucking ridiculous, because shit happens and you've just gotta move on, because Debbie is dragging Paul into the writhing mass of it, fuck it, you just gotta move on, forget shit, and maybe, even dance.

Mrs King, cradling a clear plastic beaker of gin and tonic, feels Mr Hopkins' trestle table press against her left hip.

She feels this is alright. Why shouldn't she lean against his goldfish stall? What's wrong with talking to him anyway? Who's going to guess from such things? Which passing villager would figure out that her and Jed shagged in his butcher's van last Wednesday night from the sight of this?

Drink.

Jed Hopkins is still laughing at what she's just told him about Maggie Haywire, says, She's a rum un that one. His eyes travel Sandra's red/green-lit profile as she drinks. That curve of flesh where her arse now presses against the table. That curve of her hip to her waist – not bad for an old girl. That bump-bump of tit rising from her peeking bra at the top of her dress. Her neck, her lips as she sips the drink. He makes a mental note. Try and get her to suck me off next time. Maybe after a bit of a tit-wank. Wonder if she'll swallow?

Jed Hopkins clears his throat, pats the money pouch that hangs from his belt over his groin.

Your Rose came by earlier.

Sandra King turns to look at him, smiles, frowns, says

What was she up to this time?

Jed grins. She were after me fish. Her and that Dee Dee. Tried playing a crafty one on me but I sussed 'em. Dee Dee gerrin' me to look away while your Rose stuck a dart in me bullseye.

Mrs King blows a big puff of fast air through pursed lips, blinks, is about to say something about giving Rose a talking to but something stops her.

A small plastic bag dangles in front of her face, a goldfish with a silver streak across its belly.

Give her this wi' my love, will yer?

BOOOgeeNIGHTS! aynt-no-dowt, WE-arrEAR tuh PARRRdee... With Debbie holding one hand and Sarah the other, Paul is a stiff-dancing puppet as the villagers sing, tugged and pulled by the laughing girls each time his moves dissolve into a wooden-legged shrug, his daughter now hugging him, KEEPON dancin' KEEPON dancin', her punk-Cleopatra eyes wide and bright as she shout-tells him she never thought she'd see the day (me neither, luv ... ha!) as behind Sarah, eclipsed by the happening of a dancing father, dances Natalie and Tom, Natalie happy to see her best friend happy, Tom still brooding but dancing, trying for it not to show, and as Paul flat-palms to flat-palms with Debbie Foxglove in some funny *ha-ha* daft tango, Sarah turns her attention back to Tom and Natalie, now hugging them both and shouting I LOVE you TWO! as over Sarah's shoulder Tom sees Michael cunt-face Goodman looking, leaning against the tree-trunk tent-pole by the corner of the stage, drinking, watching, and Tom feels a heat in his belly, in his skin, in his fingers and teeth and he won't look away, he's going to keep staring back just to let that pervy bastard know what's what, *cunt* ... *cunt* ... KEEPON dancin' KEEPON dancin'...

Michael thinks something has changed. Michael sees Tom staring and thinks the boy's stare is loaded. Has she told him? Michael thinks not. She wouldn't. Would she? No, she wouldn't. Never.

Look. She's dancing with him now and they're both smiling. The boy has his arms around her. The boy has his arms around her. *Bastard bastard bastard fucking bastard bastard bastard* stop, look away, don't look ... time, time ... nothing gonna stop this, nothing ... because she'll see, see it and come ... and you won't lose, you can't, it'll happen, time, time ... KEEPON dancin' KEEPON dancin'...

And behind these closed eyes Michael sees her face on the cinema screen in the half-dark, but her face isn't on the cinema screen because the cinema screen is somewhere over there, neither of them watching the film, a film near done, unwatched by her and him because kissing and kissing ... this secret meeting of him and her a train-ride from Castletor to Sheffield, to a place where no-one knows them because ... her and him hidden in the half-dark, dark-lit only by the screen where The Warriors have fought through city streets and subways while her and him kissing and kissing ... that nervous telephone call the week before, *what shall we go and see then?* both agreeing the film looked fun, his treat, as was the ice-cream and pretend Coca-Cola, tastes like cold coffee all sticky on teeth, but the ice-cream good, sharing the taste of it on a single spoon, on lips, on tongues, forgetting the probable glances of those on the row behind, and *I want you, I want you*, the kisses ever longer, deeper, hands held fingers tightening then letting go, as from the screen the sound of bottles a chink-chink, *Warriors ... come out to play-ay ...* his hand now on her leg above the knee, her hand now on his leg above the knee, and *I want you I want you*, his palm finding ladder in her tights as under the skirt hem he goes, and it's hotter under there, feeling her thigh muscles tighten as his hand keeps the travel, her hand hesitant, hesitant but, that soft bite on his bottom lip reading as *go on then, go on ...* his other hand now on her wrist, a gentle pressure a gesture of *don't be scared*, flat-palm onto him as the little finger of his other hand finds the heat of it, finding the hot line of it as she presses down, just, her fingers shaping around him, her hips rolling forward, just, as little finger is now thumb, over tights and gusset, *I want you I want you,* her shaped hand tighter, up slow down, his thumb rubbing, a press as he finds it, her breath in his mouth, his breath in her mouth, and sudden the sounds of people not screen, of seats clattering, these lights lifting as stop, stop ... NIGHT feeeVER, NIGHT fee-VER-her...

And now open-eyed to the mirror-ball universe Michael doesn't watch the end of it, of her quick-footing out of the cinema and onto the street, *her*, stopping and leaning against that lamp-lit wall, hands over face, not responding as Michael asks her and asks her *What's the matter? What is it?* on and on until finally she looks up and tells him, *Nothing ... nothing is the matter.*

Drink. He can't see her. Drink. Now he can, there ... dancing. With him. MIKEY-BOY! Michael twitches at the shout, turns to see Dennis's face three feet from his as Dennis squats down leaning forward from the stage, grinning red-faced and sweaty.

HOP UP, LAD ... NEED a PISS an' a BEER ... LET ME SHOW YER AGAIN HOW ter STICK a TUNE ON.

Dennis beckons Michael with fist and curling finger. Two steps up towards the stage and Michael feels like a fighter stepping into the ring, all eyes upon him but none really are, all except, that is, for the green eyes of Sarah Alcock, this nineteen year-old girl who pretend laughs at her dad's daft dancing as the disco lights cast blue, as the people become wind-shook trees in a blue-black forest, as something inside her screams mute, grasping at stars in a blue-black sky ... rip, rip.

48.

Getting darker, isn't it, Blackbird? Look how river is inky coal water, dot-dot-dotted with star-shine, glittery eyed by Mrs Moon. Up there, down here. Funny how things do that. Here ... there. It's like when I said about river being music, like when we played toe fish, like how putting hand on tree trunk means we touch branch up there and root down below, river same, river always music from back, back then to here today tonight right now, toe fish swim in little bit of water but little bit of water is an always was, from all way back to now. Can't go ahead though. It stays in a now all this. All and everything where going back is always back but now, now, is tick-tock this. Do you understand, Blackbird?

You hear it, which means you said it.

No.

Johnny holds his hands out in front of him, wiggles his fingers. You understand you are sat on the bank of the Went again, the place you seem to always come back to when the watching stops. Johnny's hands are now in front of you.

You can hear him laughing. You watch the fingers as they dance. The hands are now together, the fingers together, dancing together as the Went glitters black behind. Johnny sighs.

Once upon a time there was a girl who danced with a boy, and from their dance they made another girl, a secret girl, a girl who didn't know, and boy didn't know, but they were all river together, so girl was girl, and boy? He loved girl he did, felt it in his bones and heart and blood and …

Johnny is smiling at you.

His hands go over your eyes.

Look. Out of darkness, comes a girl.

49.

You comin' or what?

Maggie stands hands on hips on the bridge. Her head tilted to one side, just, as she smiles at Debbie, who stands on one leg by the Went, the other raised and crooked, a shoe upside down in her right hand as she shakes the stone from it.

Debbie slips her shoe back on, steps onto the bridge and walks towards Maggie, who tells Debbie not to go all weird, that it's no big deal, *okay?* Debbie nods, smiles a tight-lipped smile, her eyes not looking at the queen, who now puts a finger under Debbie's chin, says Hey, I'm here.

Debbie blinks, makes a quick-flicker eye contact with Maggie, who now presses her friend's nose with her forefinger, says bing-bong, says hello-hello, says Earth calling Debbie Foxglove, Earth calling Debbie Foxglove, come in Debbie Foxglove, and Debbie now laughing, for real, because Maggie is funny, because life is funny, because sometimes things happen that you don't ever think will happen, because.

Because, dear, anyone would think you to be fucking the butcher? is what Mr King would like to say to his wife, but he doesn't. Instead he glances over at the goldfish stall to where Jed Hopkins grins, giving a thumbs up to the carnival chairman who raises a slow hand in return, his wife stood beside him holding the bagged goldfish out to their daughter who hops on the spot, says thank you Mother, the mother telling her it's Mr Hopkins she should thank and not her, the excited look on her daughter's face as her and her friend Dee Dee huddle around the silver-bellied fish, these looks stopping Mrs King from adding a ticking off for the con-job they tried to pull on Jed, Rose now shouting THANK you Mr HopKINS! to the still-grinning butcher, as Sandra King glances at her husband who is annoyed she can tell, because she knows him all too well, that merest narrowing of his left eye the only clue she needs, *oh god, does he know ... not a chance ... no ...* his hand now on her back, small strokes, *pat-pat* as Alan Childlove stagger-births out the marquee entrance, his laugh the sound of a donkey being castrated, louder than the entire tent of people, louder than the Bee Gees, louder than ...

Mr King thinks the butcher to be coarse and vulgar, thinks him the sort to get a rise from stroking a moist pork chop, the sort that most probably fucks a pig carcass in his cold store during lunch-breaks. Mr King certainly doesn't like how often Sandra mentions him after the book club meetings. *Ooh, Jed said a very funny thing tonight. Ooh, Jed brought some very nice pasties to the meeting. Ooh, Jed is fucking me, didn't I tell you?*

The sweaty red face of Alan Childlove becomes a fat comma between Mr and Mrs King, a sweaty arm draped around each from behind, the drunk shopkeeper joining the select audience watching the two girls soft-prod the plastic bag of water as the little fish stares out.

Eeeee ... can I come gi' it a poke, lass?

Sandra King, in one sharp movement, releases herself from the sweaty clasp of Alan Childlove, tells the girls to be good, then heads off in the direction of the beer tent. Mr King, still draped by the drunk shopkeeper calls out to his escaping wife not to forget the speech is in twenty minutes. The girls, as one, walk off in the direction of the merry-go-round.

Eeeee ... they're gonna need a big shitty stick apiece in a coupla years them two ... lads'll be woofin' round 'em like ...

A loud sharp click like the snap of a bone. The Bee Gees stop dead. The sound of four-hundred-and-seventy-eight intakes of breath. Mr King spins on his heel, free from the sweaty grip of the shopkeeper, now staring wide-eyed into the hot black mouth of the discoless disco. Inside the marquee there is nothing but darkness, someone shouting, someone laughing, a child screaming as the twisted organ of the merry-go-round turns everything inside-out.

NIGHT FeeeVER, NIGHT fee-ver-her... Michael's heart is

beating hard as the Bee Gees start to fade, knowing as he does the time is now, and yes he's done exactly what Dennis showed him to do, the next track synced and ready to kick-in, and the record is turning, and the Bee Gees are going, gone, and, and … nothing.

There is no sound but the sound of people looking at him. And glancing up all he can do is shrug and smile as all the people look at him and no-one is dancing because there is nothing to dance to and all the people are looking at him. *What the fuck* has he … FADER! Lift the needle put it back to the start wang the fader up *fuck fuck stupid fuck* and ba-BABA-ba-BAH-BAH horns, bass, a punching god fist filling the marquee as the snare snaps the kick-in and the people are clapping the people are laughing and Smokey sings of a girl like no other he has ever, fucking, met, THANK fuck.

Watching, Sarah can't help but laugh, can't help not hearing Nat's sark of how the toilet-gone Tom would've loved that, Sarah now off to dance because she has to, and all the way from the table to the dancefloor she is looking at Michael. That hotel room in Sheffield. That lamp-lit canal below as they danced by the window. Her and him. In that hotel room. Dancing. To this. Laughing. Kissing. Laughing, so … FEE, FYE … FOH … FUM … and she remembers Michael singing it, so close to her ear she could hear the breath between words, and he's telling her to get ready … get ready … And from the stage Michael is looking. And Sarah is looking. And Sarah is dancing, there, smack bang in the middle of this where nothing else matters. That hotel room in Sheffield, that lamp-lit canal below as they danced by the window. Her and him, in that hotel room, dancing, to this. And the bath water is running, her and him, get ready … Fucking in the bath, him watching her eyes as she comes, coming inside her as she comes … get ready … And Smokey's words are Michael's words, and he's saying it to her again … she will love him, she will love him because he will make her love him … And through all this, through the memory and mass, comes Tom, to dance with his girlfriend, a girlfriend who now doesn't want to dance, needs a drink, or something, lights on/lights off, yes/no/yes, sometimes he just can't figure this girl out.

Dee Dee tells Rose to stop, to wait, to stop. Rose spins dead centre of the bridge and glares at her friend.

What?

Dee Dee, hands on knees and panting, says wait a minute, says let me get me breath back, says *hang on.*

Rose holds the plastic bag up into the air, and with one eye closed, arm outstretched, she moves the bag in front of the moon, a moon so bright it lights the bagged fish like a Chinese lantern.

Wow …

Dee Dee straightens up, stands shoulder to shoulder with her friend, the fish open closing its mouth, an eye staring out at the two girls.

God, says Dee Dee. You can see all the stuff in its belly.

From over the Went, a wide cheer, followed by a jagged throb of music, followed by a wider cheer, making the girls turn around and look. Rose frowns.

Funny … the music wasn't there a minute ago.

I want to go back, says Dee Dee.

Rose tells her she can't. Not yet. That they have a very important job to do.

She dangles the plastic bag in front of Dee Dee's face, says fish belong in a river.

Dee Dee tuts, looks up at the stars, the heel of her shoe making a dry clack on the wooden bridge. I'm not doing it … it's too dark and your mum'll go nuts if you chuck that one in.

No she won't.

Yes she will.

Fine. I'll do it myself then.

Rose turns and walks the bridge, her friend watching her go, watching her shape take on the look of a shadow as Rose takes the path left, into the trees, into the dark.

I can't believe you did that, whispers Debbie to the queen as the barmaid pours their drinks.

Just exercising my power, says the queen, not whispering.

Debbie isn't sure how she feels about what just happened. The kiss. The touching. The turning off of the generator behind the marquee.

And anyway, says the queen handing the barmaid a five pound note, I owed it to 'em, all of 'em … wankers are gettin' on me nerves.

Maggie picks one of the pints of cider up from the trestle table, sips the top half-inch from it, then hands it to Debbie.

Debbie says nothing as the barmaid hands Maggie her change. Maggie folds the three pound notes, pushes them into the top of her bra, picks the other pint up, drinks, then turns to face Debbie.

No-one likes me except you. And I'll tell you what …

Debbie feels her guts tighten. The look from Maggie's eyes feel like they're sending something hot into Debbie's head.

I love you. Everyone else can die. But not you.

Debbie doesn't know what to say. She blinks, and sees white light. The sound of heavy breath. Someone standing behind them, too close.

Kingy sent me to find yer, Maggie … speech's started … here … got yer stuff.

Dennis hands Maggie her sash, her tiara, coughs, puts his hand to his mouth too late. Debbie leans back, frowns. Maggie holds the sash to her nose, raises an eyebrow, tells Dennis he smells sweaty … piggy … oink-oink.

(Applause)

… and in these last twenty years, we have seen this village and our carnival … go from strength to strength … thanks to you, the people of Edendale … and our friends from around the Low Peak area … who have contributed so much to this, our day of carnival!

(Applause)

Rose kneels by the river, watches the mill-wheel turn. The sound is the sound of on and on, like a clock, tick-tock.

(Applause)

... Twenty years is a long time, and much has changed ... but some things have not ...

(Pause, smile)

Her anger at Dee Dee gone, Rose feels a little scared here alone. She sees the trees reach dark arms and long fingers out over her, the shadows black on the moonlit water, the moon a cracked white eye shimmering, a splintered watcher from under the black movement of water.

(Laughter)

... and indeed, some believe that this year, nineteen-ninety-nine, is the end of the world ... that we are done ... finished ...

(Pause, hold forefinger aloft to emphasise point)

Rose begins to untie the knotted bag, slowing her haste so as not to upset the fish, and she wishes Dee Dee was here, she wishes she'd not been so nasty to her, she wishes ... The knot has come undone.

(Applause)

... of dedication, of hard work ... and of community ... these singular things that have held us all together through trial and triumph ... this, our twentieth anniversary of carnival, a celebration that reaches its roots back to the very beginnings of our village ... and, ladies and gentlemen ... I believe Jeremiah would be proud ... proud that his pursuit of creating an Eden in the Dales ... is here in clear evidence today...

(Applause)

Resting the bag on the dark grass, Rose slow-opens the mouth of it, the fish still as a tiny bubble of silver air rises to the top of the water, gone, the sound of the mill-wheel's on and on the beat of Rose's heart ...

(Pause, scan audience, smile sadly)

... but, as many of you know ... this, our twentieth anniversary Edendale carnival ... is also important for another reason ... a reason that has a very special relevance to my wife Sandra ... and I ...

(Pause, take a breath)

And crackle, snap, a shape comes through the trees, a shape that becomes a body, the bag tipping limp onto its side as Rose turns open-mouthed, a scream rising from ...

(Make eye-contact)

... Twenty years ago today we lost our beautiful daughter Rose ...

(Pause)

... but ... through you ... our friends ... our community ... my wife and I have been given such strength ... such hope in the face of such a terrible loss ...

Don't scream Rose, no no ... it's only me ... Johnny ...

... and for that ... my wife and I ...

... Oh the bag the bag ...

... cannot ...

... it's okay Rose ... I got fishy ... look ... open bag ...

... thank you enough ...

... there we go ...

(Applause)

Rose and Johnny look at the plastic bag in Rose's hand.

Not much water in there, Johnny says.

Rose nods, her breath still quick.

Sorry I frightened you, Johnny says. It wasn't my meaning.

Rose looks at Johnny's face. It looks kind, soft, and nothing bad inside.

Rose tells him it's alright, holds the bag up to the moon, tells Johnny thank you for rescuing the fish.

Don't think fishy liked it in grass, he says.

Rose laughs quiet, says no, I don't think he did.

What's he called then?

Rose scrunches her nose up a little, looks up at the stars, tells Johnny the fish is called Johnny, and Johnny laughs, says shall we put Johnny into river?

Rose and Johnny are on their knees. The sound is the sound of the mill-wheel's on and on, *plosh, plosh,* like a clock, tick-tock. Leaning forward, Rose tips the bag ... *plop.*

Bye-bye Johnny, says Rose.

Bye-bye Johnny, says Johnny.

The fish, for a moment, can be seen near the surface, white belly like crocus bulb, body like orange peel, deeper, into black, then ... gone. Johnny stands, holds his hand out to Rose. She smiles, puts her hand in his, gets to her feet. They turn, walk hand in hand, slow back in the direction of the bridge. The sound of the mill-wheel growing quieter with each step. The sound of song from the carnival a muffled *bump-bump* below the whisper of the trees as Johnny tells Rose a story, a story about a girl from long ago, a girl called Blackbird who worked a loom, who sang her songs to pass time, who trusted a wrong one so got her breath took away, a baby in her belly that never was born ... girl in river, like fishy, tick-tock.

50.

Well that was surprise wasn't it, Blackbird! Now you're in story too! Did you like it?

You look at Johnny. He stands between the ash trees, and behind him, behind the trees, in the dark of the wood, you see the fog is here again. You don't want the fog to come. You have been walking for always it seems, and you don't know why, and then, you hear it, so you must have said it.

How
did
you know
me
then
there with
girl?

And Johnny is laughing. And Johnny is dancing. Between trees he skips, round and round, *and if I was a blackbird I'd whistle and sing ... and I'd follow the vessel ... my true love ... sails ... in ...* He walks over to you from between the trees, the fog now gone as he reaches out to hold your hands.

It was in whispers, Blackbird ... after Mother and Father went away and I was Johnny on his own. First it was a night, that time I heard them ... scared, scared, was Johnny on his own ... like whispering of all no people in my room so under pillow I hid, but still whispers whispered. I said to myself, it was people next doors but it was too close ... here ... like lips next to ear. It did it for nights and nights and ... Too many whispers, tangly muddle of says, things I couldn't hear but could. And then, one night, it was one say. And it told me things. It told me girl, and fish. It told me brick through window. It told me queen, king, a boy, girl that was two girls but one, where Father's rat poison was, of bad happens and fire in sky, and I saw an end of things, things that happened, and will happen, of dark bad coming from love dizzy hate dizzy, a people play of people not knowing, not seeing, not hearing music of anything else but a one ... oh, Blackbird ... you were one of these things ... it was like I knew you before I knew you ... and I'm bad inside your baby didn't happen but walk and walk you have to find ... and in these woods it sometimes is night, and in these woods it sometimes is day, but fog takes day away and makes trees into scratch fingers scratching fog sky that wants to push down, down, like fog is bad hand holding head under water ... down, down, not breathe but scream as machine spikes arm and neck and face and belly ... gone, gone, gone for silly not seeing, carried on and on like end is no end but never and ever and ...

Johnny lets go of your hands. His fingers stroke your cheek.

End is born, Blackbird, but born is beginning. Cat. Mouse. Round and round and ...

51.

Are you like, *proper daft* or what?

Dee Dee is pulling Rose by the arm onto Forgiveness Green, away from the bridge, away from where Johnny Bender stands in the half-dark leaning on the rail, waving to Rose who waves back at him, smiling, looking back over her shoulder as Dee Dee tugs her sideways into the carnival hum of light and sound and safety.

Stop waving at him you idiot! Turn around ... stop it!

Rose turns to face the way she is being led as the girls arc around the hot waft of the hotdog van. Dee Dee stops with a jolt, swings around to face Rose, now a hand on each of Rose's arms, grip firm, eyes narrowed, cheeks red, her words quick into Rose's face.

Are you bonkers what you doin' talkin' to that weirdo? Jesus, Rose! I saw you holdin' his *chuffin' hand!* Are you like ... *mad?* Don't you know what *Johnny Bender is?*

Rose shakes Dee Dee's hands from her arms. Tells her to shut up a minute.

Dee Dee glares at her friend, waiting, waiting for Rose to explain what just happened back there with that weirdo, and why, why is she smiling like that?

I'll have you know Johnny is a very nice man, says Rose, side-stepping Dee Dee, walking in the direction of the marquee, stopping six steps ahead to turn and walk backwards, still smiling, telling her red-faced friend C'mon, let's go inside the tent, Dad's talking to everyone.

And on that note, there are some people that I … that we, should thank for helping put together this very first Edendale Carnival … Firstly, the carnival committee … a team of four, of which I myself am privileged to be part of …

Mr King smiles, nods, waits for applause … wankers …

… Alongside my long-suffering and saintly wife, Mrs King …

Mr King wafts his hand to front of stage right, where Sandra stands, drink in hand, glancing down to her feet.

Don't be shy, Sandra! Take a bow!

Mrs King scrunches her eyes for a second as the applause comes, grows, crowned by a *woo-hoo* yelp from a swaying Alan Childlove as Sandra raises a quick wave into the air, looking at no-one.

… And of course, let's not be forgetting our spiritual core, the pip of Edendale's apple if you will … the Reverend Haywire … (not yet, idiots) a man ever on hand to hear out our problems both spiritual and practical alike, offering a wisdom and a goodness that over the years many of us have benefitted from …

Mr King claps, leading by example, as the Reverend waves both hands in the air and nods, looking around benevolently at his applauding congregation, a hand now on the shoulder of his wheelchaired wife who waves also, who looks around and smiles in acceptance, a quiet rebellion of *yes, I helped too*.

... And last, but certainly not least, the man that keeps our shelves stocked here in Edendale, the man who makes sure we are never short of anything, from baked beans to bottled beer, and not to mention that very particular brand of off the shelf humour he so readily supplies ... (oh *now* you sheep-fuckers get my jokes ...) our very own Mr Alan Childlove!

Alan is on a table. Bowing. Now punching the air. Now doing some kind of suggestive dance of thrusting hips and ski-pole arms. Mr King blinks, once, twice, as the applause rises, as the cheers fill the marquee. *Cunt.* Alan falls off the table, and the marquee swells with laughter. Mr King feels himself shaking his head, stops, lest they see his disgust. *Dumb fuckers love a bit of slapstick from a moron.* Mr King leans into the microphone and clears his throat. Somewhere in the distance Alan *woo-hoos* again. Laughter.

... I WOULD ALSO LIKE to THANK ... EACH ... and EVERY ... ONE OF YOU ... THAT participated in the parade ... or helped with the stalls and displays ... here on Forgiveness Green, and in the Church Hall, or by your very being here, you ... villagers and visitors alike... who have made this a wonderful day of celebration!

Mr King feels the smile tight on his face, tries to soften it,

Alan Childlove back on the table in the far left of his vision, Mr King now raising his arms and clapping high, pleased as the people mirror his gesture …

THANK YOU, THANK YOU … and so … without further ado, because I can see you're all itching to get dancing again …

Sat on the stage, behind the decks, Dennis twitches, straightens his back and glances over the table.

… And may I say what a great job our resident Edendale DJ is doing tonight … take a bow, Disco Dennis!

Mr King spins around, wafting an open hand towards Dennis, who stands, waves, bows as a chant of deh-niss deh-NISS DEH-NISS sprouts then tendrils around the marquee, led by his friends by the corner of the stage, much to the annoyance of Mr King, because no-one has chanted *his* name.

… SO! LET'S TURN DOWN THE LIGHTS, AND … GET the party started again, as our first ever Edendale carnival queen takes to the floor … Give us a wave, Maggie … isn't she beautiful, ladies and gentlemen … and Maggie has a basket of special Edendale Carnival chocolates she'll be handing out for you all to enjoy, and remember, we have an extra special event as the clock strikes a quarter to midnight … a fabulous firework extravaganza, organised by the Low Peak Council as a …

Maggie Haywire, basket of chocolates crooked in her left arm, takes to the stage and walks toward Mr King, his open-mouth paused as Maggie puts her lips to the microphone.

I HAVE SOMETHING … to SAY.

Mr King reaches out, goes to put his hand over the mic, but Maggie has already pulled the mic from its stand, crab-stepping three paces away, a flat palm telling him to stop ... wait ... listen.

The mirror-balled universe turns. A thousand eyes watching, waiting. The only sound the sound of Maggie's amplified breath ... in, out ... as she puts her basket to the floor.

The Reverend would call out her name, but the Reverend's wife grips his arm, says *wait*. Mr King would tear the mic from the mad girl's hand and push her off his stage, but what would the people think? Debbie would go up there to save her, to tell her to *come down*, that *it's alright*, but Debbie can't move, her heart a *bump-bump*, the words her friend is about to utter a hot knife-edge tracing her tongue, throat, breath. Dennis looks across at Michael who is looking at Sally, who is looking at Paul, who is watching Maggie, grinning, the voice in his head saying *go on girl, tell 'em all to go f...*

I JUST WANT TO SAY THANK YOU. THANK YOU for MAKING ME QUEEN. THANK YOU for GIVING ME A HOME in your VILLAGE. THANK YOU for my STEPDAD and STEPMUM. THANK YOU FOR BEING SO NICE TO ME when SOMETIMES I'm an IDIOT. I DON'T DESERVE THIS. IT SHOULD HAVE BEEN ROSE. SHE'S LOVELY. YOU PEOPLE are LOVELY. YOU'RE TOO NICE TO ME. I don't deserve you. I'M SORRY.

Maggie drops the mic, a BUMP then a feedback whine as she pulls the sash over her head, *Edendale Carnival Queen*

1979, a white shiver through the air as down on one knee she throws it to Rose, who stands open-mouthed and wide-eyed near the front of the stage as her hands clap around the falling sash, the marquee an eruption of cheer as Maggie jumps off the stage, takes the sash from the trembling hands of Rose and places it around the new queen, who is near-crying as Maggie hugs her, and the applause is love, and the cheers are togetherness, and the people crowd around the two queens, the old and the new, what was, and what will now come to pass, as through the throng comes the Reverend and his wheelchaired wife, to embrace their beautiful stepdaughter who has at last seen the light, the love, a stepdaughter who presses her lips to the new queen and says something no-one else can hear but her, as the Reverend lays his hands upon the penitent daughter, a kiss of forgiveness upon the head of a sinner, *amen*, as the DJ hits spin and kicks it in, and this tune is the one is the one, and everybody knows it, as Maggie picks the new queen up by the waist lifting her up, up, up upon high, and the stars will turn in this tented heaven as the grinning Dennis hits STROBE, and the/dan/cing/is/love, and the arms/in/the/air/ is love ... and all are now moving as one, living as one, being as one, and WE! are! FA-miLY! Rose crying tears of happy as Maggie eases her down, down, and WE! are! FA-miLY! and the people are cheering, and the people are singing, and GERRup EVree BOdee AND! Mr King picking the basket up, leaving the stage, mute, and WE! are! Dee Dee getting jostled further and further away as the people move in closer, I-GORRall-MAH-sisTURS-wi-ME! surrounding the dancing queens with love, and the mirror-ball turns, the stars shining bright, the voice in Debbie's head saying *who, who, who is this girl?*

Sally looks out of her window at the flats opposite. At night, in the dark, she sees little movies, little stories lit up like TV screens, unless, of course, they close their curtains on her, shut her out.

The Chinese was okay, but the sweet and sour sauce was sickly. Too sweet. Sticky almost. Inside the TV windows nothing is happening, so Sally returns to the sofa, the paused video flickering on the second-hand TV she bought last month, the bad-guy staring out of his car window with bottles on his fingers. Sally isn't sure she really likes the film. She doesn't even know why she picked it up from the video-shop shelf. A test?

She leans forward, picks up her glass from the coffee table, drinks. She doesn't like how her blue nail-polish sings too loud against the red of the wine. She doesn't like how her fingers look fat against the glass. She doesn't like how the bad guy stares, how her blue nail-polish is blue, how her glass doesn't smash when it falls to the carpet so she tells him, tells him out-loud that it wasn't her fault, over and over until she is standing, shouting the words, telling him and telling him, the upstairs flat a *bangbangbang* on her ceiling, *shut up, SHUT! UP!* dragging blue nails over the top of her clenched left hand, again, again, harder and harder until blood speckles the tracks, bottles on fingers, bottles on fingers, *War-riors ... come out to play-yay*, I am not a bad person ... I am not ... a bad ... person ... I am not ... a ... BAD PERson ... I AM NOT! a BAD! perSON! I AM NOT! A! BAD!

WE! are! FA-miLY! I-GORRall-MAH ... Paul cannot believe he's dancing to this shit. And neither can he believe how good it feels. Particularly good is the little *whoop!* that Debbie makes each time he pulls a new move, like that spin he did a second ago, telling himself it wasn't puffy cos that's what northern soulers do, yeh. And anyway, fuck it, no-one's looking, everyone's dancing, the only people seeing him are Sarah and Nat, that wet lad Tom, and Debbie ... Debbie who opens her eyes as the chorus drops into the verse, her arms slow-falling back to her sides, and now she's looking into Paul's eyes as her hips do that thing, as her waist does that thing, as her eyes close again and her hand is flat palm to Paul's, and as the chorus kicks in again her other hand is on his waist and he mirrors, that thing her waist does now against his hand, a movement finding itself as together they meet the bassline, his hand now on the curve of her hip, and this is just like fucking ... *him, fucking her* ... her doing that thing with her waist, her hips, and Paul can't remember the last time he fucked a girl, *oh yeh, that fat lass in the Roxy toilet ten years ago can't even remember her name* ... as Debbie moves her arm around him, her lips to his ear saying I'm so glad you came down Paul, and the thought hits him like a banger going off in his head as he puts his lips to her ear and says me too ... Jesus fucking Christ he has every chance of fucking Debbie Foxglove tonight, every chance, and if his hard-on is anything to go by he's gotta fuckin' relax, and he knows it, knows Debbie Foxglove is gagging for it, that if it happens he could end up shooting his load in three strokes flat, *Jesus don't let that happen, don't* … and, CUT … the bodies stopping as one as now through the speakers barks a voice of getting into it and the cheer goes up, like, like a SEX maCHINE, and as the voice counts a ONE TWO THREE FOUR … FUCK YEH! shouts Debbie, letting go of Paul as the horns punch the start of it, Debbie turning to face the stage, arms in the air shouting GO! DENNIS! as the people gyrate around her, and up there on the stage Dennis has one arm raised, headphones on, head nodding to the beat, knowing he's got them, tapping the notebook with a forefinger where the words JAMES FUCKING BROWN are biro'd big.

Sarah isn't dancing to this. She's had enough. Fine. Come down here with Dad and what does he do. Dances with that slag Debbie. Fine.

She drinks what's left of her drink, puts the plastic pint-pot back onto the table behind her. Folds her arms. Watches Nat dancing with Tom. Debbie dancing with her dad. Touching him. Wriggling her hips like she's fucking him. And look at him. Look at the look on his face. Look how she's looking at him. Slag. Now what? Where they going? Fine. Go take her for another drink, Dad. S'okay. I didn't want one. Thanks.

Paul, leant on the tree-trunk pole by the corner of the stage, does not like what he sees, and he *does not* like how he feels about it.

Sally is dancing too close to Michael. Again. She keeps catching Michael cunting Goodman's eye, there ... there ... and they keep laughing, and smiling, and copying each other's stupid fuckarse moves, and now they're fucking touching hands ... *what the fuck is* ... Paul lights a fag, tells himself everything gets fucked up anyway, and so what if Sally is a fuckarsed slag, what's it to him? He blows smoke out in a fast jet, up into the air, drinks, looks toward Maggie and Debbie who are dancing with Rose. Maggie. Right. Bollocks to Sally. Don't want to fuck her anyway. She's not punk. She's plastic. Pretend. Maggie ain't. She don't give a fuck. Look at her. Look how Kingy comes over says something to Rose, how Maggie says something to Kingy, how Kingy smiles, holds a hand up, nods, walks off. Now look. Look how Maggie is laughing with Rose. That told him. Maggie is boss. She knows what's what. Fuck Sally. If she's gonna be all slaggy wi' cuntface theer then I'm gonna be cunty wi' her. Fuck her.

Dee Dee is sat on the stage steps, watching. She doesn't like this music. It sounds rude. She doesn't like how Rose is now Maggie's friend, how Rose is now Debbie Foxglove's friend too, and no-one is her friend. She thinks about going home. Or maybe going to find Norman Standish and pretend to try and be his girlfriend because that's what Rose wants from him and *this is not fair this is not fair*. Oh. Rose is waving. Wants me to go and dance with her and her new friends does she? Pretend I didn't see her. Not looking. Not.

But Rose is in front of her now. Saying C'mon Dee Dee! Come and have fun with us!

Dee Dee tells her no, she doesn't want to dance to this. It's rubbish.

And now Maggie Haywire is here, and Debbie Foxglove is here, and all three of them are grinning, and tugging at Dee Dee, C'mon ... Come and dance with us.

Okay.

On the stage, Mr King tells Dennis that he would rather not hear songs that say things like this one. Okay?

Okay.

Mr King tells Dennis his co-operation would be appreciated, and he leaves by the steps.

Dennis slides his notebook out from under the mixer, pulls his biro out of the notebook spine, and writes JAMES FUCKING BROWN in big letters, grins, drinks, squats by the Motown case, grins again because he knows what track is gagging for up next.

Paul is watching Debbie's lips as she drinks. Out here, the sweat feels cool on his back. He lights a roll-up, then remembers that Debbie smokes too.

From the bridge, Debbie can see stars in the water.

Want me to roll you one?

She looks up at Paul, who wiggles a fag between his fingers, grins.

Nah. Prefer these, she says, half-twisting to pull a pack

of Rothmans from her small blue shoulder-bag. Ta anyway.

Paul likes how she wears her handbag. The strap crossing her breasts, from shoulder to opposite thigh like a kid might wear her schoolbag.

Paul is saying something about how lovely the sky looks. Debbie doesn't hear, not really. She's still looking into the water, at the stars, remembering.

Paul doesn't like how Sally's nose looks all shiny, how the little bumps of sweat look like ugly red freckles in the flash of Dennis's disco lights. He tells her straight. Well why don't you just go dance with Michael again then?

Sally's eyes tell him that his words stung. She blinks, looks to the floor for a second, then looks back up at Paul. I'm not dancing with Michael. We're all dancing together. All of us. It's a disco, Paul. Did you not notice that?

Paul grates his back against the tree-trunk pole, the heat rising in his belly. I thought you were punk, Sally? You know ... *punk?*

Blink.

That stung her again he thinks, feeling something like pleasure from the hurt in her eyes.

That's not fair. *You're* not being fair. I like what I like. You wear your likes like a prison. And everything else is shit, *isn't it Paul* ... Who made you the god of good fucking taste ... *ey?*

Sally feels something like pleasure from her words, from the look in Paul's eyes as she turns, looking back over her shoulder to tell him she's going to get some fresh air, that if this date is going to survive then he needs to loosen the fuck up and have some fun, and to stop-stop-stop behaving like a jealous ... twelve-year-old ... *twat.*

Pushing through the people, Sally doesn't like how the words twelve-year-old twat sound silly in her head, the way she feels about pretending she wants to carry on with this date, how she wishes Paul would just sod off, how the world isn't fair, because if it was, she could just dump Paul here and now, because he's a twat, and no-one, no-one would call her a slag if she ...

HIT IT! *BUMPF-BUMPF-BUMPF* ...

AhmJUSTa LUV! maCHINE! and Dennis is particularly pleased with this mix, YEH-heh BAY-bee ... Sex Machine, Love Machine, Dennis lad, you ... are both. He jumps from the stage three feet from where Debbie is dancing with Maggie, where Michael is dancing with Dee Dee and Rose, where Dennis will strut like a sexy chicken, elbows as wings, arse as tail-feathers, Dennis lad, you are the man ... Huh-huh ... AhmJUSTa LUV! maCHINE! Dennis now sidling up to Debbie Foxglove who does something Christ-all-fuckin-mighty with her hips, and now she sees him, Dennis, the Edendale Love Machine, yeh-heh bay-bee, how you liking this move, huh-huh ... And Debbie Foxglove stops dancing. And Debbie Foxglove starts laughing. And Dennis feels his mojo dribbling out his arse as Maggie Haywire hops into view, wraps an arm around the gasping bent-over Debbie, Dennis feeling his once-sexy chicken wings become last night's drunk-dropped chips on a Sunday morning pavement, Maggie's face now a foot from his, This BITCH is MINE, DICK ... FUCK OFF.

Bea-U-tiful ... bur-LOODY ... BEAU-tiful, yell-drawls Alan Childlove into the face of the Reverend, as all around them villagers gyrate and twist.

Yes, it was, the Reverend smiles, as Alan now projects a full plastic pint-pot grip of lager and fist towards him, froth spitting out the top and onto the Reverend's black jacket.

THAT MAGGIE ... is ... a ... DIA-MOND ... a FRIGGIN' ... DIA-MOND ... GET THIS DAHN THEE!

The Reverend Haywire hesitates, the drunken shopkeeper jiggling the slopping pint-pot in his face.

C'MON LAD! GOD'S TELLIN' THEE! GERRIT NECKED!

The Reverend's wife pats her lap as Mrs King nods, says Yes Dorothy, it was beautiful, so sweet ... and such a surprise ... I thought Jeremy was going have a heart attack up there.

Mrs King laughs, Dorothy Haywire looking up at her and pulling a twisty-lipped grimace of *oh dear*, turning her attention to Margaret Banford, who so far doesn't seem to have said anything about Maggie's beautiful moment on the stage.

Margaret Banford smiles a tight-lipped smile down at the wheelchaired Mrs Haywire.

Yes ... Dee Dee's aunt says, I'm sure my niece will be most happy for Rose.

Sandra King doesn't hear the stiff sarcasm in Margaret

Banford's tone because she isn't listening. She's looking across the heads of the benched people down the side of the marquee, down towards the right-hand side of the stage, to where in the dim flash-blink of strobe flicker she sees her husband pointing into the face of Reg the electrician, who is still dressed in his overalls, scratching his head, a shrug, her husband now jab-jabbing his finger into the old man's chest.

Paul thinks he should, thinks it's now or never as Debbie puts her cigarette out on the wooden rail that stops people falling into the Went. He takes a step towards her, the sound of his Doc Martin a soft pad upon the boards of the bridge.

Debbie doesn't hear. She is still looking into the water, at the stars, at the moon, at the glimmer of reflected lights near the bank.

Paul changes his mind, thinks not yet. He takes his tobacco pouch out of his jeans pocket and leaning against the rail, three inches from the elbow of Debbie Foxglove, starts to roll another fag. He needs to say something. This feels uncomfortable.

So ... ever heard owt from Maggie then?

Debbie blinks, says no, says let's go back, starts walking the bridge towards Forgiveness Green, says something about another drink, Paul dropping his fag-paper, now following in Debbie's wake as the Rizla slips between the boards, down into the river, held just below the surface of slow-moving water as it heads toward the mill.

52.

Tick-tock, river clock. They think Went stops, Blackbird. Away, away, around hills and villages until it gets to other river with different name so no more Went. Names, names, names. People make them, give them, so make end. Tick tock, silly dot. Water comes from sky onto hill, into cracks down, down, out of cave making river, on and on to other river, on and on to sea, then sun melts water into air, into clouds, wind blows over hill and down it comes into cracks, start again. What's end, Blackbird? Where's start? Sheep eat grass then tummy mashes it, tummy sending it to bottom hole out onto ground it sits until makes a soil, and out of soil comes grass. The quick brown fox jumps over the lazy dog. See? Father never let me have a pet. He said dogs make shits and cats bring dead mouse into house. Mother would never help my asks to Father, so I never got. Not even a fish ... and fish are important in our story ... can you tell, Blackbird?

You hear it, so you must have said it.

Yes.

Good! Then it's telling right! Breathers are catchers, most times ... they catch and put their pets in cages, to keep all for self. Prison. I don't think that right. Better friend than pet. My first friend was woodpigeon. He sat on shed roof some days. I'd open my window, slow so not to scare him. Then I'd say hello Woody, but I'd say it quiet so no-one could hear but him. Then I didn't see him for a while. Days, weeks, and snow-time came. It made me sad when he wasn't sitting on shed no more. Remembering is like pretending, but pretending tick-tock stop, everything else foggy woods, eyes open not seeing when looking in head always, this is what it was, this is what it is, again, again, again ... but then, after snow-time went and daffodil came, silly Johnny woke up once and heard sing-song, and when I looked out, there they were, all of them. Thrushy. Robin. Dove-dove. Sparrow Joe. Sparrow Jill. Chaffy. Dove-dove. Robin. Sparrow Jill. Sparrow Joe. Chaffy. Thrushy ... Do you see, Blackbird? They all fly away. All of them. But that's okay. Sometimes they come back. If they really want to.

Tick-tock, river clock. One bird gone, another one come. Look.

53.

OOOooh … AH-AH! Rose is laughing because Michael is singing to her. Michael Goodman. Nineteen years old and too old to be her boyfriend. He grabs hold of her hands and lifts them up into the air … Huh-huh … AhmJUSTa LUV! maCHINE! and she thinks she would like to kiss Michael Goodman. What would it be like? She remembers the kiss she had with Norman Standish at Claire Appleton's birthday party when they played spin the bottle. Everyone laughed. Too many people watching to feel what it was like. Norman didn't even look at her after. He just pulled a face like he was going to be sick and went *uuurgh,* blobbing his tongue out like it needed air to clean it, saying something quiet to Barry Harper when he sat back down across the other side of the circle, both of them laughing.

He didn't even use his tongue. Would Michael use his tongue? He would. He's older, and would know what to do. She thinks he must have kissed lots of girls. He's dancing with Dee Dee now.

From the corner of the stage, Michael is watching her.

All around her the bodies are moving, an insect rhythm that blocks her out, gives him a glimpse, blocks her out. He needs to get closer.

The Miracles fade, The Detroit Emeralds sliding through, a snake of bass, a snap of snare, a voice that says look at me, I'm hurting, and I'm walking towards you, now, through these nothing bodies, closer … and she is dancing, alone … no … a girl is with her … Lyndsey Palmer … that girl from Sarah's lit group, forgettable.

OH feel … FEEL the NEED in me …

And now, this close, he can see the light catch in her eyes. Like that first morning, the sun through the gap in his curtains, the kiss, *I need to go soon … no, stay, stay a little longer, don't go,* the kiss, the fuck, birdsong, the milk-truck rattle down Love Terrace, *don't leave, ever …* watching her get dressed, turned away and shy, her knickers a slow-quick up, now the bra on backwards, soft scratch sound as she twists it right-way-round, now arms through straps up and over shoulders, turn, his look caught, guilty, her smile a smile he wants to keep forever in a frame as she bends over his bed to kiss him, *I love you Sarah, I love you …*

NEED/NEED/NEED/NEED/NEED … The insect rhythm a single twitch of heads towards the stage. A sheepish grinning Dennis holding a hand up in the air as though to say sorry, wait a mo, the echo/echo of a dumb word caught in a scratch filling the tent as the people laugh, cheer, GERRIT SORTED DENNIS! as the echo dies dead, a cheer, the new sound now a princess of soft-drawn violin as the girl long-breathes *oh*, sparkles of bell ... and now the bassline, the snare and hi-hat, four/four, four/four ... MEEster ... YOR hiyZARR-fooLOV HEZZeeTAYshon ...

MISTER CHUFFIN' GOODMAN!

Michael blinks. Lyndsey Palmer has hold of his arm.

DANCE WITH US!

Mrs King watches Reg slow-weave his way between the benches, head down, on his way outside to check on the generator to get it fucking sorted, as Mr King put it so precisely.

Mrs King cannot stop herself.

Jeremy. Reg is doing this for nothing. You can't have a go at him like that. It's not right.

Mr King looks up to the marquee roof, to the stars turning, turning ...

OhhhYEHsur ... HIYcanBOOgee ...

He blows a quick draft of air from pursed lips.

Are *you* ... telling *me* ... what ... to do ... *dear?*

Jeremy King fixes his wife with a narrow-eyed glare. She has seen this before. But still, she can't stop herself.

No. I'm not telling you what to do, *dear,* but it wasn't Reg's fault the power went. And really ... the poor sod's in his sixties ... (pause, breathe out) I just don't think it's fair to go at him like you did.

She says the last part of it as soft as she can, the music too loud to speak it out without half-shout, accentuating the words with careful shaping of the lips to take the edges off, knowing as she does how not to say things to her husband.

Mr King sniffs. Raises his left eyebrow. Pause.

You'd better ... shut ... your *fucking* ... *mouth* ... dear.

Sandra King cannot stop herself. WHY? WHAT YOU GOING TO DO, JEREMY? HIT ME? IN FRONT OF EVERYONE? EY?

Sandra King is walking away. Jeremy King surveys the people, the seated, the dancing, waves to selected onlookers, smiles, laughs, straightens the Windsor knot in his tie.

OhhhYEHsur ... HIYcanBOOgee ... And Lyndsey Palmer is drunk. And Lyndsey Palmer won't shut up. And Lyndsey Palmer, hand on his shoulder, keeps yanking Michael's head to speak into his ear as they dance. And over Lyndsey Palmer's shoulder he is looking at Sarah. And Sarah is dancing. And Sarah is smiling. And Sarah is grinning. And Sarah is laughing.

Yank, yank, yank.

And Lyndsey Palmer shouts LOVED THAT CATCHER IN THE RYE! And Lyndsey Palmer shouts LOVED THAT HOLDEN CORNFIELD! And Lyndsey Palmer shouts LOVED THAT ... And Michael feels Sarah's fingers between his fingers. And Michael knows that look in her Cleopatra eyes. And Michael feels the song of all history unmaking itself, recasting into thin shards that dance in the light of this new moon dancing over a midnight sea, and ... LOVED THAT DYLAN THOMPSON POEM ABOUT NOT DYING! And Sarah's fingers clasp, saying *yes,* saying *again*, saying ... OhhhYEHsur ... HIYcanBOOgee ... and Tom and Natalie are back from the bar and Tom hands Natalie the drinks and Tom is pushing through the people and Tom grabs Sarah's arm and ... HATED THAT DAFFODIL POEM THOUGH! THAT ... were ... SHIT!

I JUST DON'T UNDERSTAND WOMEN, the crouched Dennis shout-tells Michael as he fingers through his northern soul box. Michael drinks, eyes Paul over the rim of his plastic pint-pot, there, down by the tree-trunk pole, stood mute, arms crossed, his face hard to read ... pissed off?

Dennis pulls a single out, slides the vinyl from the sleeve, holds it at an angle to the flashing lights, narrows his eyes, blows a speckle of dust off the intro groove. Like ... ONE MINUTE THAT DEBBIE LIKES ME ... THE NEXT SHE'S TAKIN' THE PISS.

Dennis stands up, places the single on the turntable. Michael tells him THIS BACCARA SONG is SHIT. Dennis frowns, puts the headphones over one ear, and bending slightly, places the needle down onto the waiting record.

It's them SEXY FOREIGN BIRDS INNIT, Dennis says, standing upright and grabbing his pint. Proper SEXY FUCKERS.

Dennis drinks, puts his pint down on the trestle table, puts both hands on his hips, leans into Michael, yowls OwwwwYEHSUR! like a camp French werewolf an inch from Michael's face.

Michael coughs cider onto the stage floor. Dennis pats him on the back. Michael takes one step away from Dennis, raises an eyebrow. Dennis puts his hands on his hips again.

Wiggles. Michael shakes his head. Dennis play-slaps him on the arm.

SO … WHAT'S HAPPENIN' wi' YOU an' that MAGGIE BIRD THEN?

Michael wipes his mouth with his shirt-sleeve, tells Dennis that Maggie is TAPPED, GAME OVER, Dennis pulling his headphones on, turning to the decks.

AREN'T they ALL fuckin' TAPPED?

Michael needs another drink. He shakes his empty pint-pot to Dennis who glances up, nods, croons a YEZZ PLEEEZ DAHLING, slow sliding faders up/down, not watching as Michael leaves the stage, not seeing Paul put an arm out in front of the passing Michael, not hearing Paul tell Michael to keep his HANDS OFF things that DON'T belong to him, YEH? not hearing Michael say WHAT? What you ON ABOUT? Paul saying THA KNOWS WHAT.

DOODaLANG-DOODaLANG … push past the bodies not looking heading out get out had enough don't look behind not looking to see if he's following, hands now together belly-button high a clench prayer of *fuckfuckfuck* fingernails dig in, scratch, scratch, pinch left hand, pinch right hand, DOODaLANG-DOODaLANG … push past bodies not looking already knowing Tom's following, Nat too probably *fuckfuckfuck* had enough *where's Dad?* NEEEDLE inna HAYstack … push past bodies past huddle not looking *get out the way* and out, out into the cooler air and, SARAH … SARAH! stop.

Tom.

WHAT?

WHAT YOU DOIN' WI' GOODMAN DON'T TELL ME NOWT COS I SEEN IT SARAH I SEEN YOU WI' 'IM ... what the FUCK'S GOIN' ON?

And off she goes again, hands together belly-button high, clench prayer of *fuckitfuckitFUCK* fingernails dig in, scratch, scratch, pinch left hand, pinch right hand, SARAH ... SARAH! stop.

Sarah stands rigid, chin down, looking down to red backs of clenched hands, to feet, to grass, to walked on candy floss flat pink dead, and here are Tom's feet.

I DON'T UNDERSTAND, SARAH. TELL ME. Tell me what's GOIN' OFF.

She feels his fingers under her chin.

LOOK AT ME.

She looks. In the red green lights of the goldfish stall she can see the tiny islands of shaved hair on his chin. The pimple by his lip.

LOOK AT ME.

There is something like hurt in his eyes. She tells him nothing is happening. She tells him that Lyndsey grabbed Goodman and got him to dance. That Lyndsey is drunk, messing about, that she was already dancing with Lyndsey when it happened, not dancing with Goodman, *not*, and that's all it was, *nothing*, and if Tom doesn't stop it he's going to spoil everything, and she needs the toilet, pinch left hand, pinch right hand, turn and walk away.

Dee Dee didn't dance for long. She didn't like the feeling

in her belly seeing Rose messing about with Maggie and Debbie, *ha-ha, look at me, these are my new friends, much more fun than Dee Dee, because Dee Dee is borrring*. So off Dee Dee went, off outside to buy candy-floss, to come back inside dodging the moving bodies, a trophy treat not started until she got near Rose, *look, look what I've got, ha ha, who needs rubbish friends like you?* and now she is eating it, *not got you one, not got you one,* and Rose is looking, smiling, waving, dancing and messing about with Maggie and Debbie, DOODaLANG-DOODaLANG ... her brand new best friends because *ha-ha, Dee Dee is borrring, borrring* ... and Alan the shopkeeper is drunk, or something, leaning over Dee Dee's shoulder saying giz a lick, DOODaLANG-DOODaLANG ... and Dee Dee nearly saying *you don't lick candy-floss you idiot* but she doesn't like the look on the shopkeeper's face, something she can't know or understand but not liking it all the same, and now the people all around her are laughing, look at the Reverend, look at the Reverend dancing daft, and the people cheer but Dee Dee sees Maggie not liking it, or something, a look in her eyes she can't know or understand, but then, Maggie liking it very much *too much* when the Reverend's skyward-bound Travolta fist hits some woman in the chin and everyone goes oh! the woman tilting wobbly, and Maggie is laughing, and Debbie is laughing, and look, Rose is laughing too.

Look down. No blood. Sarah presses the flush, rubs her thumb on her leggings, not wanting the germs from the silver fingerprinted smudgey button, looks in the mirror, at the black lips, at the Cleopatra eyes ... *who, who, who is this girl?*

Sarah washes her hands, dries them on a paper towel, opens the portaloo door, and there, stood on the steps, backlit by the carnival flicker, is Tom. Both hands on her shoulders, he soft-pushes her back inside, says he needs to talk to her, *now*. She puts her hand on his chest, but too late. He turns, twists the handle. Engaged. Now he turns to face her. The look in his eyes is something she hasn't seen before. His breath seems stunted, but faster?

Do you love me? he says.

Maggie, arms in the air, shout-tells them they're all going for a beer, to find a ride before the carnival shuts down, because she is queen, RIGHT?

Maggie looks to Rose, shout-asks if the other queen agrees. She does. Rose skips three skips forwards toward Dee Dee who stick sideways is mouthing a pink-purple cloud of candy-floss. Rose tight-grabs her hand and pulls, then pulls again. Dee Dee would ask *what?* but her and Rose and Maggie and Debbie are already a hand-in-hand choo-choo train chuffing through the bodies, NEEEDLE inna HAYstack ... hell-bent, hell-bound for exit.

His kiss is too hard, his finger too hard as it stiff-pokes up inside her. Sarah, eyes closed, is watching the blackbirds again, watching through the water of a plastic-bagged goldfish held out, hearing the sounds of a carnival from a place not here.

He is doing something to his trousers. He is pulling her hand by the wrist. His words a dry blur of hot breath against her mouth, do you love me, do you love me?

SheDOOP ... sheDOOP ... a station from the exit, the hand-in-hand choo-choo stops. Maggie turns around to see what the problem is. Debbie turns around too. Rose is looking at Dee Dee, who is looking up at her aunt. The aunt looks to her niece, to Rose, to Debbie, to Maggie, the aunt's eyes narrowing as though seeing a pickpocket's hand slow-reach into a walleted pocket.

Tom's hand is on her shoulder. Tom's hand is on the back of her head, the fingers tightening in her hair. The portaloo floor presses damp onto her knees. She thinks about her black lipstick, the mark it will leave. She closes her eyes to it. Gone. She gags as he pushes. She sees blackbirds, fish, trees, black branch fingers dancing, distorted by a shifting moon as down, down into the water she goes, and the spike is in her neck, and the fourth is the end, and the fifth will smash her ribs, and the sixth will break her spine, iron shaft that nails her unborn child to the never will, and on the seventh she will walk the bridge, fog, the sound of a crow, *now, I'm cumin ... swaller it, fuckin' swaller it ...*

SheDOOP ... sheDOOP ... Dee Dee's aunt has told Dee Dee straight. And Dee Dee has told Rose. And Rose has told Debbie who has told Maggie, who curls her lip, rolls her eyes. Dee Dee has to stay in the marquee, here, where her aunt can keep an eye on her. Dee Dee looks at Rose, hand still in hand, waiting. The hands undo. Rose tells Dee Dee she'll be back soon. Dee Dee thinks she might cry, her best friend walking out into the night, Debbie one side, Maggie the other, sheDOOP ... gone.

You okay? he asks.

She dabs her mouth with toilet paper. Doesn't look. Stands up. The knock on the portaloo door is the saddest sound that Sarah has ever heard.

Tom tells Mrs King that Sarah has been throwing up. Mrs King asks Sarah if she's alright. Sarah says yes thank you as her and Tom exit, as Mrs King enters, turns the handle. Engaged.

OO! Sally isn't talking to Paul ... oo! And Paul isn't talking to Sally ... OO! Even though Sally just brought him a drink and he's drinking it ... oo! And Sally's already said she's sorry ... OO! But Paul's thinking about Maggie ... oo! But thinking safe bet so maybe make up with Sally ... HEYey BAYbee! But Sally wants to dance have fun not watch people having fun fuck this is boring I love this song I want to dance to it not watch people dancing to it.

She turns to face Paul. Tugs his jacket-sleeve playful, smiles when he looks at her.

What? he says, the word feeling brick from his mouth.

But, stop ... Sally is sexy, right? As sexy as Maggie, maybe ...

What? he says again, smiling now, making the brick a velvet cushion.

Sat on the portaloo toilet, knickers stretched between knees, dress up around her waist, hands over her face and eyes closed, Sandra King is walking the lawn towards Rose, who sits cross-legged on the grass, pet rabbit Carrots sat nose-twitching in her lap as the dead daughter strokes her, soft-firm hand a repeat of head-to-tail, head-to-tail, not seeing her mother approach, head-to-tail, head-to-tail, and the ghost-child is singing, quiet, to herself and to Carrots, *she's a kill-errr ... queeeeen ... gunpowwwder ... jellybeans ... dy-na-mite with a lazy beam* ... and now looking up the dead girl sees her mother ... and Rose is smiling a smile that will never leave, ever, and Sandra King is sobbing, shaking in a stale fug of piss and dim fluorescent light, alone ... alone ... fingernails pressing into scalp, black bottomless pit of knowing she could have stopped it, she could've ... his grunts and stench of carcass coming back to her unwanted, and she feels sick, acid burn in her belly, rising quick, dizzy splash onto portaloo floor, and she could've stopped it, she could've ... and she is falling, always, falling.

54.

Did you ever do jigsaw, Blackbird?

You hear it, so you must have said it.

No.

Ah ... well ... jigsaw is chopped-up picture of bigger thing made small bits, and when bits are put all together you see picture of bigger thing. I think story is getting very jigsaw now, like ghost hands are putting it together quick and quicker. If it was song it'd be like song is going quicker near end to make fast-dance. There are lots of songs in our story aren't there. All people-players have own song and sometimes sing with others. Like at school assembly when we sang Jesus songs and sometimes I made my own words. GLAD THAT I LIVE AM I ... AND SKY IS POO ...

Teacher heard me once and asked me why I was being naughty. I told her I wasn't being naughty and she said yes you are Johnny because these are God's songs and you aren't singing right words and God wouldn't like you doing that. I told Teacher I wasn't sure God could even hear me and she said yes he can Johnny because God hears everything. Teacher had red face when she said it. It was more red when I told her I was thinking God wasn't anywhere anyway. Teacher breathed out and said it sounded like I didn't want to be good and go to Heaven.

Maybe that's why I walk in fog. But, I don't think so. Not Really.

Teacher made me stay in, not play out at dinnertime. Made me read Bible. Said I had to read gospels of dead people so I saw Jesus story then I would understand. She said gospel meant good news. Staying in not playing out didn't feel like good news. At all. I think it better to play out, make own gospel. Maybe our story should be called it? Gospel according to Johnny Bender ... Nah. Sounding daft. Like Jesus story. Never seen a Jesus out here. Or his dad. We should do this our own I think. Not waiting for helping god-ghost hand from cloud. Things happen anyway. Like jigsaw makes picture. But picture is already made. It just waits in box for own hand to make it so see it. Quick, brown, fox. Jumps, over, the. Lazy, dog. Did you know it said every letter? Like every bit is there but you don't see it. Can't count feathers on thrushy as she flies by can you? Too quick. Like brown fox. But in night, fox not brown, is black. Things change. And in this place night come too soon. Sun behind tor. Tor shadow dark. Nothing stop it.

Let's finish jigsaw. Fox is coming.

55.

Michael stops mid-step to take the heads off both pints, left hand, right hand, the fingers of his left wet with slopped cider, so stop again, drink another mouthful or two off each.

Here, between the beer-tent and the marquee, lit by a string of red lights, shows the grass trodden into something like a path, a path Michael is glad to be on, away from that mad-fuck Maggie Haywire who just strode into the beer-tent as he was on his way out, and of course she saw him, and of course she did that thing where she just raised an eyebrow, glancing away, pretending not to see, him, this soft-lad nowt she snogged this afternoon and now she pretends he means nothing, was nothing ... *what, a fucking, bitch* ... but hey, whatever, there's only one girl he's bothered about now, the sounds of Aretha Franklin a tug of come back, dance, and as he continues his walk back towards the marquee he knows this is going to be tricky. But stop. A girl is calling his name. Rose King, waving, ten yards to his right, stood with Debbie Foxglove, not waving.

Debbie Foxglove watches Michael Goodman walk over. Smiling at Rose. Saying Hello Rosey-Posey. Saying You comin' in for a dance? Saying Ah, right. Saying Here, have a slurp of this. Saying Go on, it'll do you good. Saying There, see. Saying Come and have a dance inabit? Saying Promise? Saying Deal. Saying You alright then, Debs? And Debbie says Yeh, Michael stooping, just, kissing Rose on the cheek, now walking away, leaving Rose looking to her feet, saying nothing.

OO! Sally has tried … oo! but. Look, Paul … I like to dance … I like dancing … and this is supposed to be a date. On a date you have fun. On a date you like each other and make each other happy. You don't stand around watching everyone else having fun. You don't not talk. Not laugh. You …

Oh … and I suppose Michael makes you laugh does he?

What?

I. Sup-*pose*. Mi …

I heard you the first time, Paul … WHAT … are you getting at?

Paul draws on his cigarette, blows smoke out fast. Says something Sally can't quite hear, aReEeSsPeeEeCeeTee … drops his fag to the floor, turns and walks away, pushing through the bodies, Sally not sure what the fuck is going on here.

Here we go girls … three lovely gin and tonics because we're lovely.

Maggie holds the triangle of drinks out to Debbie who takes the front one. Debbie grins, says ta. Maggie hands one to Rose. The bass throb from the marquee, the slurring organ of the merry-go-round, a thin scream from a far-off ride ... these are all the sounds that Rose hears.

Right girls ... down in one ... ready?

Debbie and Rose both nod, grin, echo back a ready. GO!

Through the liquid, the plastic, Rose can see the flicker-creep lights of the merry-go-round, the horses turning, and now the pin-prick of stars, an open mouth of moon, everything now gone as the gulp makes her eyes close, the sound of Maggie laughing, of Maggie shouting DO IT, Rose, DO IT, of Debbie coughing, laughing, of the red-lit grass at her feet, of wiping her chin, of Maggie laughing, of Debbie patting her on the back, of Maggie shouting RIGHT GIRLS! OCT-o-PUS TIME!

Sandra King wishes the lights were better in here. These fluorescent lights make everything look blueish. Grey. Dead. She leans closer to the mirror, dabbing around her eyes with toilet paper. She blinks, reaches into her handbag, still looking into the mirror as she feels for her foundation. Next door, the toilet flushes. The sound of a man coughing. Hacking phlegm up. Spitting?

Found it.

She unscrews the top off the tube, squirts a small curl onto her finger, returns her gaze to the mirror to work on her face as the question comes again, the same question that comes most days. Would this marriage have been better if

Rose was still here? The answer is always the same, despite the question's recurring peck.

No. Jeremy is a selfish, arrogant, insecure, shallow, *bastard*.

Does she hate him? *Yes*. Is she trapped? *Yes*. Is it her fault? *Yes*.

She squeezes another curl of foundation from the tube. Looks to the mirror. Dab. Dab. Stop. Why don't you leave him? She blinks at her own words, at the door slamming in the next cubicle, at the sound of the man hacking up more phlegm … quieter … quieter … She thinks her face looks better for the work. The upset hidden. Like the signs of age. The deeper lines, the dark half-moons under the eyes, the … Someone is in the next cubicle. She hears the door close, the handle turn, the sound of feet shuffling. She puts her foundation back into her handbag and feels for her hairbrush. In her hand, the bristles feel like spikes. The light above her hums. She works on her curls, careful not to disrupt the shape, to correct, not to spoil. Where would she go if she left him? Where? She loves the house. It keeps some things alive. It holds memories in rooms. It keeps a shadow of when she was happy. It helps her remember. It keeps some things alive.

She puts the hairbrush back into her handbag. In the mirror she is Sandra King. In the mirror she … a loud knock at the door makes her jump.

JUST a MINUTE!

Knock, knock … knock, knock.

And the octopus arm yanks them too-fast back from the outswing and I'M GONNA PISS ME-SEN HAHAhaha heads tilt left tilt right Rose squished inbetween, scream, and the octopus arm swings too-fast changing too-fast from in to back out again, Maggie's dress billowing up hahaHAHA and Rose looking up sees the stars make lines through tears HAHAhaha Debbie's hands tight between thighs I'M TELLIN' YER I'm gonna PISS ME-SEN hahaHAHA the octopus arm taking them too-fast from out to back in again and Maggie is shrieking and Debbie is laughing and Rose feels the tears cold on her face and moon is a blur and stars are a blur and the octopus arm slowing, slowing, and the air around her feels like the weight of water, and she's rising to the surface, slow, slow ...

Sandra King opens the door, feels her bones snap inside her. A light flashes, a distant scream, blur of merry-go-round like moon on water.

The ghost of her. There. At the bottom of the steps. Arm reaching out.

Eyup Mrs King ... soz to knock ... just really, really need a wee.

The girl steps up one step into the fluorescent wake. Brushes past sideways into the portaloo, Sandra King leaning into the doorway as the carnival spins around her.

A hand upon her arm. You alreyt, Mrs King?

Rose is gagging, and now it comes, an acid rise of thin sick splashing down onto the grass, speckling the sash, and

Maggie is laughing as again it comes, Rose feeling a hand on her back as she arches again, again, the red/green/orange grass spinning underneath her.

Pause. Breathe. Debbie's voice, You alreyt Rose?

Rose stands upright, wipes her mouth with the back of her hand, now flat-palm sweep across the sash, says yes, I think so, laughs, just, Maggie now coming closer, hugging her, telling her she's in the gang now, forever.

And this song sings of a river, and you, are about to drown in it. Outside the marquee, Paul feels he is on the outside of *everything*. He turns to face the Went, the moor that rises black in the dark, leans back against the corner of the village disco tent.

Fuck disco. Fuck soul. Fuck nignog shit.

He feels the bass pulse of Sam and fuckarsed Dave trembling the tree-trunk pole against him. He hears the whoops and the people buzz from inside. Hold on ... He's outside because he's an outsider. True punk. True punk til he dies. He drinks. He raises his free hand to his head, finger-twists the spikes across his hairline, flat-palm to the top checking all is spikey. Fuck disco. Fuck soul. Fuck nignog shit. Punks don't need to belong. Punks are fuck you pal, take me as I am. No fakin' it. Real. Not manufactured. Not like that puff pop disco shit. Pistols never faked it. Not packaged. Never. They happened. Cos it were needed. Proper musicians playing proper instruments and fuck you if we make a noise. Sid. He happened.

Paul looks down at his Doc Marts, his drainpipe jeans

with the rips across the knees, his Buzzcocks t-shirt, leather jacket, studs around the cuffs.

No-one looks like me in this shithole. No-one. I am what I am, and I ain't changin' for no fucker.

Someone shouts his name and Paul twitches, turns to see Jed Hopkins waving him to come over. Paul walks the short walk from the corner of the marquee to the goldfish stall, feeling himself exaggerate the swing of his shoulders, the every-other-step scuff of boot-heel on grass, the slouch ... punk. What's up, Jed?

From behind the trestle table, Jed Hopkins holds a bagged goldfish out to him.

I'm packin' up, mate ... got one left ... you wannit?

Just HOLD on ... Michael leans into Sally, says into her ear, listen, listen to the drums, the bass ... c'mon Sally it's the Stax house band ... how can you resist?

Michael moves in front of her, wiggles his shoulders in time to the snare, pulls a cartoon sad face and Sally has to laugh. He takes her drink from her hand, takes two steps forward and puts their drinks onto the stage, takes two steps back and takes her hand, and Sally is still smiling as he soft-tugs her into the middle of this, and now they're dancing, hips and shoulders mirror, looking into each other's eyes as though each is waiting for the other to say something that'll change everything, HOLD on ... I'm COMin' ... and Sally raises her hands to her neck, fingers disappearing under her hair, smiling, smiling as the dog collar comes off, now held between them as she dangles it swinging to the beat, now dropped onto the grass below, gone, a shrug as Michael puts his hands on her hips, as she puts her hands flat-palm against his chest, HOLD on … I'm COMin' … and here is the very point in their story where they will kiss, not thinking one sliver of what if, not thinking a single thought of why not, because here is right now, yesterday is gone, tomorrow not even here, just now, now, now … as now Dennis flings his arms around them both EWWWD ON! AHHHM CUMMIN! and Sally leaves not wanting to look a right slag in front of the whole village.

Sandra King steps out the beer tent, gin and tonic in hand, stops, closes her eyes, and drinks.

Eyes open, she looks up to the moon, feels herself tense, the burn in her belly more than gin as through stiff lips she tells no-one but herself that *she hates him, hates him, hates him*.

She steps to the side, away from the entrance, as a huddle of drunk Castletor Cavaliers pass by heading into the beer tent, arms wrapped around shoulders, laughing at a joke she didn't hear. She drinks. Blinks. Breathes out, looking up to the moon again, that white face in a black sky of pin-prick stars.

No. She doesn't want to go back into the marquee. No. She doesn't want to be near that fucking prick of a man, a prick of all front and no content … no … that's not right … because inside him is something for sure … a writhing snake of pettiness and insecurity, a bad nasty serpent that coils then springs on turned backs in the dark, fangs dripping a slow-bitter poison that maims any threat to his snake-made standing as Councillor King ... King ... oh, how she hates that name ... how fitting ... how not ... better he be called Snake, *SnakeSnakeSnake* ... If only they knew.

She starts to walk, to where, she's not quite sure, but she thinks of home. Rose will be fine. Jeremy will still be here anyway, even if she isn't. Or maybe she should go back into the marquee ... just ignore him ... pretend he isn't there ... dance ...

To the annoying slur of the merry-go-round organ she stops to drink again. She might just turn around, go back get another. Why not. Get drunk. Make a fool of herself. Yeh. Why not. She gulps the rest of the gin and tonic down and spins on her heel feeling a shiver in her gut, thinking two doubles pour them both into one tumbler, hears her name being called, stop.

And bang on the double-snap of the outro snare Dennis slides the faders double-quick, a razor-cut blink exit, clean as a slammed door, Sam and Dave/Dusty Springfield, bang on the double-kick of the bass drum missing out the two-second fingered bass intro, and LITTLE byLITTLE byLITTLE byLITTLE (horn-horn) this is quite possibly one of Dennis's finest moments behind the decks of ALL FUcking TIME! which turning quick to Michael is just how he yells it, a little glory dance to a song of being torn apart, rip, rip, that WAS FUcking TOP! Dennis now raising his hands in the air as something like a flutter of bird-wing cheers flap around the tent. The floor is packed. Dennis knocks back the last of his lager and nods. Nice work Den-machine. Nice fucking work.

Michael is like this: each time Dennis changes a record, or talks to him, or starts fucking about, Michael sees something like a white flash in his head, a feeling of being brought out of a trance, like a bucket of cold water thrown onto a sleeping body, dragged from unwaking life where dreams are in soft focus, a girl, not here but somewhere else, a shape he can't quite define sharply enough but he knows, and with it brings an emptiness that worsens in the waking up, an untold mourning for the loss of a living life, and if she were dead it could be no worse.

LITTLE byLITTLE byLITTLE by … Michael can sense Dennis is dancing. Michael likes this song but nothing inside him moves. He is watching the blind girl dance. There. In the middle of everything. A look on her face that Michael finds, for a moment, somehow beautiful, the unseeing girl detached from all things except the music and her own movement. Then, he sees the mother put a hand upon her shoulder, leaning in to say something into her daughter's ear. The blind queen shrugs it off, the look on her face now one of annoyance, of go away, I'm dancing, and now is now is now, go away. The mother takes one step back. Begins a rigid dance. Not really hearing the music. Not feeling it. Just pretending, taking part for the sake of being part of the flock.

LITTLE byLITTLE byLITTLE by … Mikey … MIKEY!

Back to waking life. Dennis tells Michael to man the decks again. Need a piss. Back in ten wi' more beer. Follow the notebook. Don't stray from the path. Remember what happened to Little Red Ridin' Hood. The wolf … he fucked her then ate her up.

No he didn't, thinks Michael, eyes scanning the crowd.

She is back in the room again. Somewhere. Here. The people now blood-black trees in a midnight forest under mirror-ball moon, and the wind blows hard, and the dark trees shiver, the wind carrying scent of *her* to *him*.

56.

I think it my favourite fairy tale, that one. Best bit is when he eats Grandma. I met Father's Grandma once. She was dead though. You'd have to be really hungry to eat whole grandma like wolf did. Lots of tomato sauce if I tried it. Old ladies smell a bit like wee and sweeties. Or maybe not tomato sauce but custard. Like a pudding. But I can hear myself get silly here. This is not silly time. I think bad things are coming. Bad things happen in good stories though, don't they Blackbird. Like Red Riding Hood had to have bad things happen so she could have good things happen too. Get Woodsman to chop Wolf open, out jump Grandma. I think it like happy or sad. If always happy how can it really feel like happy? How would you know? No, Blackbird … I think sad is good for sometimes. And then when happy comes … la, la, laaa … Imagine sun all time and no rain. Wouldn't work. Flowers die of laughing. And think no night-time. When would owls come out? No. Night needs day needs night. Here … look.

You are sat on the bank of the Went. You hear the noises of the people time across the river. You hear the soft-blown leaves of the trees behind you make the sound of water hush, but it isn't water hush because that is the sound of the Went, there, in front of you, but now you see something else. It is a white smiling face, a mask with black holes for eyes and a slit for a mouth, a white mask like moon, but it isn't moon, because it's there, right in front of you, held out in Johnny's hand.

Here, Blackbird. Put it on.

Johnny shakes the white moon, and you take it. Everything goes darker for a moment as you bring the moon to your face, and now, the everything is narrow and thin through the holes for eyes.

Look at me, Blackbird.

You look, and Johnny is a sad face. A white sad moon with black holes for eyes, a slit for a mouth.

See ... you are happy, and I, am sad.

You hear the sound of a fox, crying out a word you can't understand.

tick tock ... time for change.

Johnny's hand comes towards you and you feel the mask come away, the trees, the river, the lights from over the Went happening for a moment, and then, gone, as the sad mask is on you, the everything, narrow and thin through the black holes for eyes.

Look at me, Blackbird.

You look, and Johnny is now a happy white moon, his laugh, laugh, laugh, like it is coming from inside a box, and then ... one tear, black, rolling the white moon cheek, as the eyes begin to bleed black blood, and the mouth begins to bleed black blood, and the happy white moon is now black blood, and the eyes are red like fire, and the blood mouth is cracking open, teeth, teeth of a fox as a blood-black baby vomits out onto the black grass and ... Gone.

Johnny pulls the mask from his face.

It is Johnny again, smiling, now reaching out to take the sad mask from your face, the white moons now thrown into the flicker-lit black Went, side by side slow-floating towards the mill, looking up at the real moon, the stars ... the moon-masks going ... going ... and Johnny is holding your hands.

Blackbird. There is nothing to stop it. Fox must. All we can do is watch.

57.

Fucking, *fucking*, bitch.

Mr King watches from the marquee entrance as Sandra and that cunt butcher cunt stand leaning against the emptied lightless goldfish stall, ha ha, touchy touchy, why don't we just fuck right here and now because I'm a fucking slut with no shame, no shame at all that half the village can see me opening my slag-hole for some common fuck cunt of a pig butcher, why ... who cares that I'm the wife of the head of the council and live in the big house and, and ... SANDRA!

LITTLE by LITTLE by...

SanDRA! CAN I SPEAK TO YOU a MINUTE?

Sandra King and Jed Hopkins twitch like red-handed school kids caught fagging it behind the bike shed, both turning as one to look at Mr King who strides out the marquee entrance, curve-waving his arm in a beckon of come here now as he arcs around the corner of the tent.

Sandra says something to Jed, who seems to be half-minded to gesture an eyup to Jeremy King but thinks better of it, Sandra now walking a medium-paced defiance towards her backwards-glancing husband, who now turns tight-shouldered into the dark shadow cast, down by the side of the marquee.

By the side of tombola comes Maggie and Debbie and Rose, Maggie cocking a snook at the trestle table of sparse prizes as the old dear behind the stall croaks fancy a go, girls?

Maggie play-punches a sat teddy bear in the face, which flips onto its back looking heavenward, the words no ta grandma laughing their way from the crimson-lipped queen.

They walk on, Debbie with an arm around the shoulders of the other queen, who giggles at the spark and spat of her new friend Maggie Haywire, a warm glow in Rose's belly that slow-flares like a little sun, out through lungs and bones and skin, collecting onto the soft protective frame of her other new friend's arm as it gently tightens around her.

You alreyt, Rose?

Rose looks down at her sick-spattered sash and says, yeh, yeh I am ta Debbie.

The girls pause for a minute, considering coconut shy and hook-a-duck when an eyup causes all three to turn.

Paul Alcock. Grinning. Looking at Maggie.

Hey Maggie … Debs … Rose.

Paul looks like he's about to say something. The girls wait. Nothing comes. Maggie takes one step forward and kisses Paul full on the lips, steps back as the girls crackle into a shiver of laughter, hanging onto each other as Paul shades strawberry red, a voice calling CUM 'N' SMACK a COkerNUT! THREE LEFT! TWENNY PEE a GUH!

Paul shuffles from one foot to the other, laughs unconvincingly, goes to wipe his mouth but thinks better of it, his lips still smeared an evil clown slur from Maggie's lipstick.

Well? says Maggie.

Paul smiles for real, his heart beating like a Motörhead kick-drum, says: Just wonderin' if you lasses were comin' back?

He says this looking at Maggie only, and Rose feels Debbie's elbow soft nudge her. Maggie laughs, a short punch of a laugh, at first harsh then softening to an abrupt oh?

Yeh ... like ... comin' back in tuh disco?

Maggie turns to Debbie, to Rose, says whadda yer reckon, guuurls ... in a voice that sounds like a camp miner on the pull.

Rose squeaks like a mouse. Says yeh. Debbie says maybe. Maggie tells Paul they'll consider it, if he goes buy them all a vodka and orange, doubles, and goes wait for them by the stage. Paul looks at Maggie, unblinking, half-trying to suss her out, half-trying to count the cost, suddenly remembering the thing he has behind his back.

Anyrowd, he says, suddenly becoming Mr Cocky, Mr Punk, Mr Paul Fucking Lady-Killer. He holds his arm out to Maggie. In his hand dangles a plastic bag with a bright orange goldfish in it.

Happy Christmas, your majesty.

Twenty feet away, watching all of this with a little sun

in her belly that burns her ribs to blackened bastard fuck, is Sally.

She turns on her heel, heads back quick-step towards the marquee, something caught in her throat she wants to scream out into the black grass, *bastard, bastard, bastard.*

You. Don't. Do ... it.

Jeremy King's thumb and fingers tighten around his wife's neck. She steps back but there is nowhere to go, the stiff canvas of the marquee a dead stop, the song inside a punch-punch, punch-punch, yougotTHE BESTofMAHHH LUV ... as a noise rises from her gut, gets corked in her throat, WOhooWOhoo ... as the thumb and fingers tighten again, yougotTHE BESTofMAHHH ... stars, moon, blurring ...

Keep. *Your. Cunt.* AWAY. From. JED. *Fucking.* HOPkins. Or. I. Will. Take ... a KNIFE. And CUT. Your. FUCKING ... Eyes. Out.

THE BESTofMAHHH ... Sandra King falls to her knees.

Get up ... Get up, *you bitch.*

WOhooWOhoo ... Sandra King rises to her feet, slow, hands reaching down ... takes both shoes off, turns, pushing him hard in the chest, quick, quick up by the side of the marquee get out of shadows into light she will not let him see her cry, hands tightening around her shoes, and if he comes again she'll drive her heels right into his *fucking skull*, run, run into the light ... enough ... enough ... WOhooWOhoo ...

And e-*nough* is a-fuckin-*nough* ... what, what, what the

fuck she ever saw in that dickhead Paul she will never know … pushing herself through a clutter of yack-yack-fucking-yackers blocking the marquee entrance, into the starlit dark of heat, and sound, and bodies … stop, yougotTHE BESTofMAHHH LUV …

Her eyes narrow as she scans the black shapes around her. She climbs onto a bench. There. Just where she left him. And down she gets, leading shoulder-first head down past dance and dance and chatter and dance, exCUSE ME, past dance and dance and chatter and dance and …

Michael, leant against the tree-trunk pole, sees Sally weaving through the bodies, a look on her face that he can't quite figure as closer, closer, into the red/blue/orange-lit copse an arm's length ahead of him she now stands, now taking his drink from his hand, downing what's left in one, dropping the plastic pint-pot to the black flat grass, and now, with both hands on his lapels she soft tugs him back, back … back into the dancing mass.

Michael looks at Sally. Sally looks at Michael. They both are waiting, for what, they know not. Around them the trees shake and shiver. The moon turns. The constellations revolve quicker than time would ever allow in an ordinary universe. And God is a DJ. The needle a God-finger as a flat world turns beneath it, the end mere revolutions away, and yet, this God has a parallel universe within its powers, a choice of this end becoming a beginning, a seamless mix between this and that, a merry-go-round that keeps, and keeps on keeping, and look, it is he and she, caught in an orbit of each that sings … and the song is her keep running away, and he, is begging her, to stay ... The Emotions, into Four Tops, on and on no stop, he and she holding tight as the merry-go-round keeps turning, the verse drop pushing hip-bones closer, and God, is a DJ ... go across the Went and fuck.

And Jed sees her near-running, crying, shoes in hands, and so he follows, past hotdog van and dead tombola, the music of the marquee fading as ahead she moves and him following, closer, closer, SANdra ... STOP.

Sandra King twitches, turns, sees Jed Hopkins, stops, shoes dropped, barefoot stood in the pale wake between merry-go-round flicker-creep light and the darkness beyond, and she is crying, and Jed is cradling her, WHAT IS IT? WHAT? and before the slowing merry-go-round stops its turn Sandra King tells Jed to follow her home, that she's going to fuck his brains out, like a slut, like a dirty ... fucking ... *slut*.

And behind the three girls this merry-go-round is turning, on and on no stop. And they are caught between the bass throb of the marquee disco and the treble wheeze of the merry-go-round organ, that fades, rises, like a called warning from too far away, across fields and rivers, across time and space, as someone upstairs bangs a heavy fist on the floor of tomorrow, *stop it, stop it down there*, but the girls don't hear any of this, they just stand in a tight circle, not saying anything, looking at an orange goldfish in a plastic bag, opening, and closing its tiny mouth.

How can it breathe under water?

Rose and Maggie look at Debbie, who prods the bag with an inquisitive finger.

Are you thick or what?

Debbie looks at Maggie, blobs her tongue out, says, c'mon then queen know-it-all, how?

Rose clears her throat, speaks it to the goldfish in the bag, the merry-go-round, the trees beyond the river, the fox that watches from beneath the scrub as a mouse pads tentative from a hole in the dry earth, says: Goldfish rise to gather air from just above the water-line, and then they go back under where it's safe. I've already put two in the Went. A fish in a bag is wrong. May as well be dead.

Rose King looks at Maggie, and then Debbie, and then to the fish, says, fish belong in a river.

Maggie smiles, and the merry-go-round begins to slow, a called warning from too far away, across fields and rivers, across time and space, as someone upstairs bangs a heavy fist on the floor of tomorrow, *stop it, stop it down there*, and Maggie hands Rose the bag, runs her fingers slow along Rose's cheek, says yes my queen ... *yes.*

And God is a DJ. The needle a God-finger as a flat world turns beneath it, the end mere revolutions away, and yet, this God has a parallel universe within its powers, a choice of this end becoming a beginning, a seamless mix between this and that, a merry-go-round that keeps, and keeps on keeping, and look, it is he and she, caught in an orbit of each that sings ... and the song is her keep running away, and he, is begging her, to stay ... The Emotions, into Four Tops, on and on no stop, and behind the decks he stands, seeing her, feeling her, the words of a song this thin cry of fox in the darkest forest imaginable, alone, calling, and still she stands, there, by the benches to his left, her face downcast, caught in the light of this mirror-ball moon, and something is wrong, something is wrong ... and the song is her gone, and he, is left with nothing, and YOU ... keepRUNNIN' aWAY ... the boy now arriving with drinks, placing them behind her on the table, now leaning in to whisper something into her ear as her friend reaches behind her for a drink, says something laughing but the girl doesn't laugh. Look. Look at her face. What's wrong?

Look at me, Sarah, look at me ... I'm here.

And God, is a DJ. The needle a God-finger as a flat world turns beneath it, the end mere revolutions away, and yet ... this is not an end, and she ... she is looking at him, now, and Michael wants to stop this world turning, *now*, the song of all history unmaking itself, recasting into thin shards that dance in the light of this new moon dancing over a midnight sea, the seen, momentary, the unseen, deeper than you will ever know, unless, you listen not to the howls of the wind, that chair spinning out through a doorway flung wide, the shouted calls of retreat to the storm cellar, because the known world must correct itself, reform into what it was before, safe, and predictable, and *oh, come closer, please ...* for I will remake the world for you, gathered from atoms and planets, shaped from the clay that yields, that if a god loved you as I, he would give, and all this on the thin strand of seven days, and on the first day I will give you me, and on the second I will give myself, and on the third I will give you the heavens, and on the fourth I will give you the birdsong, and on the fifth I will give you the slowing dusk, and on the sixth I will give you a garden of winter, mute and beautiful, held under a glass roof where cold sun bleeds warm, where I will kiss you, and hold you, and bathe you in the waters of Eden, *and I will love you Sarah, I will love you …* and on the seventh day you will finally know …

And God, is a DJ, and this is not the end, and he, is looking at her, and she, is looking at him, and now the boy is saying something to her again, but she is *not* listening to him, she is listening to the words of this song, *Sarah, let me care for you, let me give everything I have to you*, because God, is a DJ, the needle a God-finger as a flat world turns beneath it, the end mere revolutions away and yet … and yet this is not an end, but it is, the song that was, now beginning to fade, but Michael doesn't hear, and end is coming, and end is here, the song gone, faded out, dead, and the people look towards the stage as the emptiness of a soundless universe echoes empty under a mirror-ball moon, and he, is looking at her, and she, is looking at him, Michael's mouth part-opening as though to say the words, as though to tell her here and now, in front of the whole universe, and her eyes narrow, the merest twitch of a *no, don't, please,* and God, is a DJ, but a God forgetting that this, is a long player, and as a call from the crowd shouts SORT IT OUT the next song begins itself another beginning, the end that was just a pause between acts, a snap, snap, snap of snare, a gut-kick of bass, of stings and honey bees, of favourite songs danced to all night long ... but it's the SAME ... OLD SONG ... that don't mean FUCK now she's gone ZZZZZZzzzzk ... And God, is a DJ. The almighty hand dragging this needle across the flat earth beneath, because God ... has something to say ...

Michael walks to the front of the stage, and the mirror-ball moon turns.

Michael turns the microphone on, a jab of feedback, and the mirror-ball moon turns.

Silence.

Michael looks at Sarah, says her name. The sound of it filling the marquee. Taking wings of a blackbird across Forgiveness Green. To the Went. To the tor. To the moon. The stars.

SARAH ... I NEED TO TELL THE WHOLE WORLD THAT I LOVE YOU, THAT I WOULD DO ANYTHING FOR YOU, THAT IT DOESN'T MATTER WHAT ANYONE THINKS BECAUSE ALL THAT MATTERS IS LOVE ... AND I LOVE YOU, SARAH, I LOVE YOU ...

Silence, as the universe turns.

And the universe is turning to Sarah ... looking, waiting ... and Sarah is looking back, into a dark forever ... the faces, a universe of wide-eyed open-mouthed faces, waiting ... and now she turns to face the man on the stage ... a man twice her age ... a man as old as her dad ... a man that was her college tutor two months ago, a man, that ...

I ... don't know what you're talkin' about ... Are you alreyt, Mr Goodman?

Her head shakes a wide-eyed slow no, a shrug, the look on her face now the look of soft amusement, of a punchline not quite got.

And it starts with a single rook. A caw of laughter from the back of the marquee that travels like a jenneled yell through the mirror-ball universe, bouncing off canvas and planets and solar systems, louder, louder, and if you were a blackbird looking down on all this, you would see a man alone on a stage, wilting like a dying rose, as all around the people point and laugh and jeer and call out ARE YOU ALREYT, MR GOODMAN? and onto the stage steps Dennis, now swept aside by the exiting fool, drinks clattering the wooden floor as the fool half-tumbles down the steps into the laughing jeering people, a cackle of parting sea to let the idiot pass through, going ... going ... ARE YOU ALREYT, MR GOODMAN? And out into the rook-black night he sways, near-bumping into the girl's father returning from the bar with Debbie Foxglove, who watch bemused as the wilting figure staggers across Forgiveness Green, and the people are laughing, and the fool stumbles past dead merry-go-round with horses mute and staring, and the music is gone, and the music is gone, the end.

And this is where it all begins: the kiss. Arms wrapped, holding close, closer. Moving as one in slow circle, round and round as the record keeps turning, and the music is here, now ... bones of bass and sex of drum, and this is their song, forever ... and he knows it, and she knows it, as tips of tongues press, as hands slide over hips and small of back, and this, is the beginning of all time ... for now is now is now, and God, is a DJ, and the gospel is love, and the gospel is fuck, and the gospel is a four/four beat, the words breathed into his mouth, Michael, I really like you ... don't hurt me ... *I won't, I won't* ... YOU ... keepRUNNIN' aWAY ... And if God is a DJ and the gospel is love? Then the Devil will have to rise himself up from the fire. Paul Alcock, grabs Michael Goodman by the shirt-collar, and pulls him from the girl. Michael sees Paul draw back a fist. And then, a flash ... the voice of Sally shouting DON'T PAUL, DON'T ... and the ground beneath becomes water, a river, the moon a blur above, the stars a scatter of sparks, thrown careless by a bad god of things to come, and yet here is the shape of water, on and on, this body of ever, held between banks of rock and earth, delivered as rain falling soft from a heaven not caring, down onto a green Derbyshire hillside, sinking unseen through soil into limestone bones of drip, drip ... cast out from arse-mouth into this birdsong valley, and here is the beauty of evil, and the river is deep, look.

Rose stands upon the bridge. Leaning over the rail to watch the moon tremble on the black water.

Maggie. Debbie. And Rose. The three of them, tight as mice. And Rose tells them she will call this fish Michael. And Maggie will groan. And Debbie will laugh. And Rose will tell them both to shut up because Michael is a nice name, as along the bridge she walks. Over, and onto the other side. The fish held out like a torch lighting the way. And Maggie saying Michael is a div as she grabs hold of Debbie's hand.

Kisses her cheek. Whispers I love you. The young girl ahead seeing none of this as the leaves above her shiver.

SEVEN! ... SIX! ... FIVE! FOUR! THREE! TWO ... She saw her dad coming. Looking for her. Dragging that slag Debbie Foxglove with him. Moving through the crowd, a crowd that had begun to dance again now the DJ had brought the music back, scratch right hand, scratch left hand, and this beat is a hammer, a too-loud heartbeat, *stop*, Natalie saying Goodman is a fucking nutter, Tom saying nothing ... just looking at Sarah, saying nothing, and the people are still laughing, tapping Sarah on the shoulder, doing twirly-finger gestures to temples, YOU ALREYT MR GOODMAN? and she sees her dad coming, and she needs to get out, now, cutting around the outskirts quick, don't let him see ... *What has she done?* And here she is, running out into the night, out across Forgiveness Green, out, out, crossing the bridge, knowing he came this way, seeing his dark shape cross over as she ran beyond the dead merry-go-round, looking, seeing, scratch right hand, scratch left hand ... inSTANT rePLAY! *What has she done?* And now she has gone over to the other side, and she is running, running after Michael, after the man whose child she carries inside her.

I can be daddy, Debbie can be mummy, and you can be our little girl.

The mill-wheel goes *plosh* ... *plosh* ... *plosh* ...

Rose, sat on the bank of the Went, bagged fish on her

lap, looks up to where Maggie and Debbie are stood over her, these near-black shadows, backlit by a white moon.

She crinkles her nose up, a squint. Maggie leans down towards her. Kisses the top of her head. Sings, Roh-zee-poh-zee … mah ick-ul gurl.

Sandra King, her naked back cold against the leather sofa, has her eyes closed tight.

Jed Hopkins, is grunting like a pig.

Sandra King, her eyes closed tight, is trying not to cry.

Jed Hopkins, is sweating, and he smells like carcass, like meat uncooked, and he is grunting like a pig.

Sandra King, sees dark things move, things that grunt and snuffle, animal things that are trying to sniff her out, devour her, swallow her whole down a wet throat that tightens, a wet throat that wants to carry her down, down into a dark wet belly, and she feels him lurching, flexing, a hot squirt of poison filling her up, *slut, slut, slut …*

MICHAEL! STOP!

Michael turns to see her, there, coming along the path under trees, dark bent of shadow hands reaching towards him, the black-silver Went turned by the wheel, *plosh, plosh, plosh …*

Her: Stop … Where are you going?

Him, dead eyes, a shrug.

Her: I'm sorry, Michael … I'm sorry …

And now they are holding each other, close, closer, and he is telling her over and over that he loves her, he loves her

... and now, him, pulling away: How could you do that to me?

Her, hands around his wrists: *Michael* ... how could you do that to *me*? Telling everyone *that* ... it made me want to die ... *Why* did you do that?

Her, letting go as Michael pulls her in again, him saying I just ... I just wanted you to know ... I'd do anything for you, Sarah ... *anything* ...

She puts her hands on his arms. A pressure. Levers a breath's space between them.

Michael ... look at me.

He looks at her. She looks like she might cry. Don't you *see* what you did?

He slow shakes his head in a no. He feels her hands on his arms, tight, tighter. Her words come quick. *You* ... took my *choice* away. And you had *no right* to do that ... Don't you see? Now *everyone* knows ... *everyone* ... it *wasn't fair,* Michael ... I needed time to think about things ... about *us* ... about *everything* ... and now I haven't *got* time ... because *everybody* knows ... *everyone* ... Don't you see what that makes me? *Ey?*

She lets go of his arms. Arms that hang limp by his sides. She breathes in. Out.

I'm sorry ... but ... you make me feel trapped, Michael ... I really felt something for you ... I did ... but you scare me ... and what you did tonight makes me even more scared ... Where will it stop?

He is looking to the ground. His eyes closed tight. He hears her breathing, hears her say Why couldn't we have just kept it fun? Why did you have to make it so ...

YOU SAID, you LOVED ME!

Sarah steps back. Half-stumbles on a tree root that snakes across the path. A fox cries out somewhere not here, and now he is crying, hands over his face, head tilted down towards the dark ground as the sobs cough from behind a mask of palm and finger.

Sarah takes two steps towards him, arms around him once again, close, closer.

Michael ... I'm sorry ...

The mask comes away. His arms now around her head, tight, tighter, his mouth pressed to her ear.

Please ... I can't ... do this ... without you, Sally ...

A white flash, her mother's name a firework crack of bone, and Sarah pulls back quick from his grip, back arched, step back, step back, a heel meets the tree root and now she is falling, a backwards tumble to the floor as a shadow of body moves quick past her, another white flash as she hits the ground, as fireworks explode in the sky, red and gold as Paul Alcock swings the rock down, a dumb crack of skull as Michael falls slack to the path, the heavens a crackle-spat bang of light, a cast of fire she sees in Michael's wide-open eyes, staring, as again the rock comes down, the crunch of bone, black blood a tear, black blood from nose and mouth, the head unshaped, red and gold a fire in the sky, the rock cast into water, the father now turning to a daughter not his, the words, the words, *grab his legs, c'mon.*

And red and gold the sky explodes, Rose telling Maggie again that she already has a mummy, to *stop it*, and Debbie is telling Maggie *enough*, to stop kissing the girl, and to *get off her, get off her*, and red, and gold, the sky explodes as Maggie grabs the plastic bag, the goldfish inside, tilting, red, and gold, a fire filling the sky as the bag is thrown through the air, now hitting the mill-wheel, now falling soundless onto black water, now dragged under by the wheel, *plosh, plosh* ... and Rose is trying to stand, the hand of Maggie gripping the girl's hair as Debbie shouts STOP IT, STOP IT, and Maggie is crying out, crying out the words that come as strangle, a hard hand that pushes Debbie back to the ground, red, and gold, THIS IS LOVE! THIS IS LOVE! as Rose is swung face-down into the water, head smacked hard against green-mossed rock, again, again, and the sky is a fire, red, and gold, white glint of rings spreading out across the Went as down goes the head, again, again, the queen a kneel of unholy prayer, of devils cast out as the head is held down, THIS IS LOVE! THIS IS LOVE! and the church bells ring midnight, and the people are cheering, and the people, are cheering ...

A dream.

You know this with how the Went glitters. The way your feet feel the water. Ribbons of silk. Not real. Not how water really feels.

You wiggle your toes.

This is a good dream, because you can make things happen, not like in one of those bad dreams where bad things happen and you can't do anything to stop them from happening.

Ten little toe fish. Wiggle.

You look up to the sky and see no cloud. Just a blue like no blue you know. A blue you think you can reach up and touch, your fingers in sky like toes in the glittering Went, and this dream is a good dream ... you know it.

Then, you hear it, so you must have said it.

What are *you* doing here?

Johnny smiles. He points to his feet that splash in the water.

Ten little toe fish.

And this dream *is* a good dream, because now you are laughing, and Johnny is laughing too.

Ah, Rosie-posey ... this is my favourite game ever, all little toe fish together.

Johnny is holding your hand.

Don't be scared.

And now the water is black, and the black is rising up, and you, are going under.

Oh ... I am a young maiden ... my story is sad ...
For once I was courted ... by a brave sailing lad ...
He courted me strongly ... by night and by day ...
But now he has left me ... and sailed far a-way ...
And if I was a blackbird ... I'd whistle and sing ...
And I'd follow the vessel ... my true love sails in ...
And on the top rigging ... I would there build my nest ...
And I'd flutter my wings ... o'er his lily ... white ... breast ...

Fog, white and bright like August cloud, the grass summer-green under your bare feet, and you know you must walk, on and on because, and the first spike is through your right hand, and the second is through your arm, and the third is in your neck, and the fourth is the end, and the fifth will smash your ribs, and the sixth will break your spine, iron shaft that nails your unborn child to the never will, and on the seventh you will walk the bridge, fog, the sound of a crow, ever winter the black bones of a tree, on and on, but the voice of Johnny says *stop, now is time to see it, to see all pieces of people-play jigsaw together and see it, for love is not a sing bird who lives in cage, but fly it must like sad when gone, and sad is moon but moon must come, and you are not owl, you are Blackbird, and Blackbird must sing it in sun tree or Blackbird is not, for this love is love for itself and nothing can take it, so let forgiveness be green, like April leaf always, on and on, to keep as is, and to share if others come by, and if some are trickers then trick be to them, forgive, let your moon bring night, let day bring a sun, for love will dance and song will sing it, and love is yours, Blackbird, yours ... look, she comes.*

And through the fog comes Rose, frightened, glancing scared at you and Johnny.

Where ... *is this?*

Here, Rose ... with me ... and Blackbird.

Where's ... *here?*

And Johnny laughs, quiet like breathing, says, *Here, Rose ... at beginning after end.*

And now Rose is crying, quiet like breath, and Johnny

kneels, wraps himself around her, says, *Don't be sad ... turn around ... look ...*

And the fog is moving away, a tunnel is soft making itself, a tunnel that now shows the bridge in beautiful sunlight, and beyond, the moors rise up in golden-lit green and heather, and Johnny tells it, *everything that was, has gone, for now you will walk in birdsong sun days, in rain days that wash you like flowers, and then, when night comes, you will lay side by side under blue blanket of stars, and river will sing you, tell stories of all things gone, and for always you will understand ... now, go ... both of you ... leave this fog together and go ...*

And Rose is smiling as she gives you her hand.

And you are smiling as you give Rose your hand.

And you walk, the two of you, together across Forgiveness Green, across the Went bridge into this sunlight, into this birdsong, and Rose says isn't it beautiful, and you say yes, yes it is, as now turning you will wave Johnny goodbye, but you won't, because all you see is the river, the grassland beyond where once you knew a village, and beyond this, the tor that rises up, up, into the bluest sky you have ever seen, and you hear it, so you know you are saying it: Rose, look ...

Hello Michael.

You open your eyes.

There, stood over you, face lit by a flickering lantern held in outstretched hand, is Johnny Bender.

Wet walls of rock. Dark tunnel of mine. Shadows moving.

Johnny places the lantern by your head.
You need this to see.
Gone.
Music, a drip, drip.
The flame. The flame a dance of her.

EDENDALE CARNIVAL 1979

Jackson 5 – abc
Bob and earl – harlum shuffle
Billy Ocean – Luv really hurts without you
Trammps – Disco inferno
KC and the Sunshine Band – Get Down Tonight
o'jays – Luv Train
R Dean Taylor – Ghost in my House
Smoky robinson – tears of a clown
Sister Slege – lost in music
the undisputed truth – you + me = luv
M – pop muzik
labelle – lady marmelade
~~the damned – new rose~~
CHIC – good times
Supremes – you keep me hangin on
Heatwave – boogie nights
Bee gees – night fever
The Temptations – Get Ready
Sister Slege – we are famuly
JAMES FUCKING BROWN – SEX MACHINE
miracles – luv machine
detroit emeralds – feel the need in me
baccara – yes sir, i can boogie
the velveletes – Needle in a Haystack
Aretha franklin – RESPECT
Sam and Dave – hold on, Im comin!
Dusty Springfield – little by little
the emotions – best of my luv
the four tops – you keep running away
Don Hartman – Instant replay

KINGY IS A TWAT!

Blondie – Heart of glass
Gloria Jones – tainted luv
kim weston – helpless
Shirley ellis – the clapping song
Rose Royce – Carwash
Real thing – can you feel the force?
Martha reeves and The Vandellas – Nowhere to run
elo – livin' thing
Squeeze – Slap n tickle
landury and the Blockheds – Sex and drugs and rock and roll

NORTHERN SOUL
KEEP THE FAITH

DEN + DEBS

Remeber – Birds ARE MAD!

Author photo ©Meghan Lilleyman and Scott Hukins

Dean Lilleyman is a novelist who lives in a small Derbyshire village. His first novel, *Billy and the Devil*, is the unflinching portrayal of an alcoholic, a story that has courted both controversy and praise, the Man Booker Prize nominee Jane Rogers calling it "Brilliantly evoked in all its sordid detail, black humour, demented courage, and alienation." *Billy and the Devil* was published in 2015 by Urbane Publications.

The Gospel According to Johnny Bender is Dean Lilleyman's second novel, published by Urbane in 2016.

Dean Lilleyman has been featured in both commercial and underground publications, and has performed at a number of literary events. He has lectured in creative writing and been a guest speaker on transgressive literature. He is now working on his next novel.

For more, visit deanlilleyman.com

Paperback, £8.99
ISBN 9781910692332

Billy and the Devil is the startling debut novel from Dean Lilleyman, and presents the emotive and challenging story of Billy and his battle with alcoholism.

Billy and the Devil is a shocking, compelling and intimate portrayal of isolation, sexual misadventure, and addiction. Told in a series of brilliantly rendered observations and episodes from Billy's life, this controversial story charts an all-too real descent into alcoholism. It is an unflinchingly vivid journey to a place of no return, where love is lost in the darkest of woods – a boy, who becomes a man, who becomes his own worst devil. But ultimately, what choice does Billy have?

Raw, poetic, with moments of pure imaginative visceral genius, *Billy and the Devil* is by turns funny and sad, brutal and tender, horrific and uplifting. You will be both challenged and moved by this astonishing debut novel from author Dean Lilleyman.

"This is wild stuff, very dark and very brilliant." – Conor O'Callaghan, author of *Nothing on Earth*

"Put it this way, a great novel doesn't end after you have read the last page. It reaches out after publication and plants its own mythology in the world. This is the highest achievement of Lilleyman's debut. I recommend: read this book." – Interrobang Arts Magazine

"Brilliantly evoked in all its sordid detail, black humour, demented courage, and alienation." – Jane Rogers, author of *Mr Wroe's Virgins and Promised Lands*

"Billy and the Devil *is a completely convincing character study. Said Billy is a laugh, a tart, a drunk, and more. Dean Lilleyman uses various writerly and unmannerly techniques to show us the many ages and faces of his loveable and detestable anti-hero. The book is tender, funny, sad and grotesque – but however gruelling Billy's descent becomes, it bleeds its own dark poetry. Here, dirty realism has left Los Angeles for Chesterfield, where it finds itself at a garden barbeque drinking Leibfraumilch and barley wine. Terrific."* – Matthew Clegg, author of *West North East*

"This book is not going to be everyone's cup of tea. And that is its strength. A brutal, brilliant debut. Should be read in all schools." – Push Zine

URBANE